THE UNDAUNTED

A Series of Worthy Young Ladies
Book Three

Kate Archer

DRAGONBLADE
PUBLISHING, INC.

ARE YOU SIGNED UP FOR DRAGONBLADE'S BLOG?

You'll get the latest news and information on exclusive giveaways, exclusive excerpts, coming releases, sales, free books, cover reveals and more.

Check out our complete list of authors, too!

No spam, no junk. That's a promise!

Sign Up Here

www.dragonbladepublishing.com

Dearest Reader;

Thank you for your support of a small press. At Dragonblade Publishing, we strive to bring you the highest quality Historical Romance from some of the best authors in the business. Without your support, there is no 'us', so we sincerely hope you adore these stories and find some new favorite authors along the way.

Happy Reading!

CEO, Dragonblade Publishing

**Additional Dragonblade books by
Author Kate Archer**

A Series of Worthy Young Ladies
The Meddler (Book 1)
The Sprinter (Book 2)
The Undaunted (Book 3)

The Dukes' Pact Series
The Viscount's Sinful Bargain (Book 1)
The Marquess' Daring Wager (Book 2)
The Lord's Desperate Pledge (Book 3)
The Baron's Dangerous Contract (Book 4)
The Peer's Roguish Word (Book 5)
The Earl's Iron Warrant (Book 6)

PROLOGUE

Portland Place, 1811

THE WOMEN OF The Society of Sponsoring Ladies had not thought they would see one another for some months. The season was coming to an end, and they were all rather more exhausted than they had imagined they would be.

Lady Heathway's Miss Yardley was somehow married, and somehow married to the lady's own nephew. The bizarre circumstances that had accompanied the couple to the altar were not of a kind any of the ladies would like to repeat. Lady Easton felt as if they'd all held onto their bonnets in a strong wind to get through it.

Their various households were packed up and poised to depart the town, but at the last possible moment, Lady Easton had sent a message to her friends. A rather urgent message.

As Bramley set up the tea things in her drawing room, Lady Easton smiled and wondered when Lady Heathway might ever stop crowing about Lady Gresham, née Miss Yardley. *Was* there something to crow about? To be sure, the lady had married and so she supposed that was a success, but the talk they'd all had to face down! Miss Yardley hanging from a drainpipe in the middle of the night! Miss Yardley leaving a ball alone in an unknown carriage! Miss Yardley, also known as *The Sprinter*.

And then, this was the second girl who had married a near

relation of her sponsor. First Miss Wilcox to Lady Mendleton's son, Lord Langley, and now Miss Yardley to Lady Heathway's nephew Lord Gresham.

Clara Godwin, Countess of Easton, took in a long and slow breath. At least she would not have *that* problem to contend with. Her boys were all still in school and her nephew, Lord Bertridge, was everything sensible. They had already had many talks between them, finding themselves in complete agreement that he was of such a caliber as to make a brilliant match. The Duke of Clayton's daughter was set to launch next season and that would suit their purposes nicely—a proper upbringing, a generous dowry, and very right connections. According to a friend who knew the duke's family intimately, the girl was comely and exceedingly demure, which would suit both her nephew and herself.

"What my dear new daughter-in-law, or I should just say my *daughter* as we are that close, remains unaware of," Lady Heathway droned on, "is that we have positively driven out that uncouth new viscount and she and George will have Barlow Hall."

There were audible gasps amongst the ladies. Lady Featherstone said, "Gresham has bought the hall? Was it wise, though, reinstalling the mother to her old house, Penelope? Does that not rather give Lady Barlow a leg up on the in-law side of things? Not that it is any sort of competition between you, I only say…"

Lady Heathway did not allow Lady Featherstone to finish her thoughts, as she generally had a low opinion of anybody's thoughts that might challenge her own. She waved her hands. "Of course, I did suggest they might live with me, but George was determined to reinstate his dear wife to the hall. In any case, it will be a far better arrangement. I have my own set of apartments there, as the place is a mammoth, and I intend to descend upon the house regularly. I have quite a few plans regarding granddaughters. In any case, as I have so handily demonstrated, Lady Barlow is easily overcome."

Lady Featherstone laid her hand gently over the emerald brooch she had won by solving Lord Ryland's mystery evening just weeks before. The brooch was, as far as the other ladies could see it, destined to be their constant companion forevermore. Or as the duchess had put it—*We will be staring at it until we can stare no more and the hand of death has closed our eyes forever.*

"Oh, I see," Lady Featherstone murmured, glancing down at her beloved jewelry, "yes of course you have shown Lady Barlow can be overpowered to good effect."

Lady Mendleton nodded knowingly, as if she were all too familiar with the ins and outs of the thing now that she had her own daughter-in-law.

Lady Redfield fanned herself, but one could not be certain of the cause. Lady Heathway's forcefulness often did overwhelm the lady regardless of what she was saying.

The duchess said, "There is something rather noble in returning Miss Yardley to her rightful house."

Nobody made comment on that idea. They had no need to. If the duchess named a thing noble, it simply meant that she approved.

With his usual dignity, Bramley glanced over the tea tray to confirm everything was in order and then departed the room, silently closing the door.

Lady Easton poured the cups, working up the courage to get started. Finally, she said, "In any case, you must wonder why I called on everyone to come to me. It is just that…well you see…it seems…"

She hardly knew where to begin. Her lord, always so easily managed, had suddenly decided to put forth ideas and opinions. They had always gone along so peaceably! If she wished to redecorate the house, he would find it out when he walked through the doors and tripped over a new piece of furniture. If she wished to host a ball, he would discover it when she left an invitation for him on the great hall table. Now, suddenly, he had his own ideas.

And what ideas they were! Some unheard-of baron, whose only recommendation was his interest in horses, had a daughter. At least, the baron was unknown to Lady Easton, as he apparently never came to Town and just went from one horserace to the next. This fellow's daughter, a Miss Caroline Upton, required a strong female guiding hand. Who better to firmly guide than Clara Godwin, Countess of Easton?

Why could not the girl's own mother be that guiding hand? That was not at all satisfactorily explained. All Clara could get from her lord was that there were nine children. Could the lady not keep track of them all? Was she too exhausted from having a ridiculous amount of offspring? Was that not the woman's own fault for failing to lock her bedchamber door at the appropriate time in her life?

Lady Easton still shuddered when she recalled the particular interview that had informed her of the scheme, had in the library when she was not the least prepared for it. Expecting to find her marshmallow of a husband, she'd instead run across quite another person.

Lord Easton had said quite forcefully that *she* was the one who had wished to sponsor a girl and have a dowry thrown together. She would have it and it was to be *this* girl. That was his final judgment.

His final judgment? Since when did he have judgments at all, never mind final judgments? Who was teaching him these things? Was he learning it at his club?

And then, apparently, it could not wait. The girl was to come right away. Lady Easton was expected to launch her outside of the London season. At Brighton, of all places. It had all been arranged between Baron Dunn, her lord, and the Regent.

The Prince Regent! Why was he involved? Lord Easton had not really answered that either but had mumbled something about a gentleman's word.

Her lord had been so bold as to notify her that he'd already rented Marlborough House on the Steyne, as it was in such convenient proximity to the Marine Pavilion.

Who on earth wished to be in convenient proximity to the Marine Pavilion?

As she explained it all to her friends, their expressions could not have been more irritating. And possibly alarming.

Sad headshaking from Lady Heathway, wide eyes from Lady Redfield, knit brows from Lady Featherstone, and a slow tapping of an index finger on a teacup from the duchess. Only Lady Mendleton seemed unconcerned, as that lady was far too taken up with her own affairs to care if anybody's hair had just burst into flames.

"Clara," the duchess said gravely, "this is most irregular. How does one launch a girl at Brighton? A girl may be *out* in any neighborhood, but one can hardly call it a launch. When it is locally done it is usually because the girl will inevitably marry a neighbor or the parents don't have the funds. How does Brighton fit into either of those ideas?"

Lady Easton did not yet have an answer for that. She doubted she ever would.

"Bath might be suitable. Though I think it a poor substitute, especially these days," Lady Heathway said. "But Brighton…well with the Regent and his friends carousing it is all rather…"

"But you might be quite the innovator, Clara," Lady Redfield said helpfully. "I do believe you might be the first to have done it."

"Can you not simply keep her under wraps there and then bring her to London once the season begins?" Lady Featherstone asked.

"That is precisely what I suggested to my lord," Clara said. "But he says it would be nigh impossible to keep her under wraps as she's not the sort who would stay under wraps. What can that mean?"

Nobody answered that query.

Lady Easton lapsed into handwringing, a habit that only surfaced when she was entirely beside herself.

"Now Clara," the duchess said, "I cannot envision precisely what you will face under these extraordinary circumstances. However, we must all pull together! Mrs. Belle must be contracted at once! She is the only one who will do for seaside attire. Turn it all over to her, you will have no time to mull over fabrics or design—send the measurements and think no more about it. Now, I will be in Brighton in August. Just like every other year, the Regent will send for my duke. Cecilia? What do you do?"

Lady Redfield said, "Oh, I will take the boys there to our cottage. They do so enjoy it and there are five of them and it can be so difficult for them to all agree on something that when they do agree, I cannot see how to get round it. I really do wish I could sell the house and get something in Ramsgate, or perhaps Eastbourne, but my dear baron did love his summers in Brighton."

"He is dead, though, Cecilia," Lady Heathway pointed out and not for the first time.

"Yes, but he did love it when he lived," Lady Redfield murmured.

"And you, Anne? What are your plans?" the duchess said imperiously.

"Oh yes, we will be there until the shooting," Lady Featherstone said. "You know how Lord Featherstone likes the bathing for his health, even if it grows rather cold. He finds it bracing. But I really do not see—"

"Penelope?" the duchess went on with her interrogation, not seeming to care what Lady Featherstone could not see. "Penelope, you must find a way to drag yourself away from Barlow Hall."

"Well—"

Lady Heathway had attempted to use a *well* as a *but*. Fortunately, the duchess was prepared to run over any buts, wells, howevers, or maybes. "You must do it, Penelope. Just as we pulled together for Miss Yardley, we will pull together for Miss Upton. My house is at your disposal."

"My dear duchess," Lady Mendleton said. "I believe you are

not fully comprehending our new situations in life. Penelope and I have daughters-in-law now and that, of course, must take most of our attention."

The duchess stared at Lady Mendleton. "Louisa, have you entirely lost your wits? What you two ladies have on your hands are newly-wedded couples. They have no more use for you than if you handed a bald man a comb. Furthermore, our society of sponsoring ladies is faced with an unexpected challenge. We must meet it head-on!"

Lady Easton nodded encouragingly. She did not know what the ladies could do for her in particular, but she had a vague sense that she would require reinforcements in regard to Miss Upton.

CHAPTER ONE

CAROLINE UPTON, ELDEST daughter of Baron Dunn, had been called to her father's study. While she did not know the precise reason for it, she could make an educated guess. He wished to relive the glorious races that had recently concluded. She had been there with him, and it *had* been glorious.

They had just returned from Doncaster last evening and there had been a wild celebration in the stables over their victories. Even the hands who had not gone on the trip had been mad with glee. The estate ran on horses—her father bred and sold horses, advised on horses, and raced horses. There was a little farming done, mostly just to keep them in vegetables for the table. There were of course cows to produce an endless supply of milk for the seemingly endless supply of children in the house, but horses were Dunn Hall's lifeblood.

Over the past week, the baron had won very big indeed. Likely enough to keep them going for a year.

Caroline made her way through the front hall, stepping over wooden soldiers, stuffed rabbits, hoops, and skipping ropes, all left behind by children who'd gone on to the next thing. She swerved around a carriage with the most recent arrival gurgling in it, and she presumed somebody was planning to wheel him out into the sunshine. At least, she hoped so, as she could not imagine why else he'd been left there. The constant detritus of nine children, and the children themselves, overflowed the house and was always a reminder of how necessary her father's wins were.

Nine souls were in existence already and nobody was certain there might not be a tenth coming along. Lady Dunn was always blooming, and what she was blooming with were babies.

Caroline slipped into her father's study, the only room in the house that did not contain mountains of evidence of children and their necessities.

Baron Dunn was a tall and good-looking man, fit as those who are physical in their work tended to be. He had a manly energy about him that made him popular with all sorts—he could just as easily talk to a hand in the stable or a butcher in the village as he could the Prince Regent and his friends.

"You must be in fine spirits today, Papa," Caroline said, throwing herself onto the leather sofa that sat underneath the windows that lined the study.

"Very fine indeed," the baron said, "much was accomplished this past week."

"Money in one's pocket must always be comfortable, and what a lot you did take from Lord Easton and the Regent," Caroline said, examining one of her father's snuff boxes and wondering if she dared use it while he was looking. She thought not.

"It was not only money I took from them," the baron said, looking pleased with himself. "I have made arrangements."

"Oh, Papa, you did not allow either of them to pay over time? It is always a problem, especially with the Regent. How does one dun a Prince? Nobody has yet to figure it out."

"They have paid me about half of what they owe, but it seems they are both for their own reasons in some straits at the moment. Easton has made some ruinous bets recently. And Prinny, well, he and Mrs. Fitzherbert have been on the outs but he thinks he can rekindle things by way of improvements to her house and a rather costly necklace. In any case, those two gentlemen have made up the difference in payment with something far more valuable."

Caroline could not imagine what was more valuable than

pounds and pence since any item was valued by its worth in pounds and pence. Perhaps the only thing that could not be priced was an exceptional horse, but the baron had those while the Prince and Lord Easton did not. As far as she knew, neither of them had a stud that could equal any of their own.

"Lord and Lady Easton are going to bring you out in Brighton," the baron said. "Prinny will lend a hand and show his support, making it a sure bet that you will be invited everywhere."

"Papa," Caroline said, entirely confused, "I am already out. I've been out since I was fifteen. For that matter, was I ever really *in*?"

"Ah hah!" the baron said, pointing at her. "You've hit on the problem exactly. Nothing has been done proper. You know what goes on in this house, who has the time to do anything proper? So here we are and I have a grown daughter who regularly celebrates my horseracing wins with the stable hands. It will not do. I let things drift for too long, but it will not do at all."

"Is this about the gin last night?" Caroline asked. "I very sensibly only had two glasses—one for the win and one for luck."

"It's not about the gin, though perhaps when you go to Brighton keep it under wraps that you've ever tasted the stuff. It's not a lady's drink, after all."

"Of course it is not and you well know I'd prefer a Canary or something like it but they only ever have gin in the stables. It was a celebration and one must adapt to the milieu one finds oneself in."

"There, that's another thing," the baron said, nodding vigorously. "Your milieu should not include gin-drinking stable hands. I've been very remiss about that, I'm sure I have."

"You have been remiss about nothing," Caroline said soothingly. "There is no reason I must go to Brighton and leave you with the eight of your children that provide you no help whatsoever and are only good at getting under your feet."

"They are rascals, eh?" the baron said, smiling. "I fell flat on the floor last night thanks to James. He'd ranged his toy soldiers across the front hall to guard the house again."

"You see?" Caroline said, certain she could turn her father from this bizarre plan. "You need me here to keep everything in as good of an order as it can be kept. Mama is too busy forever blooming to do it."

"She is always blooming, is she not?" the baron asked. He was exceedingly fond of his wife and though the arrival of another baby was always somewhat alarming, it was also welcome.

Caroline sat back, satisfied that she'd convinced her dear father that he could not do without her.

He drummed his fingers on the desk. "No, I will not be turned from this idea," he said. "You must go to Brighton."

"But Lord Easton, Papa? He is a pleasant enough fellow," Caroline said, "but I cannot imagine he wishes me to haunt his halls. Why should he? He does not even have daughters of his own."

"Easton will have little to do with it, I imagine. It is Lady Easton that will manage the thing. She is a respectable lady and will guide you with an expert hand."

"Guide me?" Caroline said, the dread creeping into her voice. "You've met her, haven't you? She's a stick, isn't she?"

"I have not met her, but the lady's reputation precedes her. By all accounts, she is the stickiest of sticks," the baron said. "And *that* is why she'll do very well."

Caroline stared at her father. He seemed entirely set on the idea. When he became entirely set on an idea, it was very hard to move him off it. Good Lord, was she really to be forced to spend months being bossed about by a stick?

"Do not look so glum, Caro," her father said kindly. "At least I won't have to worry that you will suddenly announce you will marry one of the grooms. Go find a fine-looking fellow with good prospects."

Caroline considered the idea. Of course, she did wish to marry and she'd seen nobody in her neighborhood that was likely. She'd thought she might meet someone at one of her father's races but that had not happened either. Her father was too prone to being in the company of middle-aged and married men. He did not have much patience for young men, he said they were far too busy proving they already knew everything to ever learn anything. In any case, he rarely went to parties or dinners and when he did it was all men. Even if there had been some young buck to encounter, she would not have been invited.

Maybe she could meet some dashing fellow in Brighton. While she had no interest in having nine children when four would perfectly suffice, she was very interested in the mechanism by which her mother was always found to be blooming.

She nodded and said, "Very well, Papa. I will go and live with the stick for a while. I will even abide by her stickiest of stick rules. But I warn you now, I will not become a stick and I certainly will not *marry* a stick!"

⫸⫷

RICHARD CAMDEN, EARL of Bertridge, strode across the wide avenue of Portland Place to see his aunt. Lady Easton had sent a footman over to inquire if he was still in town and to request his presence if he was. She had caught him at the last moment, as he'd planned to close up the house and travel to his estate in Hertfordshire on the very next day. He had been communicating with his steward throughout the season and he had a long list of improvements in mind.

For all that, he did not mind a visit. His aunt was of a very like mind and they had always got on exceedingly well. He was the only child of Lord and Lady Bertridge, now deceased. They had been a capricious and erratic couple, the house in a constant state of uproar. They drank far too much and had burned half the house down on one wine-soaked evening. They gambled excessively, took unconscionable risks with their persons, and had somehow survived three separate riding accidents and the broken bones that came with them. Finally, they had drowned after taking out a sailing boat they did not know how to sail and having failed to have the minimum of safety equipment on board by way of life rings.

He had been eighteen when the tragedy occurred. He'd been not at all surprised by it as he'd been waiting for such news all his life. The first thing he'd thought when apprised of it was: *How like them. Of course that's how they died.*

Lady Easton had never set foot on a sailing boat and he could rest assured that if she ever did, there would be an abundance of life rings. His aunt had been his own life ring throughout his childhood. He'd often spent a month in summer in her steady presence and what letters he got at school were from her. She was the very reason he'd bought the house on Portland Place—he found it convenient to have the lady so nearby.

The footman had thrown open the doors ahead of him and he made his way to the drawing room on his own. It was practically a second home to him and he had no need of being announced.

"Ah, Richard," Lady Easton said warmly, "I was afraid you'd set off for Hertfordshire already."

"On the morrow, Aunt," he said, pecking her on the cheek.

Bramley brought in the tea and a coffee for Richard. The butler looked inquiringly at his mistress, she gave him a small shake of the head, and he retreated. He had been employed in that house so long that it was unnecessary to have a conversation on whether anything else was required.

The door shut behind him and Lady Easton said, "My dear nephew, I have something very inconvenient to request. I was hoping to turn you from going to Hertfordshire and instead accompany us to Brighton. At least for a few weeks."

"Brighton?" Richard asked. "Why on earth do you go there? The place is crawling with the Prince's rather unsavory friends and the rumors of their unsavory activities erupt every summer season."

Richard paused, thinking the matter through. "It is Uncle, is it not? He wishes to go, as he does get on with the Prince and Alvanley, he somehow finds them amusing. But surely you can overrule him on it?"

Lady Easton then laid out why she could not turn her husband from this very distasteful plan. Apparently, his uncle had decided to put his foot down. The man had never put his foot down. Richard had thought he did not even have a foot to put down, so agreeable he had always been.

If that were not surprising enough, the whole scheme involved the Society of Sponsoring Ladies. He had, at first, been entirely approving of the society. A lady without means *should* have help in finding her proper place in the world. However, he had since begun to wonder if it were quite the thing. This past season with Miss Yardley under Lady Heathway's wing had verged on the bizarre.

He had at least been in all confidence that his aunt would choose a lady a deal more wisely, but now it seemed Lord Easton had chosen the girl. He'd chosen the daughter of one of his horseracing cronies. The girl would come at once and they were to squire her about Brighton, of all places. Lady Easton was to have no say in the matter.

"This is all very alarming, Aunt," Richard said. "Why has Uncle begun to have ideas?"

"I would very much like to know," Lady Easton said, "though I can hardly ask as that would point out that he's never been encouraged to have ideas up to now. I would certainly like to understand which wretched person has put the thing into his head!"

"But why does the girl come now, why Brighton, why is the Prince involved?"

"I have not been told the answers to any of those questions, though I have asked them," Lady Easton said. In a softer voice, lest someone should overhear, she said, "I have the feeling this involves some sort of gambling debt. Your uncle is over a barrel, I believe."

Richard slowly closed his eyes and opened them again. Of all the stupid reasons... He really did not know why so many gentlemen were determined to risk bankrupting themselves to win a hand of cards, or watch their horse finish first, or engage in any of the ludicrous bets that went on in his club. Why did they bet more than they could easily lose? Were they deranged? Did they somehow think it would be easier to win money than simply take the steps to ensure their estates were profitable? Why did they not notice that they rarely came out ahead for long?

For himself, he'd seen his estate's profits rise year after year through good management. He'd rebuilt everything his parents had torn down by hiring experienced people, paying them fairly, constantly reassessing his assets, and making improvements. The house had finally been brought back to what it once was. It was back to what it was always meant to be.

Along with his fields of wheat and barley, his cows and sheep, and his tenant's rents, he was making a fortune on cheese these days, though he'd only begun that operation two years before. As well, a neighbor bordering his east fences had sold off and Richard had bought it, adding almost a third to the size of his current land, which had increased his income even more. The end result was he was as rich as Croesus without having to depend upon the vagaries of a gambling hell. He might choose to bet on a boxing match on occasion, but he was well prepared to say goodbye to the money if things did not go his way.

What gentleman preferred to spend sleepless nights thinking about a mortgage or what to do about a moneylender or contemplate flying to the continent? Or worse, how to tell an eldest son it was all up?

Habitual gamblers were bored men who had no care for the generations to come. They were bored because they did not read or attempt to educate themselves beyond what had been pounded into their heads at school, and they weren't interested in real work.

His friends sometimes called him a stick for not joining them in ridiculous bets, but then his friends sometimes called him for help when they got in too deep. Along with his help would come some stern counseling and warning. He was of the opinion that some of his circle would mature and survive their wasted youth, but inevitably some would marry a lady they did not love for her dowry or slink back to their ruined estates and live as paupers in a stately house.

And of course, worse outcomes were possible. There was, on occasion, that gentleman who rashly employed a pistol to the head as a final answer to the creditors knocking on the door. The last time he'd given a friend money to clear a debt, he'd done so because he'd feared that very solution.

His uncle had always taken care of his estates, how had he fallen to such a habit?

"Naturally," Lady Easton said, "I did suggest we delay the girl's arrival or at least keep her at home until the London season but that is not to be."

"Why ever not?" Richard asked.

"Apparently, it would not be easy to keep Miss Upton at home," Lady Easton said, raising her hands as if admitting defeat. "Do not even bother asking me what that means, I do not know. Though, I feel a sense of foreboding over it."

Richard felt a sense of foreboding too. What in the world was going on? None of it made sense. Though, he could see why his aunt called on him for reinforcements. Brighton would be a difficult place to navigate. The Prince, whose morals were on the decidedly shabby side, set the unfortunate tone. It was no place for a young lady who had little experience with the world.

"You were right to call on me," Richard said. "At a minimum, we must guard our family's name while in that town in such close proximity to the Prince. Though, Edgar must accompany me. I'm sure you will not mind it, he is well-behaved."

There was the smallest flicker of revolt on his aunt's features. She was tolerant of his bull mastiff, but she had never been one to have dogs in her own house. Finally, she nodded and said, "Of course he must come."

"Excellent. I'll write my steward how he is to carry on until I feel it is safe to depart and leave you to supervise Miss Upton on your own."

"I knew I could depend upon you, Richard," Lady Easton said, the relief on her features apparent. "The girl comes to me here on Wednesday and then we will proceed to Brighton on Thursday. Lord Easton will ride ahead and he, Bramley, and Mrs. Wooton will do whatever they can to ready the house. I propose we travel to Crawley and stay at *The George*, and then proceed onto Brighton."

Richard nodded. He had been to that hotel many times to attend various pugilistic matches. He enjoyed the sport and dabbled in it himself to keep himself fit. He had even, he thought, got rather good.

"As well," Lady Easton went on, "the ladies from the society will all come to Brighton at some point too. As reinforcements."

Richard frowned. "I cannot say how much help they will be. I would have counted on Lady Heathway, but we've seen what went on with Miss Yardley this season. And her butler for that matter—who ever thought to allow that nervous fellow anywhere near a fowling piece?"

Lady Easton sniffed in agreement.

"I suppose we can depend upon the duchess, at least," Richard said. "Her duke is a sensible fellow too."

"That's just what we need," Lady Easton said, "We must bring all of our sensible ideas to the case. I really do not see how we get through it any other way."

Richard slowly nodded. "Then count on me," he said.

After all, if Richard Camden, Earl of Bertridge, was anything at all, he was eminently sensible.

AUGUSTUS BRAMLEY PRIDED himself that he worked for such a family as Lord and Lady Easton. The lady wished the house to run like a clock, he wished the house to run like a clock, and so they set the clock together. Of course, his prior employment before coming to them twelve years ago had not been nearly as comfortable. A viscount and his lady had once employed him, but their habits were not to be borne.

There were no regular times set for anything. There were no set procedures. There was no regular place for things—a letter opener might be in the desk, or it might be on the windowsill. The footmen spent half their lives looking for things. There were all manner of upsets and changes of mind. Was breakfast at seven or eight or nine? They would dine in, until the last minute when they would go out. They went through housekeepers like they went through laundry. There were maids who left before he'd even committed their names to memory. The whole household, including its master and mistress, were flighty people and he was relieved when the viscount had bankrupted himself and could no longer afford to pay him.

He'd had the idea that he would be very careful in choosing his next position, and it *was* his purview to choose. He was an exemplary butler, perhaps the very best in England, and any family would be lucky to have him. He'd turned down two offers from two households who seemed rather unorganized and unsure of how they meant to go on. But then, he'd been examined, quizzed, questioned, and interrogated by Lady Easton.

She had a strict list of requirements. She had a schedule that was not to be toyed with. There was a place for everything and everything in its place. She had a set seasonal menu and set times for meals. Her housekeeper, Mrs. Wooton, had been there for ten years and was a steady sort of lady who brooked no nonsense from the maids. Her cook was a reliable Englishman who made reliable English food and did not go in for experimenting with unknown spices from the East, newly minted French concoctions, or stewed tomatoes. The cook, for reasons nobody understood, was entirely against stewed tomatoes.

Augustus, himself, did not have strong opinions on stewed tomatoes but he appreciated a fellow who knew his own mind on a thing and did not vacillate this way and that way. The lack of stewed tomatoes in the house was a small price to pay for such decisiveness and surety of purpose.

Lady Easton and her household were the antithesis of topsy-turvy and willy-nilly, therefore it was Lady Easton who had been chosen.

Things had gone on most satisfactory until now. Nothing was a surprise, nothing was unusual, and nothing was untoward. Year after year, he knew in what location they would be, on what day, and what they would be doing. His footmen understood what was expected of them and any fellow showing a hint of cheekiness was quickly shown the door. He knew Mrs. Wooton would sail through the house and keep the maids sailing in the same direction. He knew the cook would provide a roasted beef on Wednesdays and the leftover beef would go into a soup on Thursdays.

He was of course aware of The Society of Sponsoring Ladies and also aware that one season or another, Lady Easton would take the lead and sponsor a girl. He'd quite looked forward to it, secure in the knowledge that his mistress would choose a young lady who could seamlessly assimilate into the household and that young lady would be so expertly managed as to bring acclaim to the house. Lady Easton would show the other ladies of her circle how it was meant to be done.

Now though, Lord Easton had upset the apple cart. The *lord* had decided upon the girl and the *lord* had decided they were all to go to Brighton.

Brighton. A veritable den of iniquity, according to Lady Easton. They were to go to a house he had never set foot in and he was somehow to manage it all. What were the schedules? Lady Easton did not know. What were to be the entertainments? Who was the wine merchant? Who were the grocers? What was the at-home day? Lady Easton did not know.

They were both drowning in a sea of questions and they had not an answer to any of them. All because Lord Easton had suddenly decided to have an idea.

Mrs. Wooton turned out to be little help in this matter. That good lady kept assuring him that they'd *figure it out when they got there.*

Figure it out when they got there. It was like they were a traveling caravan of itinerants, happy to ride down unknown roads with not a care for where they ended up.

As the carriage rumbled ever nearer to their unwanted destination, Bramley glanced sideways at the master of the house. Lord Easton snored softly with his head resting against a pillow propped against the window, just as he always comported himself on long journeys. He did not seem materially changed by this unwelcome notion of having ideas and opinions.

As for Bramley, he found himself very against Lord Easton having original thoughts. If Cook felt a violence toward stewed tomatoes, he felt equally strong against Lord Easton's new way of going on in the world. It was highly inconvenient.

CAROLINE LISTENED TO the comforting clip-clop of horses' hooves as the carriage made its way to Portland Place. She had long since resigned herself to going to Lady Easton and was in fact now looking forward to it. She very well knew she was on the verge of being more hemmed in than she'd ever been in her life, as Lady Easton sounded like a bit of a dragon. Or as her father had said, "If there's a way to do a thing right, Lady Easton will know what it is and insist upon it." Still, she might meet some handsome devil along the way.

Caroline's mother was amenable to the idea of the trip, though she claimed the house would feel empty without her eldest there. Caroline thought she'd been fairly successful in convincing Lady Dunn that the house would not seem as empty as she feared, as there were eight other souls making the most possible noise at all hours of the day and night.

Once she'd had time to really consider her father's plan, she did begin to appreciate all its many advantages. She'd never been to the seaside, so that was thrilling. She'd traveled with her father often, and sometimes got a glimpse of the sea out of a carriage window, but she'd never walked along it.

Further, she supposed there would be single gentlemen falling out of the trees and that was lovely to think about. And, as much as she adored her father's horses, it might be nice to attend entertainments that were not in the stables. Of course, she had attended her share of local assemblies, but they were such a small neighborhood that they never had more than a dozen couples dancing. This would be a town of some size! There might be thirty or forty couples taking the floor at a ball. More, perhaps.

And then, it would be an adventure, would it not? It would be the first time she had gone anywhere without her father. She would have a chaperone, and a strict one, by way of Lady Easton, but that was not the same as a parent. It would be her first trip as a grown woman coming out from under the wings of her mother and father.

She had frowned while she considered what to pack, on account of her dresses being out of date. They generally were out of date until modifications could be made after perusing the periodicals. She and Lady Dunn's maid had freshened up her wardrobe as well as they could, a new ribbon here, and pinched-in bodice there, and it would have to do.

Now, as the sun set over London, the carriage turned onto the avenue of Portland Place. It made its way down the surprisingly wide street and stopped outside a very handsome town house of white stone.

She was helped out of the carriage and one footman had taken her trunk while another led her up the steps. Now that she was actually here, she did feel a bit of trepidation over meeting the woman who was to be in charge of her days and nights for the foreseeable future.

Caroline took a deep breath and followed him in.

CHAPTER TWO

CAROLINE WAS LED into an elegant drawing room and a middle-aged lady dressed impeccably and sporting a rather serious expression rose and said, "Miss Upton, I am Lady Easton. Forgive our disarray—my butler, Mr. Bramley, and my housekeeper, Mrs. Wooton, have already departed for Brighton."

Caroline curtsied and made it deeper than it need be. Those sorts of little courtesies would often soothe her own neighborhood's dragon, Lady Marie, and so she thought it might have a good effect on Lady Easton.

"You are very kind, my lady," Caroline said, "in agreeing to take me in."

"I will *sponsor* you," Lady Easton corrected. "Taking you in sounds too much like you were a street urchin in need of shelter."

Caroline nodded and suppressed a giggle. Her father had named Lady Easton the stickiest of sticks and that seemed not far wrong. Even her choice of phrase was to be corrected.

"Now, you must be tired by your journey and will wish to rest. I will take you to your room. Mrs. Belle will arrive in the next hour to take your measurements before dinner. An awkward moment for an appointment, I grant, but we have so little time to attend to anything. I have been informed by the duchess that Mrs. Belle is the only one who will do regarding seaside attire."

Caroline was rather pleased that she would get new clothes. She had not the faintest idea of what seaside attire might entail, but it seemed all confidence had been placed in a certain Mrs. Belle.

"We dine at eight o'clock. It is always eight o'clock, Miss Upton."

Caroline nodded and committed it to memory. A lady did not go so far as to inform one that dinner was *always eight o'clock* unless she had very strict ideas about time. It would be quite the change from her own house, as dinner very much depended upon when her father might manage to drag himself from the stables.

As they went up the stairs, Lady Easton said, "My nephew, Lord Bertridge, will join us for dinner. He will arrive at seven forty-five and we will convene in the drawing room. He's never late, as he lives not two houses down on the other side of the avenue. We do prefer Portland Place on account of the impressive width of the street, we do not feel hemmed in as so many others surely must feel. Lord Bertridge will accompany us to Brighton as well."

Caroline nodded at each new piece of information. She supposed Lord Bertridge would not dare be late, as Lady Easton would frown upon it. Her frowns were very frowny indeed. But it might be a lively dinner after all, especially if the lord turned out to be handsome and gay.

She would put on one of her best dresses just in case.

RICHARD ARRIVED AT his aunt's house at precisely seven forty-four. He greeted his aunt in the drawing room at precisely seven forty-five and they both looked expectantly toward the door for Miss Upton's arrival.

At seven forty-six, Richard said, "You did inform her that it was seven forty-five?"

Lady Easton nodded gravely. Richard did not think that the lady being late on the very first evening was at all promising.

At seven forty-seven, they heard a clatter upon the stairs. Miss Upton was running down them at full speed. Richard wondered if Lady Easton had ever before had somebody run down her stairs. It seemed unlikely.

Miss Upton tripped into the room; all smiles as if she was unaware that she was late.

Lady Easton glanced accusingly at the clock on the mantle and said, "Miss Upton, allow me to present my nephew, Lord Bertridge."

Richard bowed to her curtsy which he had to admit was prettily done by the lady. In truth, everything about Miss Upton was rather pretty. Her hair was the richest of browns with subtle tints of gold, done up in a simple style. Her eyes were large and dark and there was something very lively about them. Her smile was ready, and he got the impression that she was more prone to smiling than otherwise.

Miss Upton's dress was simple, and he was certain there had not been an exorbitant cost sunk into it, but it was rather charming in its simplicity—a plain white muslin with a blue ribbon round the waist.

Aside from her lateness, Miss Upton seemed every inch a lady and Richard began to believe that perhaps his aunt's fears were unfounded. She did not seem as if she would be difficult to manage and she was exceedingly pleasant to look at. Certainly, it would be no trouble at all to marry her off.

A footman entered the room and turned to the clock in a very formal fashion. "My lady," he intoned, "dinner will be served in precisely seven minutes."

Lady Easton nodded. She said to Caroline, "Usually, it would be Bramley's part to keep time but, as I mentioned, he's gone ahead to Brighton. Even though we find ourselves practically camping without a butler or housekeeper, we must keep to the regular schedules."

Miss Upton nodded, appearing in full agreement. Richard hoped she was and the two-minute delay in coming down to the drawing room had only been an aberration.

"Had you been to Town before, Miss Upton?" Richard asked.

"Never," the lady answered. "I've been by and around, but never in. When I have traveled with my father to his horseraces, we always seem to be going somewhere else."

"Your father took you to…horseraces?" Lady Easton asked.

"Oh, yes, Lady Easton, I've been to dozens of races," Miss Upton said.

"Did your mother escort you?" Lady Easton asked.

"Goodness, no," Miss Upton said, "she is always too busy blooming."

Richard could see instantly that his aunt and himself had the same questions on that front. Who took a young lady who was not even out and unescorted by her mother to such places? He was not even certain that Lady Easton understood the gravity of it. There were all sorts of people mixing at a race, there was far too much drink, and thieves ambling about, and not to mention the ladies of a certain low reputation looking for business. Had she been protected in a walled off area and accompanied by Lady Dunn it might have been acceptable, but he was beginning to think she'd been in the stables with the rough sorts who cared for the horses.

For that matter, what did she mean by her mama being busy blooming? He was afraid she meant with child, especially considering he'd been informed there were nine of them. But nobody mentioned such things…

"Why should the baron take you to such places?" Lady Easton asked.

"My father has always needed me by his side on such occasions."

"Why?" Lady Easton asked.

Miss Upton gave a little shrug. "I manage the packing and make sure he eats, and I get him some medicine if his head hurts after a night of drinking."

Lady Easton seemed rather staggered by those ideas and

Richard was not less so. Medicine for when he drank too much? What sort of environments had this girl been exposed to? What sort of milieus had she mixed in?

Seeming to notice the confused looks on their faces, Miss Upton added, "Only when he drinks too much gin, of course. Brandy does not have the least effect on him."

"Gin?" Lady Easton said, her voice nearly dropped to a whisper.

"Well, you know how stable hands are," Miss Upton continued. "They mean to have one glass, but if there has been a win the celebration does tend to go on."

Only when he drinks gin. How did she know what sort of celebrations went on in a stable? Who were these people? They sounded like savages.

The footman reappeared and said gravely, "Dinner is now served, my lady."

⇶⇷

THAT EVENING BEFORE dinner, Caroline had found the modiste, Mrs. Belle, a revelation. According to the lady, all sorts of special considerations must be incorporated into a seaside wardrobe. In dresses for walking by the sea, one must sew small weights into the hem so that the sea breeze did not take hold of one's skirts, lift them up, and embarrass a lady.

Caroline took in this information with what she hoped was a suitably grave expression, though she thought it very sad information for a young gentleman hoping to glimpse a shapely calf.

Mrs. Belle's advice on footwear seemed a deal more useful. She had traced Caroline's foot and would have slippers made with a stiff and reinforced underside and a strap across the top, which would be more suitable for walking the stony beaches. She would also order half boots made of kid for walking the town or excursions to the countryside. Then, of course, there would be an array of slippers for evening entertainments.

Garments for bathing were another matter. Mrs. Belle would have a simple shift made up and it must be done very carefully. The smallest of weights would be judiciously sewn into the hem to keep the shift from billowing up in the sea, but not so heavy that it would weigh one down. The shoes for such an activity would be lightweight and double strapped so they did not slip off.

As for the materials to be used for her day dresses, white muslin appeared fresh and to good effect by the sea, but was also prone to getting dirty, so various cloaks and pelisses of sarsenet would be made. Parasols and reticules matching or compliment-ing the outerwear were de rigueur, and the colors blue and green were favored to pay homage to one's surroundings. The evening wear would be primarily light silks to better suit the heat of summer. Though, a pelisse of satin lined with batting would also be made, as there were occasions when the nights could be chilly.

Bonnets of all sorts were necessary, though a well-made straw bonnet was the staple of any seaside headwear collection.

A riding habit of light material suited to the heat would be made in a dark green with restrained braiding in the same color. Caroline was delighted to hear it as the one she'd brought with her was becoming rather threadbare.

It seemed she was to be properly turned out and she was *very* cheerful about it.

Caroline had been dressed for dinner by Lady Easton's maid and had sat by the window, gazing up and down Portland Place's outlandishly wide avenue. There had not been much to see, until a gentleman exited his house a few doors down and across the road and came striding toward Lady Easton's house.

Caroline was certain it must be Lady Easton's nephew, Lord Bertridge. He was tall, his shoulders very broad, and his hair was dark, black as night. His features were rather sculpted, though the expression on those handsome features seemed terribly serious.

She hoped he was not terribly serious, as he *was* terribly

handsome.

As she was considering his person, now disappeared under the house's portico, Lady Easton's maid Prudence flung the door open.

"Miss Upton!" she said, fluttering in like a bird landing on a branch. "It is seven forty-four!"

"Goodness, so it is," Caroline said. "Let me just make a few adjustments to my hair and I will go down."

As Caroline sat in front of the looking glass, Prudence paced behind her.

"Now it is seven forty-*five*," Prudence whispered.

"I see that," Caroline said, not entirely certain why Prudence was to keep time for her. Dinner was not until eight. She wet her finger and wrapped a stray strand round it to give it some curl. Of course, once she made that adjustment, there were other adjustments to be made.

"Seven forty-six," Prudence said. Though she had only announced the time, it sounded to Caroline as if she had said, "And now I die."

"Heavens, calm yourself, Prudence," Caroline said, rising. "I will go down this instant."

Prudence had staggered out of her way but had not seemed soothed by the information.

Caroline had run down the stairs, thinking what an odd house it was.

Of course, shortly after entering the drawing room, she'd comprehended why Prudence had seemed on the verge of a nervous collapse. Lady Easton had very decidedly looked at the clock. Apparently, it was not just dinner at exactly eight, it was the drawing room at exactly seven forty-five.

She did not fret over it long though, as she found Lord Bertridge even more handsome up close. His manner, too, was somehow fascinating. He came off proper and stiff, but there was something else underneath and she was convinced the stiffness was a façade. His shoulders were extremely broad, and she could see from the width of his sleeves that his arms were quite powerful, as if he regularly engaged in boxing or some other arduous sport. Those who engaged in that sort of close combat were always of a passionate nature, and yet here he stood as if he had never put a foot out of place. It was as if he'd put on a coat of respectability to hide a wild, beating heart and an ungovernable nature. It was very intriguing.

At least, she hoped his demeanor was a façade, as both he and Lady Easton had seemed shocked that she fetched her father medicine when he had a drink headache. They had not seemed less shocked when she had clarified it was only ever on account of gin.

Now, they had been led into a small dining room by the footman, who seemed at once stern and nervous.

"This is the family dining room, Miss Upton," Lady Easton said. "It is Wednesday, so we will be having a roasted beef, which we have every Wednesday. As you see, we require a breakfast room, a large dining room, and a small dining room in any house we occupy. It is just commonsense, to my mind, though God knows what we will find in Brighton. Probably just a room people eat in."

They were seated with Lady Easton at the head, Lord Bertridge at the lower end, and herself in the middle.

"Have you never been to the house in Brighton, then?" Caroline asked.

"We do not make it a habit to go to Brighton," Lady Easton said. "In fact, we have never set foot in it. Oh, we have friends who make it quite the habit, husbands and sons generally insisting upon it so they might bask in the royal light, tarnished as it may be. We are not so easily influenced."

"We prefer to retire to our respective estates at this time of year, Miss Upton," Lord Bertridge said. "I find it is necessary to make time for all those little adjustments and rectifications that are required. An estate cannot go on forever ignored if it is to be profitable."

Lord Bertridge did not stop there. The entire first course was taken up by the lord's planned adjustments and rectifications. Apparently, the cheese-making was going along splendidly and he planned to bring in even more cows than he had already to be able to increase the operation. He was even considering experimenting with sheep's milk.

As he waxed on about cheese, Caroline imagined him in a boxing ring. He would probably box with his shirt off. That was a regular feature of boxing, she thought.

The roast beef was duly delivered, as it *was* Wednesday, and the lord came to the end of his cheese musings.

"I suppose, Miss Upton, you will know all about my Society of Sponsoring Ladies?" Lady Easton asked.

"Indeed, I do not," Caroline said. She supposed it was some sort of charity and she'd soon find herself knitting gloves and scarves for children in unfortunate circumstances. She was perfectly amenable to the idea. Knitting was an excellent way to keep one's hands busy when there was nothing else to do and she had knitted no end of things for both her brothers and sisters and the local parish.

"Six highly placed ladies, my aunt being one of course, have stepped forward and banded together to assist those who, while qualified by their parentage, cannot afford a proper season."

Caroline had no notion of it, though she supposed that was how she'd landed here. Her father had heard of it and pushed her forward in partial payment of Lord Easton and the Regent's gambling debts.

"You see, Miss Upton," Lady Easton said, "the members of our society are all longstanding friends and we've all carried the same burden. None of us have daughters. So we thought it might be very pleasant to have a daughter for a season."

"My aunt is an excellent mother," Lord Bertridge said, nodding. "She is exceedingly steady."

Caroline imagined she was rather steady. What she wasn't though, was the warm embrace that was her own mother. Lady

Dunn was indulgent, perhaps overly so, and often distracted with one or another of her nine children, but one always knew one was highly approved of. Lady Easton was a different sort—colder, more distant, and seemingly obsessed by the minute hand of a clock.

"Of course," Caroline said, "I am ever so grateful for the courtesy, as are my mother and father."

She supposed she'd hit the right note, as both Lady Easton and her nephew nodded gravely.

The rest of the dinner was taken up with Lady Easton by turns fretting on the state of the as yet unknown house in Brighton and expressing all confidence in Bramley and Mrs. Wooton's abilities in sorting it all out.

There were some interesting pieces of information slipped in between these speculations. One, Lord Bertridge would stay in the house with them. Caroline was certain that living in close quarters would give her a glimpse of what lay underneath his stiff façade, and she was becoming more and more interested in discovering it. Two, Lord Bertridge would bring his dog, a bull mastiff named Edgar, and Caroline was highly approving of that. Her own house always had a dog running around. And three, she was to get her own lady's maid, though Lady Easton was not confident of the sort of quality of person they would discover in Brighton.

The dinner concluded with a rhubarb tart. Caroline was informed that Wednesday's dinner always ended with a fruit tart, the only change made was whatever fruit was most in season.

In the drawing room, she was sent to the pianoforte and asked to play. She had, for a moment, thought of a piece of music that was very lively. She was used to entertaining children and they were only entertained by liveliness. However, upon viewing Lady Easton and her nephew looking very staid in their chairs, she chose a series of quieter Irish airs.

After a half hour had passed, Lady Easton stood and said, "We ought to retire now. Miss Upton, breakfast is at seven and we depart at eight. Eight, sharp."

Caroline nodded, having the smallest feeling that her lateness of two minutes in arriving to the drawing room this night might haunt her forever.

IN HER BEDCHAMBER, Caroline waited for Prudence to come in after helping Lady Easton to undress. She was perfectly happy to wait, as she brought a candle to the windowsill and gazed out upon the darkened street, the lamplights making pools of yellow circles on the road. She had watched Lord Bertridge go into his house, and now he was back out again with his dog.

The dog was a beast of a creature, but he seemed well trained as he did not pull on his leash. Rather, he stayed very close by his master.

Caroline smiled. She could not hear what Lord Bertridge said, but she could very clearly see that he was talking to his dog.

It had always been her opinion that most gentlemen were rather simple creatures. They were as they showed they were, not having the guile to do anything else.

Now she was not quite as sure. Lord Bertridge seemed a different sort. There was some sort of mystery to him. It was interesting. Very interesting.

As Edgar sniffed at something fascinating he had discovered on the pavement, Lord Bertridge glanced up at the house.

Caroline waved to him, then suppressed her laughter as he promptly turned and marched back to his house, his dog nearly tripping him up by rushing against his leg.

RICHARD HAD BEEN walking Edgar, and telling him soothing things, as everybody knew the poor dog was terrified of the dark. He'd glanced up at his aunt's house, as he liked to confirm that all was in order, and there had been Miss Upton at her window.

What was she doing at the window?

And then, she'd waved. She'd positively waved.

What was he supposed to do? Wave back?

His aunt had been right to request his help. The lady spoke freely of the effects of gin, spent time at places where rough sorts congregated, and then, then, at dinner!

She'd seemed positively amused by his report on the production of cheeses on his estate. What was so amusing about cheese? She had looked...how had she looked? Well, she looked...rather pert. Perhaps even condescending. As if good cheese were some easy thing to accomplish, which he could assure her it was not!

But then, she was a bit of a conundrum. He could not claim everything she did was not quite right. She played beautifully and her table manners were highly refined.

And she was exceedingly pretty, which was both pleasant and a concern. She was marvelous to look at, but what sort of unwanted attention would that bring at Brighton? What difficulties would arise when gentlemen who were set free of the more formal rules of Town roamed the seaside?

Would she wave to those rogues as they passed by her window? What was he to do about it if she did?

He made a mental note to suggest to his aunt that Miss Upton be given a bedchamber that faced the garden, if there were a garden, so at least the threat of her waving to strangers would be removed.

Richard sighed as he sat down with a glass of brandy in his study. Edgar laid a sympathetic paw on his thigh. As he scratched the dog's ears, he concluded that this trip to Brighton would be full of pitfalls that would need careful stepping round.

It was the season when he should be quietly retiring to his estate and mulling over his papers, taking his horse out to tour the grounds, visiting tenants, and meticulously cleaning his guns for the hunting to come.

He enjoyed the London season and its general air of busyness, but it wore on him too. London could bring entertainments, but it could also bring aggravations and irritations.

Too many aggravations and irritations in one day would begin to knock on the box of his temper, which he had long kept under locks and chains. By the end of the season, he found it was entirely necessary to regroup in the quiet and orderliness of his estate. He liked looking at it in such good order and comparing it to the scenes of turmoil from his youth. It was much changed from what it had been.

Instead of going home, he was on his way to an ill-advised trip to the Prince's seaside playground.

He did not know how it would unfold. For now, he could only hope that when his aunt said they would depart at eight sharp, Miss Upton took that to be exactly eight sharp.

CHAPTER THREE

L ADY EASTON WAS somewhat mollified to find Miss Upton ready to leave the house a full fifteen minutes ahead of schedule. The girl had been to breakfast prompt at seven and had wasted no time getting herself organized. The morning had been calm and ordered, just as she preferred it.

She still could not account for Miss Upton's lateness the evening before. Was that not what clocks were for? Did they not have clocks all over the house so that nobody was at risk for tardiness?

And the things she said! Why on earth would a young lady ever have opportunity to know anything about gin, never mind what the remedies might be for imbibing too much of it?

Lady Easton was determined to forget about it, as Miss Upton had been early this morning and she did look very charming in her traveling cloak of dyed blue muslin embroidered with delicate little daisies. She suspected Miss Upton herself had sewn the daisies and it was artfully done. Further, it was not the girl's fault that her father had failed to take proper care. That would be Clara Godwin, Countess of Easton's, purview. And she *would* take proper care. She would expertly steer this ship through uncharted waters and dock it at whatever port she deemed preferable.

Richard had, of course, been precisely on time. He would ride his horse, as a gentleman always seemed so eager to do. At least, gentlemen would insist upon it until they reached that mysterious day in their life when they retreated into the comfort of a carriage forevermore.

As the carriage rumbled along, Miss Upton had been making herself very pleasant and Lady Easton found it did make the journey go faster to have a companion in the coach who was not her maid.

Over the hours, she began to grow fond of the girl. Lady Easton found that her manner was softened and she began to speak to Miss Upton as a motherly sort of person. At least, she supposed she did. One spoke to a son in a different manner so she could only make an educated guess. She might have asked Lady Mendleton and Lady Heathway how they went about it, had she been able to stand for their inevitable self-congratulations.

She pointed to a turning and said, "That is the road to Burstow, the site of many happy scenes of my youth, Miss Upton."

Miss Upton had peered down the road as they passed by it. She said, "Might you call me Caroline, Lady Easton?"

Clara was taken up short by the notion. It was very touching. Her boys never said anything touching.

"Caroline? Well, that is a pretty name, yes, it really is. Yes, I suppose I ought to use your given name, as we will be much together these coming months."

The girl had seemed pleased to hear it.

"And what may I call you?" Caroline asked.

"Lady Easton, of course," she said. She supposed that had been a joke of some sort and smiled at it. She was not particularly gifted at sensing jokes, but certainly that had been one. If Caroline were in the habit of gentle jests, she must be on the lookout for them.

Caroline had nodded. As she did so, Richard rode on ahead of the carriage. He had been behind for some time but had likely grown tired of riding through the dust thrown up by the carriage wheels. He was wonderfully straight-backed and handled his horse beautifully.

"May I ask," Caroline said, "what is Lord Bertridge's given

name? I would not presume to use it, of course, I am only curious."

"His name is Richard," Lady Easton said. "I do not suppose any nephew and aunt are closer than we are." She felt herself warming to the subject, as she always did when she spoke of her nephew. She did so wish her own boys would be more like him. They were both so wild and unruly and unpredictable. Richard was none of those things.

"We are very alike, Richard and I," Clara confided. "We see things very much eye to eye."

"He certainly seems to have been very well guided into his position as earl," Caroline said.

"But that is just it!" she said. "He hasn't been, he's raised himself to be the man he is today. His parents were silly and careless people, and I say that knowing one of them was my own sister. Richard never allowed himself to be affected by their very bad example."

Seeing Caroline watch the back of his horse disappear into the distance, Lady Easton said, "We have made firm plans between us regarding his future. I know as well as he what sort of wife will be wanted, and it just so happens that very lady will be launched next season."

"Indeed?" Caroline said. "Who is the lady? Is she one known to your family for a very long time?"

"Heavens, no," she said. "I've never laid eyes on the girl. She is the Duke of Clayton's daughter, she comes with a sizable dowry, and someone who knows the family describes her as both pretty *and* demure. Richard will want demure as a quality in a wife—he cannot abide chaos and upset."

"Goodness," Caroline said, "that does sound like a match."

Lady Easton patted the girl's hand. "A brilliant match. Now, Caroline, you are wondering about yourself, I am sure. Well, I cannot say we could shoot high as that or what we will find in Brighton. I will only say I will be rigorous in weeding out anybody who is not suitable."

The lady paused with another idea. "Though, perhaps I am mistaken about how high you can shoot, you are very pretty, after all, and many a gentleman has thrown sensibility to the four winds on account of a pretty face. A rich fellow need not even consider the size of the dowry. Perhaps you *will* make your own brilliant match. I should quite like that."

CAROLINE NODDED AS Lady Easton prattled on. She'd had no idea that bringing up Lord Bertridge would result in him being the topic of conversation for the rest of the journey. Whenever they hit upon something else, it somehow circled back to her nephew. It might have been very interesting if she'd been told of his real nature, but that was not to be. She had heard of the Earl of Clayton's daughter three times, even though all that was known of her was that she was pretty and demure.

Demure. It was a trap, she had always thought. It was meant to be a high compliment, but in order for a lady to garner such an accolade, she must forgo having opinions on anything. She must just sit in a corner with eyelashes fluttering and pretend to know nothing. It seemed a rather high price to pay for such a flimsy reward.

In any case, did anybody *really* like demure? She could not think so. Especially not the mysterious Lord Bertridge. She was certain he was not as proper as he seemed, nobody could be. Therefore, he had put on a mask. Nobody who hid their real nature, which was bound to be very wild if it needed hiding, could ever be satisfied with demure.

She suspected poor Lady Easton was fooling herself. It would not be the first time a matron was set on ill-conceived matchmaking. Lady Marie was often in the habit of it, making various pronouncements about who ought to marry who. She had never been right, but that did not seem to put her off it.

Perhaps it was only a matronly sport, and the fun was in the planning, not the result.

"Now," Lady Easton said, "here we come to the hotel. We stay at *The George*. My nephew is well-known there."

"Oh, lovely," Caroline said, "it is one of my favorite places."

"You have been here?" Lady Easton asked, her brows furrowing together.

As Caroline nodded, Lady Easton said softly, "I had forgot. With your father, I suppose."

The carriage pulled into the yard and Caroline opened the window and peered out. Lord Bertridge was already off his horse and handing it over to a groom. There were faces everywhere that she recognized.

"Hello, Jimmy," she called to the groom leading Lord Bertridge's horse toward the stables.

"Miss Upton!" the groom said, tipping his cap. "Do we see the baron coming through, nobody told me."

"He is at home, celebrating his recent wins," Caroline called.

"I heard! We all heard!"

Lady Easton laid a hand on Caroline's arm and pulled her back from the window.

"My dear, it is not…to be shouting out a window to a groom…"

The lady did not have opportunity to say more as her door was opened and she was helped down. Caroline handed a hatbox out ahead of her and got down herself.

Caroline supposed Lady Easton took exception to her friendliness with the groom. She generally was on speaking terms with everybody at *The George*, as she had been often there and her father did not like to stand on ceremony.

She smiled at the fellow handing her down, though she did not recognize him and she presumed he must be new. He was a very tall and thin fellow and he led them to Lord Bertridge, who stood at the doors.

As they went inside, the proprietor hurried toward them.

"My lord, my lady, miss…oh, it's you, Caroline!"

"Hello, Harry," Caroline said. "How are you?"

"Very well, very well indeed. Of course, we've all heard of your father's success, we are thrilled for him. May I know your friends?"

"Mr. Johnson, may I present Lady Easton, and her nephew, Lord Bertridge."

"Ah, Lord Bertridge, yes, of course, welcome back to the hotel. And Lady Easton, it is a pleasure! I have your reservations in hand, only I did not realize you traveled with our dear Caroline."

Lady Easton, looking rather icy, said, "Mr. Johnson. May we be taken to a private dining room for refreshment and then to our rooms?"

Caroline watched with interest as poor Harry began to take Lady Easton's measure. As the proprietor of a hotel that often saw the high and the mighty coming through the doors, he was no fool. Baron Dunn might not like to stand on ceremony, but Lady Easton liked to stand on the highest rung of it.

"Of course, Lady Easton. Lord Bertridge, just this way."

They were led into what Caroline knew to be the best dining room. It was commodious and faced a pretty garden at the back of the hotel. She suspected that if Harry had not thought he made a slight misstep on his guests' arrival, they would not have been given it.

Lady Easton sized up the room and nodded her approval. After Harry closed the door behind him, Lord Bertridge said, "This must be a compliment, I think. Mr. Johnson always does hold this room back when he can in case a duke or the Regent comes through."

Johnny, the most experienced waiter, came in and Lady Easton ordered the usual things to be had at a hotel—a pot of tea, ale for her nephew, a tray of cold meats and cheeses, a salad of some sort, and a basket of rolls. The waiter was then further ordered to bring a good mustard, or no mustard at all, though

Lady Easton added that she would frown upon failing to see mustard.

Caroline thought Johnny left a bit shaken and was busy calculating precisely how good their mustard was and whether it would pass muster. She suppressed a smile as she imagined her father joking about such a thing. He'd say, "So tell me, Caro, did the mustard pass muster or was the lady in a fluster?"

Caroline attempted to make general conversation though both Lady Easton and Lord Bertridge were rather quiet. She commented on the size of the room and the flowers in the garden and the famed roasted beef always served at the place.

Other than Lady Easton mentioning that it was Thursday and they had roasted beef on Wednesdays, little was said.

Caroline was left to wonder what was always had on Thursdays, though she doubted she'd wonder for long.

⤞✦⤝

RICHARD FELT A feeling that seemed nearest to discombobulation, and he did not like it. Why did Miss Upton appear to be two things at once? When he'd arrived to his aunt's house in the morning she'd been right on time and dressed in a very charming embroidered cloak and straw bonnet. She'd greeted him smiling and seemed a most pleasant lady.

All along the road he caught fragments of his aunt and Miss Upton's conversation and they seemed to get on exceedingly well.

But then they had arrived at *The George*, and she'd leaned out the carriage window and greeted a groom as if she were a local milkmaid. And then her greeting from Mr. Johnson. The hotelier had to be reminded who *he* was but had recognized Miss Upton in an instant.

As if that were not enough, the hotelier had called Miss Upton Caroline and she had called him Harry. Not Mr. Johnson, but

Harry. He did not call Johnson by his given name. He'd been to the hotel on many occasions and had never been asked to call the fellow Harry. Nor did he think he would do it if he had been asked.

It was far too familiar for any lady, much less an unmarried lady of so few years.

Something must be done. The talk of gin the night before had not been the aberration he'd hoped it was. No, later that night, she'd waved out the window at him when he'd been on the street, and now she was on a first name basis with grooms and hoteliers.

He glanced at his aunt and could see in a moment that she thought the very same thing. Miss Upton must be reined in and taught how to proceed as a proper young lady. It would reflect badly on them both if they did not rectify the situation.

Richard could not entirely blame Miss Upton for her current bad habits. A young person was the result of their raising. Except for himself, of course, as he'd understood that his parents' way of going on was foolhardy and he'd been determined to rise above it.

He supposed Miss Upton was fond of her parents and that affection clouded her judgment.

Now, it had been left to him and his aunt to set her on the right course.

The waiter came in and fortunately, he brought with him a mustard. It was labeled *Mrs. Richmond's Own* and he'd had it before at the inn, Mrs. Richmond being a local lady rather known for her mustard. Richard believed his aunt would favor it. After setting the table, the waiter silently closed the door behind him.

"Now," Lady Easton said, "I believe we will have the privacy to talk freely. Miss Upton, Caroline, we really must discuss certain…modes you have adopted. And proceed to un-adopt them immediately."

Richard could see that Miss Upton, who his aunt had taken to calling Caroline, had not the least idea of what his aunt referred to. Lady Easton, however, was ready to gallop toward the breach. He would prepare himself to act as her second in command.

Miss Upton's modes must be corrected.

CAROLINE HAD BLESSEDLY crawled into bed. She had hoped she would have her own chamber, as she usually did when she stayed at *The George*, but that was not to be. Lady Easton's maid, Prudence, had since arrived in the second carriage and would share her room. At least it was not Lady Easton herself, as she'd heard quite enough from that person for one day.

Prudence had dragged her bedstead across the room so that it rested perpendicular against the door. She explained that if any thieves or kidnappers or murderers attempted a break-in, they would have to push her bed out of the way and surely the racket of it would wake her.

Caroline did not point out the door swung outward and so the thieves and murderers could very conveniently step over her. Nor did she ask what Prudence would do once woken, but she did not imagine it was anything more effective than screaming. For herself, she was not the least worried about a break-in. Harry Johnson employed several sharp-eyed fellows who kept things in order and there had never even been a theft in recent memory.

Finally, now that she was away from the doleful eyes of Lady Easton and Lord Bertridge, she could take a breath and think things over.

What had her father sent her into? The luncheon had been one scolding after the next. She must never mention gin. Though of course her father had advised the same, she'd only mentioned it to *them*, she'd not announced it to all and sundry at a ball. And then, it was not as if she'd admitted to having tasted the stuff herself.

Further, her father would never approve of failing to greet

the staff at *The George*. They were old friends! Harry had doted on her since she first arrived at the age of eight. He was very like a second father and her own father had not had one concern about leaving her at the hotel while he ran some errand, knowing she was under Harry's watchful eye.

As a young girl staying at *The George*, she might slip into the kitchens and have a confidential conversation over biscuits with the cook, or she might drift out to the stables and size up the horses, or she might sit in the common area and have a hot cocoa in front of the fire on a chilly afternoon. She had been as safe as a hatchling tucked away in its nest.

Lady Easton and Lord Bertridge did not know her history here. And, in any case, she came from a family that did not like to stand on ceremony and that was hardly a crime. In fact, she found it a far better habit than the standoffishness those two seemed to prefer.

When it appeared they must run out of criticisms they did not. Lord Bertridge apparently frowned upon her waving to him from her window the night before, and Lady Easton had fairly shuddered over the idea. Why? It was not as if he were a passing stranger!

As if the lecture at luncheon had not been sufficient, they went over the same ground at dinner. Was she a dunce that could not recall a conversation from only hours before?

She felt herself bristle at each new condemnation. Who did these people think they were? They downright implied that her father had not done right by her. They hinted that the kindest, most wonderful man alive had not done right by her.

Was it Baron Dunn's fault that these two were wound tighter than a pair of clocks?

Oh, how she had wished to say something about their habits with clocks! And their habits in general. When Lady Easton was not correcting her, she was explaining that on Tuesdays they had fish. The lady had originally thought Fridays might be fish day but had decided it might appear papist.

Why must there be any particular day for any particular type of dinner? Was it too hard to manage consulting with the housekeeper each morning to compose a menu, as Lady Dunn always did? Was nobody to have their favorite dinner on their birthday, as was the case at Dunn Hall? Was nothing new to ever be tried?

There was something small about how they went on. At Dunn Hall, hadn't they experimented with spices? The first try, a pepper soup, they found the cook had gone too far and everybody required copious amounts of milk to tamp down the flames in their mouths. They'd kept going, though, each new dish an adventure until they'd got it as they liked it—less cayenne and more ginger.

Hadn't they laughed when the ill-advised aubergine casserole came out so wretched? Did they not still talk about Cook's disastrous mushroom picking and thank the heavens they were all still alive? At Dunn Hall, there was life and adventure, fun and laughter.

She did not, of course, deliver any of the putdowns that occurred to her. Though there had been no end of things she had liked to say.

Now, and very loud, she said, "The two stickiest of the sticks!"

Prudence looked around the room and said, "What sticks, miss?"

"Oh never mind, Pru," Caroline said. "Everything will seem brighter in the morning. At least, that's what my father always says, and I am very sure he is right! He can quite be counted on to be right, thank you very much."

BRAMLEY DARTED ABOUT the house as if he were a bird searching for an open window. He'd barely slept, trying to get the house in order, but it was nigh impossible! For one thing, where were the clocks? How was anybody supposed to know the time without clocks? Were they supposed to run outside and try to judge by the angle of the sun? Perhaps they might invest in a sundial!

Of course, he had his own fob watch to depend on. It was an elegant, enameled piece given him as a Christmas gift from Lady Easton. It had come on a black silk ribbon but the very next year the good lady had given him a silver chain for it. That was all well and good, but he was very much in the habit of checking his watch against multiple clocks. He supposed he'd have to listen for church bells like a medieval serf.

And where was the third dining room? There was only a breakfast room and a large dining room for guests. Lady Easton insisted on a small family dining room and there were none to be had at this location. What had Lord Easton been thinking, to rent a house with no third dining room?

The footmen were at sixes and sevens as they hardly knew where to be or what to do with themselves. Mrs. Wooton was doing her best with the maids, but a whole new routine must be established and how were they to do it when there were no clocks to tell them where they ought to be at any given moment?

Then, outside the front doors was not the comfortingly wide avenue of Portland Place nor the quiet countryside of Glenborough Hall, but a large expanse of a public green with people wandering around it at all hours! In the distance, across from this irritating patch of grass, was the Marine Pavilion. A den of iniquity, Lady Easton had called it. He believed it too. He supposed Mrs. Fitzherbert haunted its halls like a scandalous phantom.

One might have thought, with all these hurdles to be cleared, that Lord Easton would be on the scene and directing the preparations. But no, now that the gentleman had decided to have thoughts, he was having quite a lot of them. One of them seemed to be that he ought to be out and about very constantly and coming back a little worse for drink.

What was wrong with the man? Did he not comprehend that his wife was about to descend upon the house while nothing was in order? After all their years of marriage, did he not know how little Lady Easton cared for disorder? *He* was only the butler and *he* knew it! In truth, he entirely agreed with it.

Jonathan, the junior footman, fairly flew into the drawing room where Bramley was just now circling and fretting.

"They are here," Jonathan said breathlessly, "Charles has just gone out to the carriage."

My God. They were here. The dreaded moment had arrived.

CHAPTER FOUR

B RAMLEY HURRIED TOWARD the front doors, which had been thrown open to receive Lady Easton to Brighton. The situation, as deplorable as it was, must be faced head-on.

Lady Easton sailed into the front hall, followed by the lady he presumed to be Miss Upton. Lord Bertridge soon followed after handing off his horse.

"Bramley," his mistress said, "how have you got on?"

Before he could compose a calm and reflective answer, he cried, "My lady, there are no clocks! Not one clock in the whole place!"

He had expected Lady Easton to be staggered by this news. He was rather surprised when she said, "Fear not, Bramley, I have packed six of our own."

The relief that washed over him was quite profound. How shortsighted of him not to have guessed it, Lady Easton would never leave such a vital matter to chance.

"Have we got a third dining room?" Lady Easton asked.

Bramley shook his head sadly.

"I was afraid of that and if I could have packed our own, I would have. We will be rustics here, I'm afraid."

Bramley nodded his agreement. It would be an exceedingly uncomfortable few months, full of new schedules and procedures and no third dining room. But at least they had clocks.

God bless the clocks.

➤➤➤➤◄◄◄◄

CAROLINE HAD DONE her level best to be civil to Lady Easton in the carriage. There were moments when it had been easy, and then moments when it had been difficult.

They'd had a lovely discussion about the wardrobe that Mrs. Belle would send along. Apparently, Lady Easton had demanded that each piece be delivered as it was completed, and Caroline could expect a divine ballgown and a walking dress coming in the next days.

Lady Easton had in particular rattled on about the ballgown, which did indeed sound divine.

"I said to Mrs. Belle, it should be inspired by the seaside. Well, she does have so many very good ideas. She suggested a silk in a soft cream color, with the palest blue tulle overlay dotted with small and delicate blue glass in the shape of sea stars. It will be very like the sea's blue water and white surf. It will be ethereal, and more charming than anything Penelope ever came up with. Oh, she embraces simplicity and abhors a puffed sleeve as if it is some badge of courage."

Lady Easton had talked enough about her friends for Caroline to know that the Penelope in question was Lady Heathway. Apparently, Lady Heathway had a lot of strong opinions that she shared widely. Among other things, she was against a puffed sleeve, downright vehement regarding a spencer jacket, and had a strange and almost violent abhorrence of white soup.

Lady Easton said there was an absurdity to it, as Lady Heathway did not seem to be against having a butler who randomly shot at her houseguests. Lady Easton, herself, would decry gunfire ahead of soup and sleeves.

While that conversation had been pleasant, there were those moments in the carriage that could not pass by too quickly. There was a revisiting of complaints about gin and waving out windows.

Caroline had used all of her restraint to manage the conversation. Though, she had slipped up once. After Lady Easton had mentioned that Lord Bertridge had suggested she have a bedchamber that did not face the street on account of her waving to him, she'd said, "I only waved because he was very determinedly looking at my window. I wonder he does not question where his eyes were going, rather than my response to it."

Lady Easton had been flustered by the notion. When she gathered herself, the result was a quarter of an hour lecture on how her nephew never put a foot out of place and so of course his eyes had not comprehended where they were going.

His eyes had not comprehended, indeed.

Caroline could at least take solace in the idea that she had thoroughly discomposed Lord Bertridge as they left the hotel. In truth, he still looked rather red in the face.

As Lady Easton had directed the boy who was arranging the trunks and hatboxes, Lord Bertridge had said, "Miss Upton, I do hope you have taken my and my aunt's counsel to heart."

It was one thing to be scolded by Lady Heathway and quite another to be scolded by a lord only a few years older than herself. It felt embarrassing in a way that a matron's scolding did not. She had really grown tired of it and had no intention of taking any of his *counsel to heart*.

She'd smiled sweetly and said, "My heart remains my own to manage, Bertie."

He'd then stared at her as if she were the devil in flesh as she was handed into the carriage.

Despite her irritation with both of them, she did not quite know what to make of Lord Bertridge. He could not possibly be as stiff as he pretended at. Perhaps he was a terrible rake and took extra care when in polite society? How better to do it than pretend at being the stickiest of the sticks? How better than to attempt to boss about other people in his vicinity regarding the correct way of going on?

She could not know all the facts, but she was determined to

find them out. She was also determined to let the man know that she was not taken in by his pretenses. She would force herself to put up with Lady Easton's vagaries, but she need not be so careful with the lady's nephew. Or *Bertie,* as she'd decided to call him. Her father had not handed her over to Bertie's care. Her father would likely take a dim view of how Bertie pretended at being so straight-backed. In fact, she was certain her father would pronounce the habit tedious.

They had arrived to Brighton and Caroline's mood began to lighten. It was a lively town, with jolly people coming and going and crossing streets and laughing. Mrs. Belle had been right, the ladies wore an awful lot of blue or green pelisses over fresh white muslin with complementing parasols and there were straw bonnets everywhere. Caroline could smell the salt in the air and there was something invigorating about it.

Seeing all the many people reminded her that though she had so far been cloistered with Lady Easton and her nephew, she would not always be. There would be parties and balls and excursions to the seaside. She supposed she might even actually go into the sea.

Caroline knew how to swim well enough. There was a lake on her father's estate, very deep in the middle. She had spent half her summers swimming and helping the younger children practice how to do it and her father had called her Lady Swim Fish. Baron Dunn taught all of his children how to swim at the earliest possible moment, as he had been rather haunted by the tale of a friend in Yorkshire losing a son to drowning. He had been vastly relieved that they'd all taken to it so far.

Their own lake, though, did not have waves but for the ripples kicked up by the wind, so it would be very interesting to swim while bobbing up and down in swells.

The house Lord Easton had rented was very elegant and fronted by a charming expanse of a green that seemed a popular promenade spot, which would be most convenient. From the front of the house she could see the roofs of the Marine Pavilion.

Caroline hid her amusement over Bramley's panic about the lack of clocks and then his gratitude over Lady Easton having saved the day by bringing her own clocks. It seemed this house was to go on as her other houses did and they would have beef on Wednesdays, gathering in the drawing room at precisely seven-forty-five.

"Now," Lady Easton said, "we will get settled and rest from our journey. Then, tea in the drawing room." She'd turned to Caroline and said, "We have tea at four o'clock."

Caroline had nodded, understanding that the lady meant four o'clock *sharp*.

"We will wish to have a quiet evening in, to recover from our journey," Lady Easton went on. "Bramley, do tell me that our usual Thursday dinner is on offer?"

Bramley had nodded gravely. "Chickens have been procured, my lady."

Lady Easton appeared vastly satisfied to hear that the chickens had been got, and Caroline wondered what she'd have done if they hadn't been. Goodness, they were at the seaside, they should be enjoying the sea's bounty at every opportunity. Instead, they would have chicken.

"Has my lord gone so far as to assign rooms?" Lady Easton asked her butler.

By the look on Bramley's face, Lord Easton had not gone so far as to do much of anything. He shook his head, seeming to be in a state of grief over the question.

"Then I shall do it," Lady Easton said, "Everyone, remain here while Bramley leads me up to view what I am left to deal with."

Lady Easton sailed up the staircase while Bramley jogged ahead of her.

"Well Bertie," Caroline said, "I suppose I am not to have a room with a pleasant view of the green on account of waving. Though your aunt insists you were only looking at my window because your eyes did not comprehend where they were going.

Do they often get away from you and act of their own accord?"

One of the footmen snorted at this salvo and quickly turned away and fussed with the trunks to hide his laughter.

Lord Bertridge huffed and said, "Miss Upton, this taunting way of going on is not to be borne!"

Caroline shrugged. Whether Bertie could bear it or not was his own affair. Though, she had to admit he looked rather handsome in his fury. Almost as if she'd got a glimpse of what was underneath his careful façade.

Lady Easton appeared at the top of the staircase. "It is all arranged." To the two footmen, she said, "Bramley will direct you with the trunks." She turned and said, "Caroline, come with me, Bramley will show Richard where he is to be."

Caroline picked up her skirts and flew up the stairs, leaving the huffing Lord Bertridge behind.

Much to her surprise, Lady Easton led her into a charming bedchamber that overlooked the green.

As Caroline peered out the window, the lady said, "Now I know we had that little dust-up about waving and Richard did advise a view to the garden but it is a very dreary view as you would mainly be staring at the house behind this one and I cannot like it for you."

Caroline was rather touched by that. "Thank you, my lady. I shan't wave to anybody."

Lady Easton patted her arm and said, "I know you won't, my dear. Now, Prudence will come in after she's settled me and unpack for you. There is a little shelf in the corner there and so you might pass the time with a book. I have reviewed them all and do not find any of them offensive or inappropriate for a young lady."

With that, she hurried to the corridor and closed the door behind her.

Caroline walked to the bookshelf and read through the titles. There certainly was not anything offensive, or anything interesting either. Most were dry tomes on military campaigns, there was a copy of Fordyce's sermons that did not appear to ever have been opened, and the most exciting book was one with pastel drawings of the flowers in the area.

She hopped to the window, that being a far more interesting pastime.

One of two young bucks strolling along the path round the green near the house glanced up. He nudged his friend, and then the two smiled and waved at her.

Caroline sighed and closed the curtains. They looked genial, but she could not very well start waving out the window before she'd been in the house an hour. Lady Easton was at least counting on her for *that*.

She amused herself by thumbing through the book on flowers and it was rather interesting. It seemed the seashore was a difficult master and only the hardiest of plants could survive the wind and the salt spray.

Prudence eventually came in and the first thing she did was place a small mantle clock above the fireplace. "Mr. Bramley has looked it over and pronounces it accurate," Prudence said meaningfully.

Caroline laughed and said, "Do not upset yourself, Pru. I fully intend on being in the drawing room with at least a minute to spare."

Prudence nodded and said softly, "You might even make it two minutes, just to be safe."

"Very well, two minutes," Caroline said agreeably.

Though the strict adherence to time by the minute had its irritations, it also had its amusing moments. On hearing her agree to two minutes, Prudence looked as if a physician had just told her she was not dying after all.

Goodness. What a household.

RICHARD HAD STORMED and stewed all afternoon. He'd even resorted to having a brandy, which had seemed to alarm Bramley to his core. There was no help for it, there were times when he was faced with so much aggravation that the temper he had so carefully boxed up in his youth threatened to make a reappearance. He'd had the urge to throttle Miss Upton, and so he must have a brandy to shore up the box.

And to stop thinking of *her*. She was positively daring! And rude. Who was she to make fun of what his eyes were doing? His eyes had not been doing anything at all but checking on his aunt's house. It had not been his fault that Miss Upton had been sitting at her window.

To try to suggest that he, that he had been what? A peeper? It was outrageous. She was outrageous. What had his aunt dragged him into? For that matter, how on earth was Lady Easton to control such a person? Miss Upton was glib, she flouted the rules. She did not even take rank seriously.

He was Lord Bertridge. The very idea that she would have the effrontery to call him Bertie—it was undignified and far too familiar.

And here they were, in Brighton, where there would be no end of opportunities to find trouble. Alvanley and his set were here, he was certain. Where the Regent went, they went. They were careless men, overly impressed by their own wit, as if wit were the highest accomplishment a man could strive for. They were all unrepentant flirts, which he found very distasteful. What good could be said of leading a lady on? Or worse, meddling with a gentleman's wife? When he determined he should pursue a lady, there would be no mistaking his purpose. It would be direct and proper.

Of course, he had not yet done any such thing. The Duke of Clayton's daughter was not out until next year. She was a far different sort than Miss Upton. She had been described as demure and wouldn't that be a nice change from what he had recently been subjected to.

If Miss Upton had been raised demure, what a lady she might be. She might have every respectable gentleman at her feet. Not himself, of course, as he was firmly set on the duke's daughter, but most everybody else. Who would not gravitate toward a lady who was demure and also the owner of a remarkably pretty head of rich-toned brown hair, large and dark eyes, and a ready smile? She was everything lovely, until she spoke. Then, the effect was quite ruined.

He briefly thought of telling his aunt of Miss Upton's latest outrage. But then he'd thrown over the idea. He ought to be able to control Miss Upton himself and if he were to tell the tale, it would appear as if he could not garner the necessary respect on his own. No, that would not do at all.

He had managed to mollify himself somewhat in the ensuing hours. The brandy certainly helped in that regard, but a welcome arrival helped even more. His man had turned up with his dog. His valet expertly managed the unpacking and ironing of his shirts, while Edgar engaged in an extremely enthusiastic reunion. Richard had often noticed that it did not seem to matter if they had been parted for five hours or five days, Edgar launched himself at his master as if he had been convinced they would never see one another again.

Kingston had brought Edgar's bed along, a wood box filled with layers of blankets, and set it up in the corner of the room. At home, Edgar would sleep on the ground floor, as he did like to get up and have a walk around the house to check on things, but knowing his aunt's lack of interest in dogs, it was better he stay confined.

He could not confine him always though, so Edgar had happily trotted at his feet as he made his way to the drawing room at precisely two minutes to four.

He was rather pleased to have Edgar by his side. The dog was notoriously fearful of strangers. Though Richard knew it to be fear, Edgar would appear to anybody else as if he were merely standoffish. Perhaps even disdainful. If he could not insult Miss

Upton himself, let Edgar turn his nose up at her.

To his surprise, Miss Upton was already in the drawing room.

To his further surprise, she had dropped to her knees upon seeing Edgar and said, "Come to me, you darling dog!"

Edgar trotted rather joyfully to the lady, threw himself on the ground and exposed his abdomen.

What was the dog doing? He was supposed to be insulting Miss Upton, not paying her the highest respect of showing his undercarriage! Was there nobody to count on anymore?

"You sweet thing," Caroline said, rubbing Edgar's belly. Whatever she thought of Bertie, his dog was a different matter altogether. He was wonderfully built—solid as a brick house. His coat was tawny and lighter on the underside and he had a very silly, drooly mouth.

Caroline, always living amongst dogs in her own house, was well aware that most reacted very well to enthusiasm and praise. Let them think you approved of them over all other living creatures and they would very much approve of *you*. Or as her father would say, *dogs adore those that love them and abhor those that don't.* Edgar was a beast of a dog, but his mind was no different from any other.

Bertie did not seem to appreciate his dog's current adoration and Caroline supposed he was one of those owners who preferred their dog to love only them. Or perhaps he did not like how undignified Edgar looked in his current position—on his back with his legs straight in the air, tail wagging back and forth like a runaway pendulum.

Lady Easton came in and took in the scene. From her gentle sigh, Caroline surmised she was not fond of dogs herself. And likely not fond of finding her charge on the floor with one.

Caroline bit her lip to keep from smiling. At least she had not been late.

Bramley brought in the tea at precisely four o'clock and Lady Easton said, "Caroline, do come and sit by me."

Caroline gave Edgar a last tummy pat and scrambled up from the floor, brushing the telltale dog hair from her skirts.

As they sat down, Caroline presumed they were to embark on a rather dreary tea, likely peppered with things she should not say or do. Perhaps Bertie would be disappointed to discover that she'd been given a bedchamber facing the street and might wave to anybody she liked.

However, before any of that could unfold, Lord Easton turned up.

"My dear," he said, coming into the room and lightly kissing his wife's cheek. "Miss Upton, charmed to meet you, though I've seen you from afar so often as you've been by your father's side. You do look well, the sea air must agree with you. Richard, how do you get on?"

Caroline had risen and curtsied, thinking he was a very genial gentleman. He might be a terrible gambler, but then she could not fault him for that as it had so often been to her father's advantage.

"Easton," Lady Easton said, "I have made various arrangements and you will find everything in order now. You will hardly notice we are not at home—it is Thursday and so we will have chicken as always. Bramley has seen to it."

As Lady Easton apprised her lord of her arrangements, Edgar slinked to Caroline's feet and looked up longingly until she scratched his ears. She was rather startled by Lord Easton's response to his lady.

"There will be no need for chicken tonight!" the lord said with an enthusiasm that did not seem warranted. It sounded rather like chicken was an unnecessary burden that had been happily shaken off.

Caroline was certain he'd been somewhere drinking something—he had that air about him that she recognized in her father's friends when they were not yet worse for it, just a bit more cheerful than was their usual habit.

"What can you mean, my lord," Lady Easton said, her brows coming together as if they had long searched for one another. "It is Thursday."

"Bah," Lord Easton said, "we are at Brighton, we cannot cling to the regular schedules here."

"Can we not?" Lady Easton asked, appearing entirely mystified.

Bramley had just entered the room with an extra tray of cakes. He appeared shocked to his shoes over hearing of schedules being thrown over.

Caroline looked back and forth between the parties with interest. Was the chicken really to go out the window? Or would Lady Easton restore order? It was very like watching a play unfold.

"Certainly, Uncle," Lord Bertridge said, "you cannot mind a chicken."

Lord Easton looked at his nephew quizzically. "I don't *mind* a chicken, we just have no need of one. The Regent is throwing a rout, and he positively insists we attend. I just saw him on the Steyne and he positively insists."

Both Lady Easton and Lord Bertridge shook their heads at this news. "A rout, Uncle?" Lord Bertridge said. "Surely, all of Brighton will squeeze in and nobody would ever notice we did not attend."

"Prinny will notice," Lord Easton said. "He wishes to be introduced to Miss Upton. He takes a particular interest in her future."

Though Caroline was aware that the Regent had gone in with Lord Easton on her launch due to the money owed her father, she had not thought he'd actually do anything.

"Why, though?" Lady Easton asked. "Why does the Prince Regent concern himself with Caroline's future?"

Lord Easton waved his hands as if wishing that question

away. "Gentlemen's talking and all that," he mumbled. "In any case," he said more loudly, "we go at nine. Have something to eat beforehand as you never can tell what will be on offer. Have the chicken if you like. Yes, there, you see? You can have the chicken after all."

With that, Lord Easton strolled out of the room.

"This is all most irregular," Lady Easton said.

Bramley cleared his throat and said, "My lady, if I may? Perhaps we could move the chicken from eight o'clock to seven o'clock."

Lady Easton slowly nodded. "I suppose so, though it will not be the same."

Bramley shook his head in sad agreement, while Caroline wondered if that meant she ought to reappear in the drawing room at six forty-five sharp.

"What has got into Uncle?" Lord Bertridge asked. "A rout? At the Pavilion? It will be an unpleasant crush of people, and so many of those people the Regent's friends."

Caroline could not guess why the Regent's friends were deemed unpleasant. Perhaps they were not stickiest of sticks enough for Bertie. If that were the case, she supposed she might like them.

"And why does the Regent involve himself in Caroline's launch?" Lady Easton mused. "Caroline, do you know anything about it? Did your father happen to say anything about the Prince?"

Caroline had easily surmised that Lord Easton had kept his lady very much in the dark about his bets, and the Regent's bets, and the fact that Mrs. Fitzherbert required improvements to her house and some expensive jewelry. She would be the last person to expose either of them.

She said, "I do not know any particulars, my lady."

Lady Easton appeared satisfied with the answer, as if it were the answer she had fully expected. "For that matter," she said, "I do not know Brighton at all, what does a launch here even entail?

I wish to do my best in the effort, but I feel very much at sixes and sevens."

Caroline felt some amount of sympathy for the lady. She was one who had so far lived her life on a strict timetable she could rely on and now she hardly knew what to do next.

"Perhaps, my lady," Caroline said, "things will become more clear at the rout. Perhaps the Regent will communicate some sort of reason for his involvement and some plan he might have?"

"A plan?" Lord Bertridge said derisively. "From the Prince?"

Lady Easton suddenly blinked. "I just thought, did you notice, that Easton called him Prinny? You do not suppose that he has become…an intimate of that circle? Could that be why he suddenly has ideas and opinions? Did *they* put the notion in his head?"

Both Lady Easton and Lord Bertridge appeared horrified by the idea.

Caroline concentrated on keeping the smile from her face and scratched Edgar's ears. She did not know if the Regent had encouraged Lord Easton to have opinions and ideas. She did not know if the Regent had any plan regarding her whatsoever. What she did know, though, was that she was going to a rout.

That was quite enough to know for now.

CHAPTER FIVE

RICHARD HAD RETIRED to dress for the blasted Regent's rout. A rout, of all things. It was the worst sort of party to take a lady like Miss Upton. She was at once bold and naïve to the ways of the world. A rout presented far too many ways to get into trouble far too easily.

What outrageous things he had viewed in routs past!

He had seen unmarried ladies slip off with some young buck and eventually come back again decidedly disheveled. He'd wait for the inevitable marriage announcement, it never came, and then the lady hurriedly married another.

He'd seen married ladies cavort with gentlemen who were not their husbands, the husbands often not even present! Behind draperies, in alcoves, exiting servant's closets, it seemed no location was off limits.

And that was just what he'd seen. There were the things he'd heard the following day but had not witnessed himself. Lord Mantinay discovering his wife in the arms of Mr. Bruster, which had resulted in a duel and Mr. Bruster's now permanently damaged arm and even more damaged reputation. Mr. Jacobs meddling with a female servant. Sir Michael attempting to lure a duke's daughter out of view of her mother. What else had gone on that nobody even knew about?

He would have to keep a close watch on Miss Upton. He would not allow her to sully his family's reputation. He did not think she would purposefully do something shocking, but he very much thought she was a lady ruled by her passions and might fall into something she would regret.

As Kingston worked on his neckcloth, Richard looked dolefully at Edgar. "And you," he said, "you have been a traitor of the highest order. One would think I don't feed you. I was very much counting on you to ignore Miss Upton, not to throw yourself at her like a long-lost friend."

Kingston, well-used to him talking to his dog, did not betray any surprise at hearing of Edgar's traitorous afternoon. As for Edgar himself, he only wagged his tail.

Kingston finished his cloth and brushed his coat one last time. Richard sighed and went to Edgar, patting him on the head. "Now, no barking while I'm out. Neighbors never like it and we don't even yet know who they are. Kingston, if you hear him, do come and get him and take him to the servants' hall until I return. I pray it will not be late."

As he jogged down the stairs, he met with some confusion in the great hall.

Lady Easton said, "But I do not understand why we must take two carriages when we can all fit in one very easily."

"The Regent wishes me to introduce Miss Upton," Lord Easton said. "He was very particular about it. I will take Miss Upton and then you and Richard can follow behind. It is not far, after all!"

Despite the explanation, Richard had not the faintest idea of why his uncle and Miss Upton should go separately. He wished to inform his uncle that it was not ideal. He needed to keep his eye on Miss Upton, not be separated in the crush, though he could not very well say so with the lady standing there.

As for Miss Upton herself, she was dressed neatly in a white muslin with a bright green ribbon at the waist, topped by a pelisse of pale green satin that he was sure was Lady Easton's. Miss Upton's hair was done beautifully, taken up and with soft curls allowed to frame her face. She really was wonderful looking, if only she could be persuaded not to speak.

"But Easton, this is all very irregular," Lady Easton said.

"Throw over your habits and schedules, my dear," Lord Easton said cheerfully. "We are in Brighton now." He held out his arm and said, "Miss Upton?"

Miss Upton took Lord Easton's arm and they sallied out to the first carriage.

Richard reached the last step of the stair and entered the hall. As his uncle and Miss Upton disappeared into the first carriage, he said, "What is going on?"

"I have not the faintest idea, Richard," Lady Easton said. "It seems nothing is as it should be and we are living in a topsy-turvy world. I feel quite off balance."

Richard agreed with that assessment. It felt as if the ground beneath his feet was not as solid as it had been.

"I really do not care for Brighton, Richard."

"Nor I, Aunt, nor I."

⊰⊱⊰⊱⊰⊱

CAROLINE HAD BEEN seated across from Lord Easton after their very odd departure from the house. She did not mind it, she only thought poor Lady Easton was entirely confused.

The carriage started up and the lord leaned forward confidentially. "Miss Upton, I wonder if it were possible, that is, I would not like my wife to be intimately acquainted with any wagers I may make…or have made in the not very distant past…"

The lord had trailed off, though Caroline understood him perfectly. She said, "You do not wish Lady Easton to know of the bet with my father. Or the Regent's bet, for that matter."

"Yes! Yes, that is it exactly," he said, looking vastly relieved that she had caught on so quickly.

"Of course, I will say nothing," Caroline assured him. "I have already been asked why the Regent should involve himself in my circumstances and claimed I know nothing about it."

"Excellent! You are a very good sort of girl. Of course, Dunn's daughter would be a good sort. But I say, there is my nephew too. I would not want him to be privy to any details."

Caroline could not repress a giggle, "Goodness no," she said, "Lord Bertridge seems a bit of a stick."

The lord roared with laughter. "Yes! That's it, that's what he is. I am fond of him, naturally, but a stick, yes, Lord Stick would be very disapproving."

Caroline nodded. "He has already been disapproving of *me*, I shan't allow you to be thrown into the mix."

"Has he? He can be like that, yes, he really can. I suppose it was some minor infraction he blew up to ridiculous proportions?"

"Exceedingly minor and extremely ridiculous," Caroline said, feeling the utter relief of talking to someone who viewed things as she did.

"Yes, I see how it was. I do tell him, from time to time, to loosen up a bit. But then, he had an unusual childhood—his parents were a couple of lunatics. I know it was very good of him to go in the opposite direction. But, sometimes one may go too far in the other direction."

This was the second time Lord Bertridge's parents had been mentioned and Caroline could not imagine what they'd been like. However, Lord Easton was right, one could course correct too much for their own good. Or don a mask too severe for one's own good. She still was not certain which one it was.

"Lord Stick, that is amusing," Lord Easton said. "Though, we'd better not repeat it outside of ourselves. It is so accurate that I'm afraid the moniker would become quite permanent."

"Lord Stick would *stick*, I think you mean to say."

"Hah! You have your father's wit, I see."

Caroline smiled and said, "I am in no danger of repeating Lord Stick, as I have got used to calling him Bertie."

"Not *to* him, did you?"

"Yes, directly to him."

"Oh, he must have been irate. Probably still fuming over it. Bertie, hah!"

"He really did earn it," Caroline said.

"I bet he did. I tell you what," Lord Easton said, "if we are to survive this summer at all pleasantly, we must be allies."

Caroline smiled. "Conspirators."

"Accomplices," the lord said.

"Abettors," Caroline added.

"Yes! All of those. Well, I must say I very much like this way of going on. I had quite given up on advertising my ideas and opinions, you know. The canaries did me in all those years ago. So now, when I decided to put forth some strong ideas, I wondered if the very roof might not fall down on my head. But then it didn't. I feel quite liberated."

Caroline had not the first idea of how canaries could do a person in, but she did not much care. "Count on me to act as your second in any matter but an actual duel, Lord Easton," Caroline said, happy to have a friend in the house.

Finding themselves of one mind, they pleasantly schemed all the way to the Regent's drive. Lord Easton said gleefully, "Those two will not know if they are coming or going! Now that I have opinions, they're coming at me hard and fast!"

Caroline was delighted with Lord Easton. Though Lady Easton was convinced that her lord had only recently developed ideas and opinions, it turned out he'd had them all along and just kept them under wraps.

The wraps, it seemed, had been entirely flung off.

RICHARD PEERED OUT the carriage window. His uncle's carriage had surged ahead, his own having had to give way to another coming round a corner.

It seemed every vehicle in Brighton was headed toward the

Marine Pavilion and a long line had formed on the drive.

"As I suspected," he said to his aunt, "it's going to be an annoying crush."

"I so dislike these things, in general," Lady Easton said. "It borders on the uncivilized, having to practically shout to be heard. A dinner is so much more pleasant, one can have a rational and extended conversation with another person, not these ships passing in the night."

If that was all his aunt thought happened at a rout, she had not attended many or had not had her eyes open when she had.

"I do not like to lose sight of Miss Upton," he said. "There are too many ways to go wrong at a rout. It is too unconstrained. What on earth was Uncle thinking?"

Lady Easton sighed, loud and long. "It appears, Richard, that your uncle has been harboring ideas and opinions for quite some time and now he's decided to spring them at me all at once. Worse, he seems to have not the slightest care for whether his ideas and opinions are correct. Which, of course, they aren't."

Richard shook his head. "He would be better off if he allowed you to guide him as you always have done."

"I never saw things coming to such a pass," Lady Easton said wistfully. "In the very beginning of our marriage, he did try to put his foot down here and there. However, my mother had warned me of the likelihood, so I was well-prepared. At such moments, I would lock myself in my bedchamber and weep. Loudly. His attempts eventually petered out and I really never thought to be revisited by the inconvenience."

Richard was a bit startled by this history. He'd had no idea that mothers might warn daughters about such things. It made him wonder what else they talked about.

"I do not believe Easton has tried to put his foot down since seventeen ninety-six," Lady Easton went on. "It was about the canaries. He swore he would go mad with their insipid singing all the time and he could not bear it. I cried and told him what he really could not bear was for anybody to be happy."

Richard stole a sidelong glance at his aunt. "But you've *always* had canaries."

"Yes. You see? That was that."

Richard declined to inquire any more into it. It was rather disturbing to understand that so much went on in a woman's mind.

As he peered out the window again to see where his father's carriage was in the long line ahead, he blinked.

"Good Lord," he said, "Alvanley and Pierrepoint are helping Miss Upton from the carriage, though they are not even at the head of the line. Did the Regent send them out to discover her? And there goes Uncle with them. They are laughing. Why are they laughing?"

"Those people are always laughing," Lady Easton said. "Though why your uncle and Caroline should join them in it, I am sure I do not know. But then, what do I know these days? My own husband has gone quite independent—I do not know what he'll think of next. I suppose he'll want roasted beef on Thursdays instead of Wednesdays."

Lady Easton sighed again and it sounded to Richard as if everything she knew to be true had been upended. He could not dwell on it though. Miss Upton had disappeared into the house.

It was going to be a long and arduous evening.

As THEY'D WAITED in the carriage, Lord Easton had told Caroline that the Regent was in talks with the famed John Nash to re-do Marine Pavilion and it was almost certain that in the coming years it would cease to be a house and be turned into a palace. An exotic palace, if Lord Easton's information could be relied upon. Apparently, the Prince was intent on onion domes on the roof like any maharajah's residence.

Lord Alvanley had announced himself at her carriage door as

being a special envoy from the regent. Or as the lord had amusingly put it—*to retrieve the recent for the Regent.*

Apparently, she was the recent. Lord Alvanley seemed to know Lord Easton very well and Caroline was happy to know him too. He was a comely gentleman not past twenty-five, seemed perennially smiling, and had a good-humored sparkle in his eye. What he was not, unlike some other person she'd recently become acquainted with, was a stick.

The jolly party made their way through the doors and Caroline gazed around her, catching glimpses of the room through the throngs of people milling about. Though the crowd blocked much of her view, she caught peeks of it. The building itself was of the neoclassical style, decorated on the exterior with cream glazed tiles. The interior was far different. The walls were covered in a bold red Chinese paper and what chairs she could see were black lacquer, the seats a robin's egg blue silk embroidered with gold thread.

Lord Pierrepoint was collared by some elderly lady who needed his opinion on the history of a painting on the wall. Lord Alvanley suppressed a smile and whispered, "The poor dowager, she's entirely besotted with Pierrepoint."

Caroline did not respond, though she found great mirth in the idea of a venerable old woman developing a youthful infatuation over a dashing gentleman. Mirth, but also the idea that perhaps feelings of romance never really died, even though society would like to think so.

Lord Alvanley expertly steered Caroline through the gathering, with Lord Easton on her other side.

"Just this way, Miss Upton," Lord Alvanley said.

He guided her to where the Prince held court, surrounded by people who wished to converse with him. Caroline had seen such things before—when a duke turned up to the races, men flew toward him like moths to a flame. The Prince's flame burned brighter than even a duke's, and so it seemed that all that stepped into the pavilion wished to place themselves nearby.

"Make way—coming through with a looked-for delivery," Lord Alvanley said.

The crowd did make way, which surprised Caroline. She supposed Lord Alvanley's own flame must burn bright too.

"Ah, Alvanley," the Prince said cheerfully.

He was a large man with a distinct paunch. Though, Caroline thought, *paunch* might be a very kind description. Her father would say he appeared to have swallowed the world. His clothes were very fine and did an equally fine job of holding in the swallowed earth.

"Miss Upton," Lord Alvanley said, "I present you to His Royal Highness, the Prince Regent."

Caroline curtsied as low as she could possibly manage without falling over.

"Charming," the Prince said. He looked around at the sea of faces who leaned toward him and said, "Is she not charming?"

There were various nods and affirmations, as if they were all in agreement regarding Miss Upton's charms.

Caroline, herself, only smiled and hoped she did not blush under such scrutiny. She was not at all in the habit of that feminine art, but there were times her cheeks got away from her despite her best efforts.

"Easton," the Prince said, "you bring to us a lovely addition to our party."

Lord Easton bowed and said, "It is my pleasure to escort Miss Upton this evening, Your Royal Highness."

"Everyone?" The Prince said, peering around, "Miss Upton is lovely, is she not?"

Again, the crowd was in full agreement with the Prince.

"Your Royal Highness," Lord Alvanley said, "might I suggest I take Miss Upton around to meet your friends?"

"Excellent notion, Alvanley," the Prince said. "Easton, let us discuss the private matter between us in the library."

Caroline was certain the matter between the two gentlemen was the lost bets to her father and sponsorship of herself as partial payment of the debt. Fortunately, she did not believe anybody else would know it.

With that, the prince set off with Lord Easton while Lord Alvanley held out his arm. Between introducing her to this person and that and letting all know the prince had named her charming and lovely, Lord Alvanley amused her with his comments.

"I thought to get you away once the deed was done," the lord said. "One tends to stay in the Prince's good graces by not *overstaying*."

"The deed being to publicly wrest a few compliments on my person, I presume?"

"Precisely," Lord Alvanley said. "Now that all of Brighton has been told what to think, Miss Upton will be invited everywhere."

"He was very kind to do it," Caroline said.

"I have been wondering, of course, why he was so set on it. Do not mistake me, you are everything charming and lovely, but he does not generally take such an interest in a young lady being introduced to society."

Caroline very well knew why the Regent took an interest but would hardly own it. Rather, she said, "It has been my experience that any man keen on horses is just as keen on my father. Perhaps the Prince does the baron a favor?"

"Ah, yes. How stupid of me to forget you are Baron Dunn's daughter. He is a talented fellow when it comes to horscflesh. And witty too. Rather pleasant to be around."

Caroline smiled. "And then, I did hear that he has a lovely and charming daughter, so that's something."

Lord Alvanley laughed. "I had thought, when I was sent on the errand to find you in the line of carriages, that I would come upon a blushing miss who could hardly account for how she got there. I am glad to be mistaken."

For some reason, his words stung just the smallest bit. It reminded her of the celebrated duke's daughter who was described as demure. She did not wish to be a blushing miss, or demure either. Why did people expect it?

The pinprick drove her to speak, as pinpricks often did.

"Lord Alvanley," she said, "if those ladies exist who are so unsteady that they have trouble understanding where they are and attempt to remedy the situation with pink cheeks, I can only celebrate that I am not one of them. It seems a tedious existence."

"Brava, Miss Upton," Lord Alvanley said, appearing surprised. He paused for a moment, then he said, "I am holding a small dinner on Tuesday, my dinners are generally held to be amusing as we always have a few wits at table, why don't you and Easton come?"

"I am not certain I could keep up with a wit," Caroline said.

"Oh, I think you'll do just fine, and as for Easton, he's a rather wonderful audience. After all, what would be the point of wit if there is not an appreciation of it? Easton's always been an enthusiastic appreciator."

"Then I must be too," Caroline said. "But tell me, when you say Easton must come, do you mean Lord Easton? Or Lady Easton?" Caroline said teasingly, though she knew perfectly well who he'd meant.

"Save me from peril," Lord Alvanley said laughing, "the *lord*, if you please. I'll send round an invitation."

As if mentioning the name of Lady Easton had called her from the spirit world, the lady herself popped in front of them. "Caroline, there you are, I have been searching the place for you. Have you been presented to the Prince yet? Lord Alvanley, how do you do?"

Lord Alvanley bowed and said, "Lady Easton, I have done the honors and the Prince names Miss Upton charming and lovely."

Lady Easton appeared remarkably pleased to hear it, as if the compliments had been given to herself. Caroline supposed that, as her sponsor, the lady was happy to take credit for anything gone well. She was not sorry for it, as a few things had not gone as well.

Lord Bertridge soon made his way into their circle. He

seemed to be perspiring, as if he had been running round the room, rather than walking.

"Alvanley," he said stiffly.

"Bertridge," Lord Alvanley replied. He smiled as he said it, and there was absolutely nothing wrong with the way he said it, but Caroline sensed that he was not over-fond of Lord Bertridge.

"Miss Upton," Lord Bertridge said, "do allow me to introduce you to some people you ought to know."

Caroline was not particularly inclined to leave Lord Alvanley's company, as he was so amusing and lively, but she did not see how she could say no. Lord Bertridge held out his arm and she reluctantly took it.

As they moved off, she heard Lord Alvanley say, "The people one *ought* to know are invariably a chore."

She suppressed her laughter and pretended she did not hear it. She could not imagine what Lady Easton would think of such a comment. Bertie, however, was disinclined to ignore it.

"Alvanley always finds himself so amusing," Lord Bertridge said sullenly.

"I did think he was, actually," Caroline said, not being able to resist defending her new acquaintance.

"Oh yes, he can turn a phrase, but that is hardly what makes a man. I only say, Miss Upton, that I find his set rather, well they are rather…rather…"

Caroline nodded sagely. "It is always so important to know if a gentleman is a *rather*."

Lord Bertridge ignored that comment and instead introduced her to Lord and Lady Carruthers, a middle-aged couple who seemed as empty of mirth as Lord Bertridge himself. Fortunately, their conversation did not last long, especially since it centered on some new accounting method the lord was finding impossible to understand, though his steward had explained it three times.

Out of the corner of her eye, Caroline spotted Lord Alvanley pointing her out to his friends and it was not a moment before young bucks on acquaintance terms with Lord Bertridge came one after the next, looking for an introduction.

And so the evening went on. One moment Bertie was introducing her to another sticky person she ought to know, the next she was smiling at a lively gentleman. It was a virtual dance of the boring then amusing, staid then fun, dull then bright.

Caroline could not be unhappy with it, though. It was more amusement than she'd had since accompanying her father to Doncaster and she had met so very many new people.

CHAPTER SIX

RICHARD ARRIVED DOWNSTAIRS early for breakfast and Edgar quietly settled himself under the table to be on the lookout for anything dropped. It was one of Edgar's favorite activities, as he seemed to enjoy the mystery and suspense of waiting to discover what might come raining down from the sky. He supposed he'd encouraged the habit, as he could not bear for Edgar to end disappointed and always did drop something in the meat variety toward the end of the meal.

The rout had been everything Richard had thought it would be, and perhaps a little worse. Why should the Regent pronounce Miss Upton lovely and charming? The Prince did not even know the lady and, if he did, he might revise the charming part of it. Lovely and *alarming* would be better suited for accuracy.

Why was Alvanley involved? Why should he go running to Miss Upton's carriage like a footman? The man was considered respectable, but that was mostly on account of him being an intimate of the Prince. Richard really did not see how respectability was conferred by being friends with that old heathen.

Of course, he would never say the Regent was a heathen aloud, but he was free to think it and certain he was right. He was also certain he was not alone in the opinion.

As the Prince had made public his approval of Miss Upton, they were bound to be swamped with invitations. At least that might take Miss Upton out of Alvanley's way part of the time—

there would be some who would leave that particular gentleman off their invitation list, as they did not like to be found the victim of his famed wit. It was bad enough to have to stand for it as he said one of his stupid bon mots, but then it would be endlessly repeated. Somehow, those who repeated the man's quips seemed to think they had made themselves as clever as Alvanley himself.

And then, there were so many other gentlemen pushing through the crowds to be introduced to Miss Upton. Some he knew, some he did not, some were friends of Alvanley's that he did not really care to know. Were any of them seriously looking for a wife though? That was the whole point of this absurd exercise. Get Miss Upton creditably married.

Alvanley certainly was not looking for a wife. He was an outrageous flirt and Richard suspected he would never marry until he came close to the threshold of becoming repugnant in his old age, which would be quite a few years yet. Richard could not approve of Alvanley as a suitable acquaintance for a girl just out in society.

She was just the type he'd flirt with though. Despite all her outrageousness, she was exceedingly pretty. And maybe even *because* of her outrageousness—it was just the sort of thing Alvanley would favor.

His uncle came in, looking hale and hearty, despite the fact that they'd not returned to the house before three.

"There you are, Richard," Lord Easton said. "I suppose you enjoyed last evening?"

Richard could not bring himself to prevaricate about it so only shrugged.

"Cheer up, old fellow," Lord Easton said, "I've heard of something that will interest you. The Prince is bringing in Gentleman Jackson for some sort of exhibition to raise funds for mothers and children in Brighton who find themselves less fortunate. I do not suppose the Regent has given those poor people much thought, but it seems Mrs. Fitzherbert has and he is determined to please her."

"I thought he'd had the decency to be done with that woman," Richard muttered.

"Oh, you know how those two go on—they're done and then they're not, and then they are. In any case, I said you'd be interested."

Despite his disapprobation of Mrs. Fitzherbert, he *was* rather interested. He'd only had the opportunity to train with Jackson once, a few years before, but he'd learned a lot in the session. Jackson went about things in a very scientific fashion, which suited him very well. There was a method to adopt, not luck to pray for—it was full of practicality and sense. Further, he favored boxing for its ability to burn off any temper that might be knocking on the sides of his box. At the moment, there was plenty of irritation that he might pummel out of himself.

"When will it take place?" Richard asked.

"Wednesday, next," Lord Easton said. "It is to be public and down on the beach. It will be quite a spectacle."

"Public? I really do not—"

Lord Easton waved his hands. "Yes, I know, you won't like it being public but it would hardly be an exhibition if it were not. As well, it is for a worthy cause and if that is not enough to spur you on, you'd curse yourself if you sat on the sidelines."

"I do not suppose the magistrate will approve the thing going on so publicly."

His uncle laughed and said, "I very much doubt Prinny asked, I suspect he told the magistrate that he can keep his thoughts to himself. Jackson arrives sometime today and trainings are to begin on the morrow."

His uncle was right, the Regent could do what he liked. Further, it was too big a chance to miss.

"The Prince has told me that all interested gentlemen are to turn up on the green behind Saint Nicholas church at eleven in the morning to begin the training. That location is private enough so you will only be in the public's eye at the exhibition. On the day, I'll be your bottle man and Kingston can be your knee man.

I'd be your knee man myself but let us be realistic—if you actually sat on me, we'd collapse to the ground in a heap."

Richard ignored that embarrassing picture. Of course he would go. He could not like the public aspect, but four days training with Gentleman Jackson was a chance not coming round twice.

Miss Upton tripped into the room, looking as if she had not been out until the early hours of the morning. Richard supposed she was one of those creatures for whom sleep was a hobby, but not a necessity.

She brightly said good morning and took a plate from the sideboard. As she approached the table, she glanced underneath it.

"I see Edgar has joined us," she said. Richard watched her as she went back to the sideboard and added extra pieces of bacon to her plate.

He well knew what she was doing. She was planning on cementing her friendship with his dog by way of a rasher. Unfortunately, he was also certain the strategy would work all too well. Whatever Edgar's standards were, he threw them over for any sort of meat.

Bramley brought in the morning post and handed it to Lord Easton. He flipped through the letters and then stopped at one.

"Ah hah!" he said, tearing it open. "Alvanley writes, and he's wasted no time about it. Not even franked, he must have sent a servant to drop it off."

"That's probably about the dinner party," Miss Upton said.

"What dinner party?" Richard asked, as his uncle read the sheet of paper.

"At the rout last evening, he mentioned that he wished to extend an invitation to dinner," Miss Upton said.

"Did he?" Richard said, drumming his fingers on the table. Why would Alvanley think Lord Bertridge and his family would deign to attend one of his juvenile parties? Richard had never been invited to one, but he had heard of them and firmly decided if he ever *did* get an invitation, he would decline. It seemed the time had finally come.

"Oh I see," Lord Easton said. "It is to be a very small affair and he's only got room for two more."

"I hardly think my aunt will wish to accompany you," Richard said, a bit singed that he was not included though he had firmly vowed to decline.

"No, no," Lord Easton said, "he thinks of myself and Caroline."

"What?" Richard said, dumbfounded.

"Yes, it says right here, the charming and lovely Miss Upton and her escort Lord Easton. Well, you know, he does say he's only got room for two."

"Who has only room for two?" Lady Easton said, coming into the breakfast room.

"Alvanley," Richard said, practically spitting the name out. "He's having a dinner."

"I am afraid I am not *at all* interested," Lady Easton said haughtily.

"Excellent," Lord Easton said, "that solves all difficulties then. He wants myself and Caroline."

"What?" Lady Easton asked. "Why, that is…" She turned to her nephew and said, "Richard, do help me out."

"Dashed strange, is what I think," Richard said.

"Yes, strange. And not at all…what we would wish. After all, Alvanley…" Lady Easton trailed off.

Richard had no intention of trailing off. "See here, Uncle, it's all well and good for *you* to associate with the Regent's crowd, but I hardly think it's the thing for an innocent young lady who knows little of the world."

Miss Upton appeared to bristle at the idea that she knew little of the world. She might bristle all she liked but it was perfectly true. It was ever the case with those who could not conceive that there was more to know than what they had so far seen.

"I cannot imagine what sort of dangers would lurk at a dinner," Miss Upton said. "Does Lord Alvanley keep crocodiles under the table, or perhaps dose a dish with arsenic and we'll have to guess which it one is?"

Lord Easton snorted. "Hah! That's funny, it really is, oh the picture I get from it. Everybody's feet up to avoid the crocodiles and hoping somebody else finds the arsenic first!"

Richard and his aunt both stared at Lord Easton. Who was this person? Who were they both?

"Uncle, you know perfectly well what I mean," Richard said. "It's a forward sort of set. Too forward."

"Yes, that is it exactly. He skates the line of respectability and I am certain he will cross it one of these days," Lady Easton said. She'd sunk into her chair and nodded to Bramley to bring her tea. "In any case, Easton, why should you be escorting Caroline anywhere?"

"Why should I not?" Lord Easton asked. "She is our guest and the daughter of a great friend of mine."

This was the first Richard had heard of his uncle being *great* friends with Baron Dunn.

"I only say that it should be me escorting Caroline," Lady Easton said.

"And it would have been, my dear," Lord Easton said, "had you been invited."

Richard was certain the world had gone mad. Bramley went to the door where one of the footmen was waiting for him. They conferred together and then Bramley returned to the table.

"My lady," he said, "the agency sends word that the candidates for Miss Upton's lady's maid will arrive beginning at eleven o'clock."

Lady Easton pressed her hand across her forehead as if she had a headache.

Miss Upton said, "Lady Easton, I may do the interviewing if you like. You do seem tired."

"No, no, if I am not to accompany you to dinner, the least I can do is see to your maid. I have very particular ideas about what is required from a lady's maid."

Lady Easton looked at the opposite wall, seeming as if her thoughts were far away. She suddenly jerked forward. "Something touched my foot," she cried. "Is there a dog under my table?"

Before Lord Bertridge could account for Edgar, Miss Upton said, "Do not fret over it, Lady Easton, I have taken extra bacon and will fortuitously drop it and Edgar shall stay by my side for the rest of the morning."

Lady Easton considered this plan and murmured, "Bramley, do fetch me a willow bark tea. And add some laudanum to it. I feel a terrible headache coming on."

CAROLINE FELT A ripple of guilt that Lord Alvanley had not invited the entire household to dine. But then, she really did not think either Lady Easton or Lord Bertridge would have had a very good time.

As for herself, she was planning to have an excellent time.

Despite Lady Easton's headache, or perhaps because of the salubrious effects of the willow bark and laudanum, the lady was able to carry on with the interviews for Caroline's lady's maid.

Caroline did not know what, particularly, the lady looked for, but she suspected it was something very buttoned up and somebody willing to come to Lady Easton if she noted the least thing out of line.

A woman of twenty-two years, native to Brighton, was finally hired that afternoon. Her name was Bemmy Smith, which Lady Easton had at first thought too unusual a given name to put up with. She was mollified, however, in discovering that the maid's real name was Jenny but her younger brother never could pronounce it as a child and had called her Bemmy. The name had stuck. Lady Easton, being an eldest sibling herself, had been very sympathetic to the idea. And then, on further conversation, Lady Easton was convinced that Bemmy had just the right attitudes about things.

Conveniently, the maid was eager to start that very day and so Lady Easton had led her to Caroline's room and made the introductions, then had left them alone to get started on whatever needed doing.

As soon as the door closed, Bemmy hooked her thumb toward it and said, "She's a bit of a dragon, ain't she? She wants you guarded close and careful. I spun her a marvelous story 'bout my strict habits. One thing I know is to give a person what they are outright telling you they want to hear. So I did."

"Then," Caroline said slowly, "do you say you are *not* strict, after all?"

"How should I know?" Bemmy said. "I've never been a lady's maid. We'll just see how I go on. I never did think of myself as a strict sort of person, but then who can say? The feeling might steal over me as I settle in."

"But Bemmy," Caroline said, thoroughly confused, "if you've never been a lady's maid, why did the agency send you?"

"What agency?" Bemmy asked.

"Mrs. Brown's Employment Agency," Caroline said. "They sent all the other women."

"So that's where they came from," Bemmy said, nodding and looking for all the world as if a great mystery had been solved.

"Yes," Caroline said, "that is where they came from. If you did not come from the agency, where did *you* come from?"

"It was like this—I was lounging round the Steyne and I noted them women comin' and goin' from the house and I finally asked one what she was doing. She told me all about it, thinking she had the lead on the hiring. As she rattled on, I started thinking that acting a maid to a lady sounded pleasant so I knocked on the door and told that stern fella who opened it that I was arrived for the position. He never did blink over it."

Caroline attempted to parse what Bemmy was saying. She'd

never been a lady's maid and had been wandering around the park and noticed the women coming and going, and then had…just strolled in.

"Your lady was fascinated to hear 'bout the time I stopped a certain young miss from an unfortunate elopement, draggin' her back into the house with my own two hands," Bemmy said. "She liked that one terribly good."

"But, there really was no young miss or unfortunate elopement?"

Bemmy shrugged. "There probably was one sometime and somewhere, though *I* wasn't there for it. Oh, and I told her of another young miss caught mooning over a groom and how I slammed the door shut on that flirtation. She nodded ever so approvingly over that story."

Caroline heaved with laughter. The situation was absurd. Oh, how her father would be amused by it.

She took a deep breath and said, "I cannot imagine what Lady Easton will say when she discovers you were not sent by the agency."

"Why should she discover it?" Bemmy asked, looking truly confused.

"Well," Caroline said, "for one thing, Lady Easton will tell the agency who she hired when she sends over the fee."

Bemmy snorted. "Don't you worry 'bout that," she said. "I know Lacy Brown well enough, that old fishwife. I'll send one of my brothers over to see her and apprise her of the situation. She'll take her fee and lips buttoned."

"I see," Caroline said, delighted with the maid's ingenuity. "Now, Bemmy, if you are going to pass yourself off as an experienced lady's maid, we have quite a bit of work to do."

Bemmy nodded enthusiastically. "I don't mind hard work and I pick things up quick. Just tell me how I'm to handle that sour-face downstairs in the hall and we'll be right as raindrops."

"That is Mr. Bramley," Caroline said. "Perhaps, until you acquire more experience, say as little as possible. That would probably go for everybody except for me, for now."

Bemmy pointed at her head with her index finger, which Caroline supposed signified she was committing the advice to memory.

After an hour of discussion, Caroline thought they might actually carry off the ruse. It turned out that Bemmy was the eldest of a large family and an expert at sewing and polishing and generally keeping her brothers and sisters well turned out. She was all confidence that she could do something with Caroline's hair, and if not, Caroline could manage that herself.

Of course, there were some new things that Bemmy had not thought of, such as sleeping in the servants' quarters and eating with the staff and waiting for a bell to be rung to know when she was wanted. However, she took it all in stride and claimed it would be an adventure.

Caroline could not say if Bemmy would have an adventure, but she was fairly certain she was in for one herself. For all that, though, she was rather delighted with Bemmy Smith of Brighton.

LADY EASTON HAD gone to lie down after taking Bemmy to Caroline. She had fretted a good deal about the possibility of finding just the sort of lady's maid she looked for in Brighton, but all fears had been laid to rest. Bemmy was of the dragon variety of maids and she was certain the woman would come to her if even a toe were to inch out of place.

Of course, that had not been her only worry. Caroline was so…spirited. And seeming to have a lack of understanding of rank and where she stood in it. Clara could still not quite get past the vision of Caroline at the inn, practically hanging out the window to call to a groom as if they were friends. Calling Mr. Johnson by his given name as if he were her family. Of finding her on the floor in the drawing room with that dog of her nephew's.

She supposed those sorts of bad habits took root when a girl was too influenced by her father. Especially a horseracing sort of father. The lady of the house must lead a daughter forward, not the gentleman.

Lady Easton sighed very softly and noticed she had taken to sighing quite a lot recently. There was her own gentleman to think about. What had happened to him? He'd gone from easily managed to all decisiveness. She might not mind giving way on matters of no importance, at least she imagined so though she had not tried it very often. But Easton was making decisions that were both important and wrong.

She'd been forced to bring Caroline to Brighton and somehow arrange a launch but she did not know how to do it. Her circle of acquaintance was not large here, there were so many who were of a different set. Was she to simply wait for invitations? She supposed they would come now the Prince had advertised his approval.

And this dinner at Alvanley's! That was no place for a girl on the marriage mart. What she sought for Caroline were eager young gentlemen seeking wives, not the self-satisfied so-called wits that haunted Alvanley's table. Then, she doubted her husband's ability to be a strict guardian, he was a little too jolly these days.

Clara sat up. She required reinforcements. Certainly, Lady Featherstone and Lady Redfield had arrived by now. She would send out a desperate call for assistance. She needed to keep Caroline going in the right direction and she needed to turn Easton from the new direction he'd taken. Her nephew was always a comfort to her and helpful when he could be, but these delicate matters required a female mind on the case.

CAROLINE HAD NOT minded that they stayed in the evening

before. They had been very late to the Prince's rout and she found herself tired by the end of the day. At least, they'd all stayed in aside from Lord Easton who announced he was off to a card party somewhere. Dinner had been quiet and had been chops on account of it being Friday. In the drawing room, she had played a little. It was very dull and Lord Bertridge seemed especially glum. She had been certain they would all be brighter in the morning.

She could not say whether Lord Bertridge had been brighter in the morning as he did not appear at breakfast and it was said he'd already gone out. Edgar had been left behind in his room but set up such a howling over it that the lord's valet had to let him out. Edgar had trotted straight to the breakfast room and happily settled himself under the table.

After breakfast, Caroline was full of energy and wishing to get out of the house. She called for Bemmy and they went to see Lady Easton in the drawing room.

"My lady," Caroline said, "I wondered if Bemmy could escort me on a walk. She is a native of the town and knows of a charming street with shops not so very far from here."

Lady Easton had seemed on the fence over the idea until Bemmy had said, "Mind, only the most reputable shops with proprietors well known to my family and eminently respectable. I wouldn't stand for anything less."

This had seemed to soothe Lady Easton a great deal and, in any case, she appeared to be entirely taken up with writing letters. They had tied on their bonnets and were out of the house in a trice.

As they made their way down the street, Bemmy said confidentially, "I did tell a bit of a story just now."

"Did you?" Caroline asked. "Do you say, then, that the shop-keepers are *not* respectable?"

"Oh, no, they're all right," Bemmy said, laughing. "Only, I don't think that's where you'll want to go. You see, I heard some fascinatin' things in the servants' quarters last night and one of them is that the Prince has brought Gentleman Jackson to town and all interested gentlemen are to meet him on the green at Saint Nicholas church for a practice and Lord Bertridge was one of the interested fellows."

"Goodness," Caroline said, though her thoughts were fuller than that single word. She had been convinced, the very first time she'd met Lord Bertridge, that he must engage in some violent sport. She was right, after all. Was he not so buttoned up as he seemed, then?

"I heard it is customary," Bemmy said, "that the fellows take their shirts off when they train. At least, that's what my brother says."

"That was my understanding too," Caroline said. She was not at all shocked by the idea. She'd seen enough stable hands shirtless. However, it would be quite another thing to see Lord Bertridge shirtless. For all his stiffness, he could not entirely hide his well-made physique under starched shirts and sober coats. She had perhaps noticed it more than she ought.

"And it so happens," Bemmy went on, "that I live hard by Saint Nicholas and I know how we can slip in and observe from the tower. I spent many a day runnin' round that place in my youth and my younger brothers and sisters still tiptoe in sometimes."

"That does sound more interesting than visiting shops," Caroline said. Of course, she knew perfectly well that Lady Easton would not approve. But on the other hand, visiting a church could hardly be criticized and if one were to by chance see anything interesting out a window that could not be called a crime. Nobody could be faulted for what they saw out a window. For that matter, one was not required to tediously recount what one may have viewed through any amount of windows in a day.

"What do you say?" Bemmy said. "It is not a quarter hour from here by foot."

Caroline smiled. "Very well. We will visit a church, which is very proper. If we happen to see anything surprising out of any windows, we can hardly be blamed for it."

Bemmy winked and they set off at a fast pace down the road.

CHAPTER SEVEN

BEMMY HAD BEEN right, at the pace they walked they came into view of Saint Nicholas church closer to ten minutes than fifteen. It was clearly very old and Bemmy said her father reckoned it had been there since the fourteenth century. All manner of things had tried to destroy the church, first the French some time in the fifteen hundreds, and then the great storm of 1703 took part of the roof and another storm in 1705 took the rest of it. For all the enemies trying to destroy the place, it always got rebuilt and she supposed it would be there always.

The tower that Bemmy had spoken of as their viewing point could not be missed—the shadow of its dark stone loomed over the green.

They strolled by the line of carriages, including the Prince's own, as if they had no interest at all over what might be occurring on the grounds. Just a lady and her maid, out for a walk.

"Now, we'll just slip round the back so as not to be observed," Bemmy said, taking her hand.

They skirted round the church and slipped into its quiet confines. Like all churches, it had its own particular atmosphere. It was far cooler than the out of doors and smelled of years of burned candles and generous amounts of linseed oil.

Bemmy led her through to the bell-ringing chamber and then up the stone steps to the top of the tower. There were two windows, side by side, and they dashed over to them.

A crowd of men gathered round an exceedingly tall gentle-man. Even from this distance Caroline noted his sloping forehead, exaggerated aquiline nose and ears that appeared to be pointing in two different directions. He was not a handsome man but a very well put together one, tall and broad-shouldered, and he seemed to have a presence that drew men to him. Caroline could not name what that presence was, exactly, but her father had it too.

None of the men were in their coats or waistcoats, having thrown them off to waiting grooms and footmen.

Caroline scanned the gentlemen—there was Lord Alvanley, and there his friend Lord Pierrepoint. A few of the gentlemen she did not know. The Regent had set himself on a sturdy chair to view the proceedings, a range of servants standing by to fetch him whatever was needed. And then, there was Lord Bertridge.

He too wore only a shirt and Caroline thought it suited him very well. His casual attire softened him, or hardened him, she could not tell which. It just made him…less a stick.

"Your Lord Bertridge holds up well amongst them," Bemmy said.

"He is not *my* Lord Bertridge, Bemmy," Caroline said.

"That's a right shame," Bemmy said. "He's a looker and a lord, what else could you be huntin' for?"

"For one thing," Caroline said in as scolding a tone as she could muster, "I am not *hunting* for anything."

"Ain't you?" Bemmy asked. "I thought that was what all proper ladies do. They hunt around for a husband."

"Well, of course, I will eventually marry…" Caroline said, trailing off.

"But he ain't good enough?" Bemmy asked.

Caroline looked down at Lord Bertridge, his hands on his hips and expression full of concentration. "He's a bit of a stick, you see. At least it seems so. I cannot make him out and I cannot like that I cannot make him out."

Bemmy snorted. "Now if he were *beatin'* you with that stick, I could understand your complaint."

Caroline had to admit that Lord Bertridge did not look very like a stick at the moment. "You know, Bemmy, I have held a suspicion that Lord Bertridge might be hiding his real nature under the façade of being a stick."

"Ah hah," Bemmy said, "and was you to find it out, then you might be interested after all."

"No, no, I do not say that," Caroline said hurriedly. "In any case, it would hardly matter what I thought. Lord Bertridge takes no interest in me whatsoever. If anything, I believe he rather disapproves of me."

Bemmy did not appear to understand that idea at all. "You are a pretty lady with a lord as a father. God in heaven, what do fancy people want out of life? The rest of us see somebody the right age and with a little coin in their pocket, look each other over, and say, fair enough, let's amble on to the church."

Caroline did not dwell on this alarming picture long, as Mr. Jackson had given the gentlemen some direction or other and they were moving off in pairs.

They seemed to be practicing stances and it was not very exciting. "I suppose there will not be much to see, after all," Caroline said.

"I don't know about that," Bemmy said. "It's a warm day already, noon is on its way, and there ain't a sea breeze stirring. I expect shirts off in the next half hour."

As it happened, Bemmy was right. Mr. Jackson put the men through their paces, and Caroline could see that their shirts began to cling to them from perspiring under the hot sun. Lord Alvanley struggled out his shirt first and the rest, seeing the Regent did not seem opposed, followed suit.

Despite the many shirtless gentlemen in her line of sight, Caroline could not take her eyes off Lord Bertridge. He was powerfully built and had seemed to throw off his very buttoned up persona. He was rather magnificent, a Greek God could not look more masculine.

"Are you sure you can't like him?" Bemmy asked, leaning a little further out the window. "I, myself, would ignore any little parts of his nature I found irritating and just think about what he looks like."

"Bemmy!" Caroline said. "I am sure you should not talk that way." Though she claimed she was sure, she also could not ignore that her own thoughts had been drifting in the same direction for a moment. Only a moment, though. And only because he was so very handsome.

Was Bemmy right? Could she ignore that he was a stick? Or could she hope that on further acquaintance he was not such a stick? Her idea that there might be a wilder version of Lord Bertridge had begun to waver over the days, mostly because of how often he seemed to disapprove of her *not* acting the stick.

Who was he really? Caroline sighed, thinking she might never know.

Lord Bertridge had paused in his practice. He shaded his eyes. And he looked at the tower. Then he leaned forward and squinted.

Caroline grabbed Bemmy's hand and pulled her away from the window. "He's seen us! Bemmy, he's seen us up here!

Bemmy fell into a fit of laughter over the idea.

"Stop laughing this instant!" Caroline whispered. "What should we do? How can we get away?"

Between heaves of laughter, Bemmy said, "We go out the way we came, he won't try to catch us, he don't even have his shirt on."

"Excellent," Caroline said. "Excellent idea."

"Then we'll go to a shop and buy a ribbon and claim we were never anywhere near this church."

"Yes," Caroline said, feeling as if she were grabbing a pole that would pull her out of icy water. "Let us hurry, we must be gone from this place."

This peeping out the tower window had seemed like such a lark when they'd done it unobserved. But to be seen!

And, to be seen by Lord Bertridge, who already looked down upon her way of going on.

Though, why should she care for his opinion and his approval?

She did not know, but somehow his opinion rankled.

Bemmy led Caroline down the stairs, her maid's quiet laughter echoing along the stone walls of the tower.

RICHARD SAT IN the tub that had been brought into his bedchamber and filled with icy water, soaking his sore muscles from the day's exercise. It had been a blasted hot afternoon and though the bath was a shock to the system it was also a relief.

He had gone back and forth over what he'd seen. Or thought he saw. In the middle of the boxing practice, he'd paused to catch his breath and glanced up at the church's tower. He'd sworn he'd seen Miss Upton and her maid at the window, at least, he was very sure he recognized her bonnet. But then the two heads disappeared from view in an instant and were not seen again. Over time, the notion began to seem farfetched. Was she there? Or had it been the heat?

Were it any other lady, he would have come down firmly on the side of his imagination, fueled by excessive heat and not enough to drink. But it was not any other lady. It was Miss Caroline Upton, for whom no thing could not be dared.

Viewing men shirtless! Viewing *him* shirtless!

Well, if it was her in that window, at least none of the other gentlemen had noted it. Particularly not his sparring partner, a cousin of Alvanley's. Mr. Landon proved to be just as glib as Alvanley himself, though with not much that was of substance to bolster his bravado. He was the second son of Baron Tisdale, but as he said, "My brother is unmarried and drives his phaeton far too fast, so you never know. Perhaps he'll kick off and then *I'm*

Lord Tisdale, dancin' through the daisies."

Though Richard had been convinced he'd indicated his distaste for the gentleman and his comments, Landon would persist. He had all sorts of questions about Miss Upton, none of which were answered.

It seemed Mr. Landon admired Miss Upton's father exceedingly and had heard from the Regent that his daughter was expected in town. Landon claimed to have a keen eye for horses and, in the event that his elder brother did not kill himself in his phaeton, he thought he might like to go into business with a gentleman like the baron. He then found the effrontery to wonder if Richard might arrange an introduction to Baron Dunn.

That idea was met with a cold stare.

Richard could not have obliged in any event, as he did not know the baron, but thought Baron Dunn would be ill-advised to join any venture with Mr. Landon.

Richard had never met a less likable fellow and would say a prayer that the eldest son stay alive long enough to have his own sons and cut that jackanapes out of the inheritance line all together. Let Mr. Landon commission in the navy, and then jump off a ship when he encountered deep and shark-filled waters.

He briefly wondered if he should tell his aunt that he'd thought he'd glimpsed Miss Upton at the church, but speedily ruled against it. What if he were wrong? Or what if she claimed she'd been only touring a local church and then been shocked at what she'd seen out the window. Then it would somehow be his fault for being out of doors without a shirt on.

She was so much trouble. He really did not know what was to be done about it. He supposed he should simply be grateful that his own future had been mapped out satisfactorily. The duke's daughter would be no trouble at all, as it was quite confirmed that she was demure. All he need do was meet her next season and set off on a course of wooing—calls, flowers with increasing meanings of affection, the proposal, the duke's blessing for the match, the wedding, and then some sort of trip to cap the whole thing off. He was certain it would unfold smoothly, with no unpleasantness associated with it.

Miss Upton would do well to take a page from that demure lady's book.

⤜⤛⤛×⤜⤛⤛

LADY FEATHERSTONE AND Lady Redfield hurried into Lady Easton's drawing room.

"We came as soon as we could," Lady Featherstone said, "we were only delayed in that Cecilia seems to be without a carriage at the moment, necessitating my trip clear across town to fetch her and bring her here."

Lady Redfield shrugged and said, "I have the carriage, but with so many sons, well, they are always off in different directions and I found myself without horses. I suppose they've lent out a few…"

Bramley, having anticipated the ladies' imminent arrival, led the footmen in with the tea service. He expertly laid the things and retreated, closing the door behind him.

"However you have got here," Lady Easton said, "I am grateful you *are* here."

"Clara," Lady Featherstone said, "your note did sound almost frantic."

"Or lively, one could call it," Lady Redfield said, always looking to soften the blow.

"Certainly," Lady Featherstone went on, "you have not been here long enough to encounter any serious difficulty. What has happened?"

Lady Easton poured the tea and said, "Easton, who you will remember has suddenly become insistent on having ideas, decided we must go to the Regent's rout."

"Oh dear, I do avoid them myself," Lady Featherstone said.

"My eldest is always keen to go, though he has yet to be

invited as he is not quite elder enough, even though he's the baron now," Lady Redfield said.

"The point is," Lady Easton said, hiding her irritation, "we were forced to go and the Regent pronounced Caroline charming and lovely. Now Alvanley has invited her and Easton to dinner. Only them, mind you! Not me! Apparently, there is only room for two more people. And then, it has come to my attention that Caroline does not fully understand how a young lady is meant to comport herself and even if she did, I do not have the first idea of how to launch her in this swamp. It is all most irregular and not at all what I planned. The only thing that has gone at all smoothly is the maid I hired for her. *She*, remarkably, is an absolute treasure."

"I see your problem, Clara," Lady Featherstone said.

"You bear it wonderfully well, though," Lady Redfield said, her tone all encouragement. "And, how lucky to find a treasure of a lady's maid. This is something, is it not?"

Clara ignored the encouragement. Cecilia would encourage an elephant to fly to the moon if she felt it had its heart set on it.

"Cecilia, Clara does not wish Miss Upton to be pulled into the Regent's set by way of Lord Alvanley," Lady Featherstone said.

"Yes, exactly," Lady Easton said. "What am I to do about it?"

"We all know the Prince rules in Brighton," Lady Featherstone said, "and that's about the only rule there is in this town."

"I do wish I could convince the boys that we ought to go to Ramsgate," Lady Redfield said wistfully, "but then my husband always did love it here."

Clara ignored Lady Redfield. After all, how many times could it be pointed out that the man was dead? Who cared now what he once loved? As for her boys' opinions, Cecilia had been better served to get in the habit of telling them what to think, rather than allowing them to willy-nilly come up with their own opinions.

Lady Featherstone said softly, "Your baron won't care about Brighton now, Cecilia."

Lady Redfield nodded and said, "I suppose it's a shame there is not another leading set she might be pulled into. Then you might just switch the sets."

Clara considered the idea. For once, Cecilia might have hit on something. "Perhaps that is the answer. We put together our own set. A set hallmarked by sedate dignity. There must be dozens of people who would delight in escaping the Prince's entertainments. Or at least, have a choice when one felt not quite up to royal high jinks. I am certain Richard will help us weed out the undesirables on the male front, and as for the female, well, we know what we're looking for."

"Should we put it about?" Lady Featherstone asked. "Let people we deem acceptable know that we put together a rival set."

"Certainly not," Lady Easton said. "We must not be seen to challenge or insult the Regent. It must be done subtly. We will simply have a dinner with all the right people. The thing will take off on its own and we need say nothing."

"It's very clever, Clara," Lady Featherstone said. "Surround Miss Upton with respectability."

"Yes, indeed," Lady Easton said. "She will meet someone suitable to marry and she will pick up those good habits she sees an example of. Yes, it will be quite the thing."

The ladies were enormously satisfied with the idea and went about making a list of the new set. Between them and what Lord Bertridge was able to add later, they pieced together a guest list of twenty exceedingly staid people known to be in Brighton. It was a very good start.

CAROLINE ADMIRED HER dress in the looking glass and Bemmy fussed with her hair. Mrs. Belle had promised Lady Easton that she would send dresses as they were completed and three had already arrived. The one she wore this night, a silk of the palest blue with a delicate white gauze overlay dotted with embroidered shells in silver thread, was everything denoting the seaside.

The past days had been rather thrilling. She and Bemmy had been given leave to walk everyday and had made it a habit to slip into St. Nicholas church and peer out the windows of the tower. Whatever small sense of guilt or uneasiness Caroline had experienced that first day had been soothed away by Bemmy's assurances. After all, it was just in good fun and they did nothing particularly scandalous. At least, not scandalous to a rational person.

Naturally, they were far more careful now and were not spotted by wandering eyes again. There had been one exciting day when the Prince's chair faced in their direction but, as he never did look up, they got through it wonderfully well. Lord Bertridge, on the other hand, did sometimes glance their way and it became a bit of a game to avoid being spotted.

The boxing practices had progressed to longer sparring matches where Mr. Jackson selected a pair of gentlemen and then gave them pointers as they worked. Both Lord Bertridge and Lord Alvanley held their own very well, though Caroline thought Lord Bertridge had a slight edge. Alvanley was athletic, but he had not the height or broadness of shoulder that Lord Bertridge had.

Caroline's feelings about Lord Bertridge were mixed and confused and jumbled up. He was both the physical man on the green and the buttoned-up gentleman to be found in the house. She could not make him out. She could not make herself out. She did notice, however uncomfortably, that she thought about him quite a lot. She thought about him boxing, and she thought about him talking to his dog.

She'd several times overheard him having a conversation with Edgar. It seemed the beloved dog could not do wrong, even when he was doing very wrong. There was something stirring about Edgar being so approved of by one so generally disapproving. It was as if anybody meeting with the lord's approval must somehow feel the distinction of it. It was also as if Lord Bertridge could drop his guard and make allowances for those he loved.

Caroline gave herself a little shake as Bemmy made the last arrangement to her hair—a lovely, enameled comb of sea green placed artfully among her curls. This evening was Lord Alvanley's dinner and she was determined to enjoy it. She was a little irritated with herself that she found herself wishing Lord Bertridge was to attend.

"Well," Bemmy said, stepping back to admire her work, "if this get-up don't slay the fellows, I don't know what will."

"I am not setting out to slay anybody," Caroline said.

"Right, right," Bemmy said. "Cause you ain't looking to get married. What was you planning? You weren't set on being a governess?"

"No, I am set on no such thing," Caroline said. "I will, of course, marry. When I meet the right gentleman."

Bemmy sighed. "The right one is under your nose and in this very house. As my ma says, a bird in the hand is worth two in the bush."

"Indeed," Caroline said, always finding Bemmy too amusing to scold her over her sauciness. "And who is *your* bird in hand, I wonder?"

"Ah, that be Jimmy Smithson. His pa has got a small farm and he'll take it over someday. All last summer we were walking out and come fall, I said, Jimmy, I'll have ya if you like. He said, alright Bemmy. It's all settled, we'll marry once his pa gets an extra room built on the house so we can live all comfortable-like."

"The whole procedure sounds very…efficient," Caroline said, delighted with the story.

"No muss and no fuss," Bemmy said. "A habit you fancy types might want to examine."

Though Caroline could only appreciate Bemmy's way of going on in the world, she could not quite imagine marching up to a gentleman at a ball and declaring, *I'll have ya if you like.*

"Now, I reckon Lady E has had some of the farm's cheese

stocked in the larder, as everybody knows it's quality—a blue but not too pungent as some are. I won't mind having a wheel of that in my house for everyday and Jimmy says I'm to learn all about cheesemaking."

Caroline giggled and said, "Perhaps Jimmy ought to consult with Lord Bertridge. On the night I arrived, he told me no end about his cheeses."

"Blast! There's a burned biscuit, look at the clock!" Bemmy cried. "You got about half a minute to be downstairs. Even if Lady E ain't goin' nowhere, she'll be put out if somebody who is goin' sets out late. She don't like late."

"No, she does not," Caroline said, hopping up from her chair.

CHAPTER EIGHT

B RAMLEY HAD GOT on as best he could in this wretched abode they found themselves in. Everything felt topsy-turvy, despite the comforting ticking of Lady Easton's clocks.

For one, the staff were not at all used to arranging bracing cold baths and now suddenly Lord Bertridge required one every day. Naturally, there would not be anything convenient like an icehouse on the grounds to cool the tepid water of summer, so he'd been forced to make inquiries throughout the town. He'd had encounters with no end of alarming people! They were all so familiar, as if they and he were on the same rung of the social ladder. He was butler of a great house, where was the respect and awe?

Lord Bertridge's boxing had seemed to have led to the bizarre habit of sitting in cold water. While Bramley must always look upon the sport as something noble, he could not approve of all these baths!

For another, Lord Easton had seemed to have lost his wits. They had gone on so regular for years and now suddenly he had become an entirely new individual. Why was he so jolly all the time? Why was he always coming and going and thinking everything a joke?

And especially why had he suddenly no regard for how they liked to go on? Just this very morning, Bramley had asked the lord if he preferred coffee or tea, knowing full well he would say coffee as he always did. The only reason Bramley had asked at all was that it was a courtesy—no self-respecting butler fell into the habit of presuming.

He asked, putting his hand on the coffee pot handle, and then Lord Easton had said, "Surprise me."

Surprise him. Indeed. Augustus Bramley had never surprised anyone in his life. Surprise was antithesis to his very core of being. Lord Easton was served coffee and, while *he* may have been surprised by it, his butler was not.

Bramley had heard that some men reached a certain age and revolted against fleeting youth, temporarily returning to their wild younger days. Bramley himself had never had any wild younger days so could not empathize with the sensation. He could only pray that Lord Easton's transformation *was* tempo-rary. Mrs. Wooton claimed it was a pleasure to see the lord so jolly these days. Mrs. Wooton had grown suspiciously jolly herself and claimed the sea air was good for her aches and pains. Was jolly really a wished-for state in an elevated house? Was not quiet dignity and seriousness of purpose more the thing?

Then of course there was Miss Upton to contend with. She was not at all what he and Lady Easton had wished for. She was very…something. Perhaps she was just too everything—too direct, too adventurous, too careless, and entirely too friendly with Lord Bertridge's wretched dog.

The dog, though his master thought him good in all things, spent half his day leaving fur on furniture, chewing table legs, barking at a window, or slinking into the kitchen to harass the cook. They had already lost a mince pie to the creature.

As if all of this were not enough to contend with, there was the new lady's maid. Some two persons reputed to be her parents had named her Bemmy, of all things. Lady Easton was so approving of her, but he could not understand why. The girl said the most outrageous things at the servants' table. How many disreputable stories about disreputable people did she know?

And now, here was Lord Easton and Miss Upton prepared to

set off to a dinner that, as far as he could gather, was entirely unsuitable. Lady Easton had made her opinion known about this Alvanley character and her opinion was not favorable.

Lord Bertridge and Lady Easton had come into the great hall to see them off, though neither of them looked particularly approving.

"Now Caroline," Lady Easton said, "you do look ever so charming and of course I wish you to enjoy yourself. I only caution you and put you on your guard. Be mindful of defending your right to be treated always as a lady. Men like Alvanley and his set can overstep on occasion."

"Do not allow anybody, particularly Alvanley or his cousin, Mr. Landon, to take any liberties," Lord Bertridge said.

"They think they are so full of wit," Lady Easton said, "but the danger is, they may drift into dangerous territory in pursuit of it. Further, whatever occurs at that dinner will be much talked of, as it always is. Do not be a subject of gossip."

Lord Bertridge practically recoiled at the mention of gossip. "Nothing can kill a lady's chances faster than an unfortunate story making the rounds. And, of course, it would reflect on the family."

"Reflect poorly," Lady Easton said.

Miss Upton had only smiled and said, "But I do not go alone. Lord Easton will be there to chaperone."

Lady Easton nodded, but it was a very slight nod, indicating she did not have much faith in her lord at this particular moment in time. She looked at the clock and said, "He is late."

Bramley was certain Miss Upton suppressed laughter at that comment. What on earth was amusing about being late?

He was a sane man trapped in a madhouse.

RICHARD HAD WATCHED Miss Upton and his uncle leave for

Alvanley's dinner. He and his aunt had done their best to warn Miss Upton, but he did have the feeling that she'd not taken them at all seriously. She should have, she might well be walking into a wolves' den. Who were the other ladies to attend? Were they respectable? He did not approve of Alvanley and even less of his wastrel cousin Mr. Landon. Who knew who else would be at table.

He really believed that Miss Upton needed to be protected, as she was not very inclined to protect herself. She was at once too innocent and too forward—a lethal combination.

As well, she did not seem to have the first idea of how she appeared when she left the house, lovely in that fantasy of a dress, her hair effortlessly swept up, her color high and her eyes bright. She was a magnet for every rake in town.

And what of his uncle? When Lord Easton had finally come down the stairs a full three minutes past the time, he'd laughed off his aunt's scoldings about it. Then he'd really laughed off her warnings about Alvanley. He'd kissed his wife's cheek and turned to Miss Upton. "Come, Caroline, it is time to escape the magistrates' grips."

Who were the magistrates? Was it meant to be him and his aunt?

It was ludicrous that anybody should think that of him. He was not the enforcer of laws. Yes, he of course was careful in his dealings and wished those around him to be equally careful. But that hardly made him the Sheriff of Nottingham!

He felt himself tightly wound, his fists were clenched and he would like to box somebody at that moment. He did not like the feeling. It was familiar to him, as he'd often felt it in his youth and it still came to him from time to time. As a boy, he'd been in an almost constant state of it whenever he was not away at school— it would fade and then he'd be subjected to something that would bring it on again.

On his birthdays, year after year, his parents never remembered, though they used it as a promise often enough. They would do this or that on his birthday. He was eight when he finally concluded that all that would ever happen was that he'd get an extra biscuit at tea, and that was only courtesy of the cook. Twice while he'd been at school, they'd forgotten to send a carriage at term end and he'd spent a humiliating few days with the headmaster. Once, they'd set the house on fire and promptly saved themselves, looking surprised to find him also on the lawn. Perhaps the worst of it was the way they often looked through him, as if he was not there at all.

In those days, he'd wanted to rage until the house fell down around them all. He'd never raged though, it would have been too like his parents and their ungovernable emotions. One moment they were madly in love, the next they were trying to scratch each other's eyes out, the next they were drunk and loudly proclaiming their adoration, and the next they were throwing books at one another. How many mornings had he come down the stairs to find empty decanters strewn everywhere and a room nearly destroyed? He had vowed he would never be like them and so he had placed his rage in a secure box and never allowed it to see the light of day.

The box that constrained his temper had held steady all these years because he'd created a life that allowed it to be so. If one were careful and arranged things in an orderly fashion, one's box need not be disturbed. Or, if it was disturbed, one could retreat to one's orderly house in the country to restore calm once more. He'd managed the London seasons just that way, enjoying the entertainments and then when he occasionally found it all too much, shutting the door on Portland Place. And yet, ever since he'd arrived to Brighton he had seen the box shaken and the lock rattled. There was nowhere to retreat to, as the house itself was turmoil.

Perhaps he should just leave. He might retreat to his estate, where all was calm and peaceful. He would spend his evenings on the back lawn with a few candles lit, a book, a glass of brandy, and Edgar by his side. He would look up occasionally and see the stars above and the faint lights of a tenant cottage in the distance. Sometimes, if the wind were right, he might catch muffled laughter from the tenant's children. Those sorts of evenings had always acted as a panacea, the remedy after his box had been shaken in London.

So much was right at his estate, and so much was wrong here.

LORD ALVANLEY'S RENTED house being also on the Steyne, it would be no trouble to walk. However, Lord Easton said it would be the sort of thing that would make them the target of wit. He could not say how, exactly, but it might be something along the lines of arriving on foot like peddlers. Alvanley was a friend of Brummel's and had adopted some of his attitudes regarding standards. It was Lord Easton's understanding that Brummel was currently on the outs with the Prince and most definitely not in town. He was not sorry for it, as he found that gentleman to be a poser of the highest order who did not believe half the things he said. Furthermore, Alvanley's wit was far more amusing because it did not have the same meanness or bite to it. Alvanley might gently bruise, but Brummel drew blood.

Caroline was not sorry Mr. Brummel had absented himself from the Regent's circle. All England knew that that gentleman could reduce a lady to tears by one disapproving look at her person. It was not so much the man's disapproval that would cut, but how talk of it would spread. Her father had told her of an instance when Lady Felicia had arrived to a ball in a rather elaborately decorated gown and Brummel had commented, *It is a dress, I suppose.* The baron said the poor lady had been shaken and tearful. Caroline had no wish to test herself against that over-critical fellow.

Alvanley's house was well-appointed, having been taken for

the summer months from some lord or other from the north who had grown bored with the place. What made it stand apart, though, was not its accoutrements but its atmosphere. Caroline had noticed it as soon as they had entered the drawing room—it was decidedly lively.

Perhaps she noticed it so distinctly because it was everything Lady Easton's house was not. It was loud and it was jolly, rather than quiet and ordered.

Lord Easton took her round and she met the Prince once more, but this time accompanied by a lady he introduced as Mrs. Fitzherbert. Of course, Caroline was aware of who she was, but was not over-shocked to know it. There were unhappy marriages all over England and on occasion one of those unhappy persons sought solace elsewhere. She neither approved nor disapproved and was only grateful to have come from a home in which the gentleman did not wander.

Caroline had traveled with her father enough to have seen the desperate gambits of some middle-aged married ladies attempting to gain his attention, but the baron never wavered as he loved his wife. He had once told Caroline, though she was sure he should not have, that men who wandered might well bring a disease back to their wives. That, he would never do.

She had curtsied low to Mrs. Fitzherbert, giving the lady as much due as she would give the Prince's real wife. In truth, Mrs. Fitzherbert probably deserved more, if reports of the Princess's behavior could be believed. Caroline's show of respect seemed to please both the Regent and his companion. The Prince pointed out that Mrs. Fitzherbert lived next door to Marlborough House, Lord Easton's current accommodations. Caroline had nodded and smiled and prayed there would be no suggestion to call, as Lady Easton would certainly go mad over it.

Another thing Lady Easton would not care for was that there were so few ladies in attendance. It was only herself, Mrs. Fitzherbert, and a certain Mrs. Jordan. If Caroline had not been particularly shocked to encounter Mrs. Fitzherbert, she could not quite say the same for Mrs. Jordan. The lady was an actress and long-time mistress of the Duke of Clarence. The duke himself was not present and Caroline could not make heads nor tales of it. She *did* know what Lady Easton would make of it and it would be nothing anyone would care to remember hearing. Lord Bertridge would have a few things to say about it too.

On the other hand, it was not Caroline's purview to approve or disapprove of the Prince's friends. And then, Mrs. Jordan had been invited by Lord Alvanley and she was the leading comedic actress of the time, so perhaps she was the exception to the rule. And certainly, Lord Easton would take her home in an instant if he thought any of it were at all improper. In any case, she found Mrs. Fitzherbert kind and Mrs. Jordan was a clever lady, surrounded by those who wished to hear her wit.

Lord Alvanley approached and said, "Easton, how do you? Miss Upton, I am delighted that you deigned to attend my little dinner."

"Deigning is for kings and queens, I think," Caroline said. "I have only come."

Lord Alvanley laughed and said, "There, that is just the thing. You have a certain wit about you, Miss Upton. I do always wish my table to be peopled by people with wit."

"Except for myself," Lord Easton said.

"Oh, no, Easton, never think you are alone. Mr. Crafton must be your companion in that. But, you are such an agreeable audience that I think you are never left out of these things."

"I do enjoy a good joke," Lord Easton said, "though by the time I think of my own I am in bed in the dark."

"Miss Upton," Lord Alvanley said, "what we all like about Easton is that he is so invariably pleasant. I have never heard an unkind or snide remark from him—it is a refreshing quality not often encountered. And then, it would be very hard to dislike a fellow who so delights in a good joke—nobody has more fun at the thing than he does."

Caroline nodded her approbation of the sentiment and

thought she was gaining a clearer picture of Lord Easton. He did seem to be so well-liked wherever he went and he was invariably pleasant. And then, when he was delighted, he was exceedingly delighted.

"Not like that nephew of yours, eh, Easton?" Lord Alvanley said, laughing. "He's always looking askance at something or other. Though, I should not joke about Bertridge, as I have discovered he is no joke in a boxing practice."

"He does take the sport seriously," Lord Easton said. He paused then said softly, "The poor fellow takes such a lot seriously."

There was a hint of sadness in Lord Easton's tone and Caroline hardly knew what to make of it. She had been holding out hope that Lord Bertridge's stickish demeanor was just a façade, a cover for polite company. But certainly, if it were so, other gentlemen would know the truth of it. That did not seem to be the case, though. They saw Lord Bertridge just as he portrayed himself.

She found herself exceedingly vexed over the idea. She had really begun to hope that the man she viewed on the boxing green—fists flying with abandon—might be the real man. She startled herself as she realized she had grown fond of that illusory man.

Lord Alvanley's butler had arrived at the drawing room door and looked meaningfully at his master.

"Ah," Lord Alvanley said, "we go through. Miss Upton, take my arm."

CAROLINE FOUND HERSELF seated between the Regent, who headed the table, and Mr. Landon, a cousin of Lord Alvanley's. The method of seating was opaque, but it seemed that there was no hostess, and so Lord Alvanley and the Prince hosted together. She might have thought Mrs. Fitzherbert would do the honor, but that lady seemed well-pleased with her current location.

The party was only fourteen and Caroline found it a pleasant arrangement. Rather than having to keep track of when to turn to one's opposite partner, much of the conversation was had by the whole table at once.

If Caroline had any doubts about Lord Easton's value as an audience, those doubts were washed away in a sea of laughter. One person would make a witticism and Lord Easton's deep laughter would nearly shake the room and he would be heard saying, "Yes, that is all too true, goodness I have never heard it expressed so, oh, I will be laughing myself to sleep tonight!"

He also found a moment to recount Caroline's retort when it was suggested that Alvanley's table might be too forward for a young lady and there was much laughter over the idea of crocodiles underfoot and a secret dish dosed with arsenic.

Mrs. Fitzherbert and Mrs. Jordan were both contributors to the general jollity, though Mrs. Jordan, being an actress, was particularly gifted at mimicry. She did a marvelous imitation of a high-placed lady looking about a shop with the utmost disdain and asking for impossible items, such as a shawl of silver metal. Her disappointment after being informed that it was not to be had was positively inspired.

At those moments when conversation was had amongst dinner partners, Caroline found both the Regent and Mr. Landon entertaining in their own ways. The Prince had his own attitude that was very amusing, he seemed not particularly interested in what the world made of him. After all, he said, he could not be dismissed from the job.

Caroline certainly hoped not, as those kings who *had* been dismissed generally went on their way via violent means.

Mr. Landon was at once entertaining, complimentary, and solicitous. Never had the world seen a dress so charming or such a charming person wearing it and never was her wine glass to be found empty. She felt rather giddy from the wine's effects and she was certain Mr. Landon was very taken with her.

Her high spirits began to wonder if something would come of it. He was a good-looking fellow, though not anything to compare to Lord Bertridge. What he might not have over Lord Bertridge in looks, he certainly made up for with his conversation. His household was bound to be filled with laughter and gaiety. And after all, she must marry at some point and probably ought not to dismiss a likely gentleman over wishing that Lord Bertridge was other than what he appeared to be.

As she reminded herself, one could not marry an idea or a hope or a phantom. For all that she pretended to Bemmy that it was neither here nor there that she was to marry, she was not such an idiot as to believe it. If she were not to marry, she would end a spinster in her brother's house, always second fiddle to his baroness, whoever that lady turned out to be.

Mr. Landon was a second son and so was likely bound for the military or the clergy, though he did not say what his plans were. She did not mind that his prospects were not elevated, she only hoped he would choose the military as she had no interest in becoming a clergyman's wife. She thought he must favor soldiering, as he seemed entirely unsuited for the church.

Of course, she was getting far ahead of herself in her speculations and the champagne with dessert no doubt helped her on her way. She reminded herself that Mr. Landon only seemed taken with her at this moment and many a gentleman was taken by a lady for an evening with nothing to come of it. Further, she did not know him half as well as she would need to if such a serious matter as forevermore were to come up.

She did wonder why Lord Bertridge had singled out Mr. Landon to warn her against. He was such an entertaining fellow and all happy smiles.

Perhaps that was it—Lord Bertridge did not approve of all the happy smiles.

THE ENTERTAINMENT OF the evening had slipped effortlessly into the drawing room, as the men did not bother staying over their port but brought the bottle in with them. Both Mrs. Fitzherbert and Mrs. Jordan took a glass and, as there did not seem to be any tea tray arriving, Caroline did too. She sipped it very slowly, conscious of how much wine she'd had at dinner. She'd often sat with her father in their own dining room, savoring a fine port, but generally not to cap off three glasses of wine and one of champagne.

Blessedly, nobody seemed interested in pushing her toward the pianoforte. She was competent enough on the instrument, but did not love playing in public. She also thought that one missed a great deal of conversation when they were providing the entertainment and the conversation at this particular party was not to be missed.

The rest of the evening was spent playing out scenes, where Mrs. Jordan was the performer and the rest of the party made guesses. She was a baker who had made a mistake with the yeast, she was a lady's maid who had singed her mistress's wig, she was a young buck slyly courting a daughter despite her mama's disapproval.

The last amusement of the evening was listening to Lord Easton laugh all the way back to the house. Caroline thought she had not been entertained so much in all of her life.

She fell asleep both lighthearted, and with a nagging feeling about Lord Bertridge. He would not have approved of the party at all. Further, and despite all her rationality, she could not help but think that he might interfere in her thoughts when it came to a practical decision about her future. She could not help but think it, as every time she considered another gentleman like Mr. Landon the lord did creep into her mind.

He was becoming very irritating about it.

CHAPTER NINE

L ADY EASTON HAD not been pleased to watch her husband and
her charge saunter off to Lord Alvanley's dinner the evening
before, but that began to feel a pleasant interlude compared to
what she faced now.

As the sun streamed into the breakfast room, she stared at her
husband through the dust motes that always seemed to be
floating in the air in this wretched town.

She was staggered. Clara Godwin, Countess of Easton, was
positively staggered.

"As you might imagine," Lord Easton went on, "it was all
rather jolly." The lord paused and set down his toast. "What is it,
my dear? You look as if you might tip over."

"I feel I do not understand you properly, Easton. Did you
mean to say that Mrs. Jordan, Dorothy Jordan of the stage,
attended the dinner? At the table? She was not some hired
entertainment?"

"Yes, that's her, and of course she was at the table," Lord
Easton said cheerfully. "And then after dinner, well, I cannot even
describe, I thought my sides would split, I really did, it was that
amusing."

Though Lady Easton was *mentally* staggered, out of the corner of her eye she noted that her very sensible butler was
physically staggered. He held his hand out to steady himself on the
sideboard. What mad world did she live in, that her butler had

more sense and decorum than her husband?

"She is an actress!" Lady Easton cried. "An actress! An actual actress!"

She could not think of any further description than to point out that the woman was an actress. She fanned herself and Bramley hurried over with the teapot.

"One of the finest actresses in the land," Lord Easton said, nodding.

"An actress!" she repeated. "You have exposed Caroline to an actress!"

"Now, it's perfectly fine, my dear. Neither Alvanley nor the Regent turned their noses up at her and the Duke of Clarence quite favors her."

"As well he might—she's his mistress!" Lady Easton said, fanning herself. "She is an actress *and* a mistress!"

"Yes, yes, but we are at the seaside. Things are more relaxed here. Times have changed, you know," Lord Easton said.

"Times have changed, have they?" Lady Easton said. "The times. They've changed. I see. And where have I been while the times were so helpfully changing?"

"Well, I suppose—"

"Do not even answer that!" Lady Easton said. "I'll have you know, the times have not changed that much, nor will they ever."

Edgar trotted in and looked hopefully around the table. Noting Lady Easton's glare, he turned around and trotted back out again.

"I put my foot down, Easton. I put my foot down firmly and with determination. It is bad enough that my husband would allow himself to dine with an actress, but I will not allow Caroline to be dragged down to the gutter. Lord help us if there is talk about this. What will her father think? You will have ruined her chances!"

"Nonsense, I—"

"Do not say another word," Lady Easton said. "All I can do is attempt to repair this situation. No more Alvanley. No, he is finished. I am arranging a dinner on Thursday and all the right people will be there and you will be there and there will not be an Alvanley in sight! There will be no jolly times in the presence of an actress. Not under my roof!"

"Now, my dear, you are never particularly jolly anyway and technically, it's not our roof, but very well, if it pleases you."

"Nothing pleases me at the moment," she said sulkily. Never in her life had she had such a great urge to throw a plate at her lord's head. It was maddening!

Edgar trotted back in again, though this time he brought reinforcements by way of Lord Bertridge.

"Richard," Lady Easton said in a controlled fury, "you are to know that your uncle and Miss Upton dined with an actress last evening."

"Surely not," Richard said.

"It was not just any actress," Lord Easton put in, "it was Mrs. Jordan. She is quite renowned, you know."

"Renowned for being the Duke of Clarence's mistress!" Richard said.

"I rather think that might be over," Lord Easton said, "at least, I have heard so."

"What difference would that make?" Richard asked imperiously. "My God, they have heaps of children between them. How many? Ten? A dozen? More?"

Lord Easton shrugged, as if he was not concerned over the precise number of illegitimate offspring that might have been produced by that union.

"I have told your uncle about the dinner we planned," Lady Easton said. "We will have the right people. And from now on, only the right people."

Lord Easton sighed, as if he knew well enough that the right people would not be nearly as entertaining as the wrong people.

CAROLINE HAD BEEN at the top of the stairs and intending to go down to breakfast when she heard the ruckus going on in that room. Lady Easton had just been apprised that Mrs. Jordan had attended Lord Alvanley's dinner.

She was not surprised that the lady did not take the news very well. It was indeed unusual that an actress should have been there. But then, Caroline had convinced herself that it must be all right on account of the Regent's approval. And Lord Easton's approval, too.

She tiptoed back to her bedchamber and found Bemmy sorting through pairs of gloves.

As she entered, Bemmy shook her head. "I can hear 'em from here. What do they think? A swell will turn to stone by breathin' the same air as them that tread the boards? I reckon we ought to slip out of the house and be on our way."

"I think so too," Caroline said. "But it is too early for the boxing practices, where shall we go?"

"Down to the seaside," Bemmy said. "You ain't been there yet and it's a mite strange, seeing as you're living in a seaside town."

Of course, it *was* strange, and Lady Easton thought Caroline had been to the water's edge several times when in fact she'd gone to the tower to watch the boxing.

"I'll change my shoes," Caroline said. "Mrs. Belle had a pair made specially for walking the beach as she says it is hard on one's feet. They are grey in color so as not to show the dust and they have a strap across the instep."

Bemmy rummaged through a trunk, softly chuckling. "Fancy types," she said, "they got shoes for every occasion."

Caroline had never imagined herself particularly fancy, but then she supposed having special shoes for one particular part of the geography of England might make it seem so.

Their intent was to quietly descend the stairs and out of the house without being observed. It was now a set thing that they walked in the mornings and so it would not be necessary to inform Lady Easton of it.

Their first foray to the top of the stairs was unsuccessful, as Lady Easton was in the front hall speaking to Bramley in low tones. Caroline could not hear all of what was said, but just bits and pieces: *outrageous, ill-considered, vexed, nonsense, wit's end.*

All of those things were said by Lady Easton, as Bramley only lent a sympathetic ear and nodded in grave agreement.

Finally, the lady exhausted herself of her outrage and wandered into the drawing room while Bramley looked toward the breakfast room with something like steely determination and strode through its doors.

Bemmy took Caroline's hand and they flew down the stairs and out the doors.

It was a glorious morning—the sun was bright, the breeze gentle and bringing the scent of salt with it. They turned a corner and then took East Street toward the King's Road.

As they strolled along, they passed by two matronly ladies, one of which Caroline had seen at the Prince's rout but had not been introduced to. Caroline smiled in acknowledgement.

The lady whispered to her friend and then they passed Caroline by without meeting her eye.

"What did you go and do to those two stiff-necks?" Bemmy whispered.

"Nothing," Caroline said. "I do not even know them."

"Hmm, I reckon they're disapprovin' of you being young. It's my experience that plenty of ladies past their prime are resentin' of any who ain't."

Caroline did not know if that were true or not, but the sight of the sea dismissed thoughts of the two women and their pursed lips.

"Bemmy!" Caroline cried. "It's glorious! I have seen it in the distance from a carriage on occasion, but not up close. Look how big it is."

"Aye, but not big enough. Dieppe is but a hop and a jump and them rogue Frenchmen *have* jumped over here from time to time. My pa swears that you can see that blasted land from the beach on a very clear day, but I never did see it. I reckon it's only on the clear days when he's had a few too many gulps of gin."

They hurried down to the beach and Caroline was at once appreciative of Mrs. Belle's good sense in designing footwear. More delicate slippers would not have done at all as they walked over the stones.

The water was entrancing—a deep blue such as a painter might create by carefully mixing in a hint of green. The waves rolled in, their white tops tumbling over, as if an unseen giant's hand in the distance pushed them forward. Caroline watched the bathing machines wheeled in and out of that glorious expanse. She must try it someday soon, she really must.

A very stout older woman had just taken hold of a lady coming out of a bathing machine who seemed not very enthusiastic about the operation. The older lady was the dipper and she talked sternly to her charge until the poor thing submitted to getting in the water.

"That's old Martha Gunn," Bemmy said. "She's been dippin' people as long as I can remember and the Prince does favor her. It's said that she's got the run of his kitchens when she likes it. She's a clever one, only working the warm months and then puttin' her feet up all cozy-like through the winter."

"She seems rather fearsome," Caroline said.

"Aye," Bemmy said. "She said to me once, when I was lookin' into the career, she said, Bemmy, you got to be strong in body and strong in mind and overcome all their yipping and yapping 'bout how they've decided they won't go in. Get 'em in and they'll be grateful for it. The *ton* don't know their own minds half the time."

"Were you really thinking of taking such employment?" Caroline asked.

"Not for long. For one thing, I ain't the best swimmer, and for another, I don't fancy being cold and wet. We ain't in the tropics, after all."

Caroline suppressed her laughter over the idea that Bemmy would have for a moment considered the job though she was not a good swimmer.

They turned around and made their way back the way they'd come. Caroline could not help looking at the sea. It was so vast. It seemed incredible that men would board ships and sail out into it. She wondered about those first intrepid souls who'd ventured it. Who was the first to look at the expanse and decide to find out what was out there? Who dared brave sailing out into water that might be leagues deep? Who left their family, not certain they would ever return? Who got out of sight of land, and then kept going?

Bemmy pulled her thoughts from her reverie. "Just ahead," she whispered, "there's a gentleman standin' there staring and he's been starin' for a while. I'll run him off if you like. When I was younger, I was called Bemmy the Basher on account of I would pay back nonsense with a bloody nose."

Caroline followed Bemmy's gaze, hoping whatever situation was developing would not actually result in blows and bloody noses.

She laughed as she saw that it was Mr. Landon. "It is all right, Bemmy, I was introduced to the gentleman last evening."

Bemmy relaxed her balled up fists just as they reached him.

"Miss Upton," he said bowing. "Charmed to see you again so soon."

"Good day to you, Mr. Landon," Caroline said, "Do you often walk along the sea in the mornings?"

"I try to avoid walking anywhere so early in the day," Mr. Landon said, "but my cousin was up at dawn and making all sorts of noise and I found I must make my escape. Alvanley is determined to shape himself up for the boxing exhibition and apparently those efforts must be very loud and initiated at unconscionable hours."

"You do not have an interest in the sport yourself?" Caroline asked. She was perfectly aware that Mr. Landon had attended Mr.

Jackson, having observed the exercise each day, but she would never admit to the knowledge.

"Oh, I am very interested in boxing, Miss Upton," he said, turning to walk with them. "But I find I do not like practicing a thing ad nauseum. It's all very jolly when Mr. Jackson puts us through our paces, but Alvanley is running round the house to increase his wind and lifting statues to increase his strength and the sight of it gives one a headache."

Mr. Landon made a quick feint to insert himself between Caroline and Bemmy, but Bemmy blocked him with determination. He ended up slipping back and coming to Caroline's other side. Bemmy seemed suspicious of the arrangement, but the maid could not work out how to be on two sides at once.

"He must be very keen to show himself well," Caroline said, doing her best to erase the picture of poor Lord Alvanley racing round his house clutching statues.

"Very keen, indeed," Mr. Landon said. "He never wishes to look the fool as it is his career to make others look foolish."

"If that is not *your* career," Caroline said, "have you settled on what would be?" She thought it had been a rather graceful way of inquiring if he would join the military or the clergy and she very much hoped he was not set on becoming the neighborhood vicar.

"Ah, the second son's dilemma, what to do with oneself. I have perhaps thought of something out of the usual way. I find, when I look about myself, that my sole interest is in horses. That is what I wish to do, Miss Upton. I wish to breed and race fine horses."

Caroline was surprised by the idea, but not displeased with it. It was, of course, the only life she'd ever known.

"My father is fairly well known for his horses," Caroline said. "Baron Dunn?"

Mr. Landon tripped over a flint stone. "Baron Dunn? Fairly well known? Miss Upton, you are too modest on your father's behalf. He is the first amongst horsemen. Nobody questions that he sits at the pinnacle of the sport, especially not after the recent races at Doncaster."

"Were you present, Mr. Landon?" Caroline asked. She had not seen him there, but that did not mean he had not attended.

Mr. Landon shook his head. "Sadly, no. I had a family obligation. But, there is nobody interested in the sport who has not heard of his victories by now."

Caroline was very much enjoying the conversation. How wonderful that Mr. Landon did not choose to be a clergyman. How wonderful that he wished to follow in her own father's footsteps. Were he to be someone significant in her future, she might have a life she knew well, and enjoyed.

"Tell me, Mr. Landon," Caroline said cautiously, "how do you view ladies who take an interest in horseflesh?" She almost held her breath for the answer, for it would be something indeed if he held the same views as her father.

"The poor ladies," he said, "everybody is always wondering if they should have this or that interest. My own view is the female mind is just as discerning as the male mind. In fact, with animals of all sorts, a lady has a slight edge, I think. If there is any real difference between the sexes, I think it is that females better sense the intangibles. They are better able to understand a horse's feelings. Some might dismiss how the horse feels about things, but I do not. I believe it affects their performance mightily."

There could not have been any answer more perfect than the one Mr. Landon had just delivered. While she had been intrigued to hear of the gentleman's interest in horses, and even wondered what that sort of future might hold for her, she had also wondered if she might not be left behind because the activities would not be deemed suitable for a wife. It seemed Mr. Landon had no such qualms. Just as her father had not.

"My father feels as you do," Caroline said. "I have often accompanied him to races and was present at Doncaster."

"What a privilege you have, Miss Upton," Mr. Landon said, "to be able to glean so much knowledge and experience from your esteemed father. Anybody wishing to be in the business of horses must rejoice to have a partner so well versed."

Caroline blushed deeply, at least she thought she did as her cheeks were very hot. Had that been a hint of his interest in her as something more than a friend and acquaintance? It certainly seemed so.

"May I escort you somewhere?" Mr. Landon said.

Before Caroline could answer, Bemmy said, "We'll be goin' to visit the vicar. He'll be wantin' people to deliver some poor boxes."

Caroline was well aware that Bemmy had decided they must rid themselves of Mr. Landon and proceed on to the boxing practice. She was not entirely sure she agreed, but there was not much she could do about it.

"Well," he said, as they reached the road, "I ought to be off myself. Mr. Jackson does not approve of one arriving late to his instructions. I suppose you will attend the Prince's musical evening on Thursday?"

"I am afraid not," Caroline said, "Lady Easton holds a dinner that evening."

"I see, well, perhaps Alvanley can be convinced to host another party on a different day."

Caroline smiled, but she did not answer. She did not believe Lady Easton would allow her to step foot in Lord Alvanley's house again. It was a shame, but it could not be helped. She was dreading what Lady Easton would have to say to her regarding her first foray into it and having dined with Mrs. Jordan.

"And of course, you must attend the ball the Prince hosts on Tuesday next at The Ship Inn. Everybody interesting will come, surely Lady Easton will insist on being there."

Caroline was not so certain of it, though she did have hope of it. "I hope so, Mr. Landon."

"And I *pray* so. Good day to the charming Miss Upton and her…rather stalwart companion," Mr. Landon said with a tip of the hat.

Watching him stride down the road, Bemmy said, "Now

there's another fella in your pocket. What do you think of that one?"

"He seems a very genial gentleman, but there are no gentlemen in my pockets," Caroline said.

"I bet there is," Bemmy said, "if you would only have a rummage through them."

Ignoring that last comment, Caroline said, "Let us proceed to the church for the boxing and let us take a different route from Mr. Landon as you have so helpfully outlined that we are meant to be visiting a vicar. And let us not pass by our own house as we would not like to be seen and called in."

"Right you are," Bemmy said, "*You* don't want to hear about Mrs. Jordan from Lady E and *I* don't want to hear about her from Bramley. If Lady E is unhappy, he's unhappy. All over an actress, bless their nervous souls."

Caroline was determined not to laugh—Bemmy was entirely outrageous at times. She was not very successful at it, though.

⇻⇺

THAT AFTERNOON, LADY Redfield and Lady Featherstone had not, to Richard's knowledge, been expected to the house. Yet, here they were and looking a bit crazed.

Lady Featherstone had not even paused to remove her bonnet. For that matter, the lady had not seemed to pause when she'd donned it, as it sat askew on her head in an unflattering attitude.

Lady Redfield's eyes darted around the room and settled on nothing, like a bird who was certain a cat was hiding in every corner.

Richard stood and bowed to the ladies and prepared to take his leave.

"Do stay, Richard," his aunt said. "I am certain Cecilia and Anne come to me to assist in the dinner arrangements. We will want your opinion, too. Everyone we have asked has accepted and we will wish it to be perfect."

Lady Featherstone shook her head emphatically and whispered, "It's not about the dinner. It's about the talk. The talk about Miss Upton."

Richard paused his stride and stood stock still. He wished to be at once away and staying. What had the girl done this time? What could she have done that caused gossip? Were people already talking about Alvanley's party and the fact that Mrs. Jordan had attended?

Lady Easton sank into her seat. Softly, she said, "Do stay, Richard. Whatever it is, I shall require your strength."

Bramley brought the tea in, which they had been waiting for anyway so that Richard might fortify himself after the boxing practice. Bramley had only to gather more cups and saucers and plates and, Richard thought, recover from the sight of Lady Featherstone's disheveled headgear.

"Do give your bonnet to Bramley, Anne," Lady Easton said. "It is decidedly off-kilter."

Lady Featherstone reached for her headdress and felt around it. "Goodness, I quite forgot I had it on," she said, untying the ribbons.

"It does look very charming when it's on straight, though," Lady Redfield said kindly.

Bramley left the room carrying the hat as if it were a live viper.

As the door closed, Lady Featherstone said, "When Cecilia came to me with it, I said, Cecelia, we must race to Clara's side this instant."

"With what, though?" Richard asked. "Is this about Alvanley's dinner?"

Both ladies nodded vigorously, and Lady Redfield looked particularly relieved that he'd deduced the thing so quickly.

There was a long sigh coming from the direction of his aunt and Richard noticed her wringing her hands, which she only did on the direst of occasions.

"I knew it!" she said. "I told Easton he'd made a grave error and he just laughed me off. The man has gone over the cliffs of insanity."

Whether his uncle had gone over any cliffs might be up for debate, but Richard was not particularly interested in debating it at the moment. Instead, he said, "What, precisely, is being said?"

"Oh well, you know," Lady Redfield said, staring at the door as if she might make a run for it, "my son mentioned the dancing."

"What is wrong with dancing?" Richard asked.

"Nothing, nothing at all," Lady Featherstone said. "Unless it is on a table with ankles showing?"

A stunned silence settled over the room. It was not possible.

"And then the other thing you heard, Cecilia," Lady Featherstone said encouragingly.

"Oh, the other thing. It seems there was some sort of game?" Lady Redfield said, "A scavenger hunt? Of people? In the dark?"

Lady Easton tapped her fan in sharp and fast raps on the arm of her chair. Richard felt his temper pounding on the sides of his box.

Miss Upton had all but ruined herself and embarrassed them all. How could she be so foolhardy? How could his uncle be so foolhardy?

Lady Easton practically jumped from her chair. "Easton!" she bellowed, louder than any hawker on the street.

CHAPTER TEN

B RAMLEY THREW OPEN the door to the drawing room at Lady Easton's shout.

"Bramley," Lady Easton said in a fury, "find my husband and bring him here. I do not care where he is, I do not care if he must be fetched from Bombay. He must be found and brought to me this instant!"

"He is above stairs, my lady," Bramley said rather breathlessly.

"Get him," Lady Easton said coldly.

They sat in silence as they waited for the lord's arrival. There were several times when Lady Redfield attempted to rise and flee the house, but his aunt would not allow either of the ladies to go.

Lord Easton finally strolled in, looking as cheerful as ever. "Ah, ladies," he said, "it looks like quite the party."

Lady Easton ignored that comment. Rather, she said, "You failed to mention a few details about that dinner, Easton. You failed to mention dancing on tables and a scavenger hunt in the dark."

Lord Easton looked quizzically at his wife. "Whatever are you talking about?"

"Oh, I know, I have heard. Everybody has heard," Lady Easton said. "Caroline was dancing on a table and I cannot fathom how she came to be so and why you would not stop her. And then, hiding in the dark where anything might have happened? Her reputation is in shreds, as is our own."

"I have not the faintest idea of what you are talking about," Lord Easton said. "There was no dancing and no scavenger hunt. There was a dinner, and then Mrs. Jordan acted out scenes while we guessed at what they were. The scenes were not at all scandalous, a baker who'd used too much yeast was typical. That is the sum total of the evening."

"But then why..." Lady Easton trailed off, but it was not necessary to finish her thought anyway. All in the room knew what she meant. If it were not true, why would somebody create such an outrageous story?

"I can guess what happened," Richard said, "Some ridiculous young dandy who attended the evening tried to impress his friends with a wild story, having no care that Miss Upton must be tainted by the tale."

"If it is so, that is very unfortunate," Lord Easton said.

"Not unfortunate, Uncle," Richard said. "It is all very predict-able when one chooses to associate with the likes of Alvanley and his friends."

"They are not bad people," Lord Easton said, "really, they are not."

"Not for you, to be sure," Richard said.

"Well, it's water under the bridge now," Lord Easton said, "I'll tell you what, I'm on my way to see the Regent. I'll find out who put the tale about, he won't like it one bit on account of Mrs. Fitzherbert. I'm certain he will quash any more talk about it."

"Mrs. Fitzherbert was there too?" Lady Easton asked incredu-lously.

"Oh, yes, didn't I say?" Lord Easton said. "She lives right next door, by the by. Anyway, I best be off if the thing is to be put aside quickly."

With that, Lord Easton strolled from the room not appearing any more shaken than when he'd come into it.

"Do you see what I mean?" Lady Easton said, staring at the door her lord had just made his exit through. "Who is he? I no longer know who he is. Mrs. Fitzherbert is our neighbor? Does he think she might call on us? Or worse, did he tell her *we* would call on *her*?"

Lady Redfield nodded sympathetically. "I believe, Clara, that when some gentlemen reach a certain age, they encounter a…rough patch. Did you know that one time, my baron dyed his hair black as night. It was ever so alarming, as if there was a stranger in the house. I shrieked once, encountering him in a corridor. I suspect he only gave it up because it kept staining his neckcloths."

Nobody had any comment about the departed baron's experiments on his hair.

"I think what is needed," Lady Featherstone said, "is some practical action. We must take steps."

Richard thought Lady Featherstone was right, but what steps? What on earth could they do to salvage Miss Upton's reputation? She had, as it turned out, been falsely accused and he felt a moment's pang of guilt over so easily believing the story. Further, though he had said it was bound to happen when associating with the likes of Alvanley, Miss Upton *had* been escorted by his uncle. She should not have been there, but he could not in good conscience say that it was her fault for being there.

"We need all the ladies here," Lady Easton said. "Lady Mendleton, Lady Heathway, and especially, the duchess—they must come to us immediately. The three of us will write letters to them, stating that fact in the strongest terms. And Cecilia, when I say strong, I mean strong. Do not write your usual letter of vague hints couched in compliments. You must be straightforward and forceful. We do not make a request, we make a demand."

Lady Redfield's brows knitted together and Richard was certain the lady had never been forceful in her life. No doubt her effort would end entirely incomprehensible.

"I'll help you set the right tone," Lady Featherstone said to Lady Redfield.

Lady Redfield nodded enthusiastically over that idea.

Richard thought it was as good a plan as any other. For himself, his only plan was to bide his time until he could box off some of his anger and frustration at the exhibition on the morrow. He might pummel a gentleman into nonexistence if he were to discover the inventor of the story while he was in his current state.

He was determined to do well at the exhibition. That meant he must be well-rested and in control of his body and his mind. He could not allow the near-constant disaster that was Miss Caroline Upton to occupy his thoughts and distract him.

CAROLINE HAD THOUGHT to go down for tea and had got as far as the landing before turning back around. Lady Redfield and Lady Featherstone had blown into the house with some urgency and speeded toward the drawing room.

Their arrival would not have been anything to put her off, but the manner of the two ladies had seemed less than genial. Lady Featherstone had practically thrown her pelisse at the footman and marched in with her bonnet slipping sideways and still on her head. Lady Redfield had flown after her in fluttery nervous steps like a chick after a hen.

Caroline had very sensibly retreated to her bedchamber and took up some sewing. As a usual thing, Lady Easton would be perturbed that her charge was not on time for tea, but she was certain that was not the case now. She would be far too taken up with whatever emergency her friends had arrived with, probably to do with the dinner.

She could not entirely ignore her disappointment. Lord Bertridge would be in the drawing room too. Caroline was certain she'd heard his footsteps on the stairs a few minutes ago. She did not wish to be drawn to that scolding person but somehow, she was. He had been magnificent at the boxing practice. Lord

Alvanley may have been running round his house and lifting statues, but it seemed Lord Bertridge had no need of it. He fought with some sort of ease, as if he never tired, though it was clear enough he wore out his opponents.

Bemmy burst into the room like a gust of wind.

"I was just in the servants' quarters and it's abuzz with the exhibition on the morrow. Bets are being laid in town and Lord Bertridge is favored."

Caroline sighed. "How I wish we could view it, though Lady Easton would never allow it."

"She can't disallow what she ain't been asked about," Bemmy said.

"Certainly, she would find it out. People would talk, Bemmy. A lady is not meant to view such things."

"Right you are," Bemmy said. "But the rest of us can view just fine and if you were to look like the rest of us…"

"Are you saying I should go disguised?" Caroline said. It was an outrageous idea, and yet a very interesting idea.

"Easy as rollin' dough," Bemmy said nodding. "Tomorrow, we nip out for our walk and go straight to my pa's house and get an old cloak I got there. It's drab as anything, and I'll set you up with a threadbare bonnet too. Then, we take ourselves down toward The Ship Inn. I heard they've leveled the beach and laid boards down to make a proper ring. Nobody will give you a second look."

Caroline set down her sewing. On the one hand, it would be glorious to watch the result of all the practicing the gentlemen had done and she was sure the gamblers were right—Lord Bertridge was bound to do well. And of course, she would be interested to see how Mr. Landon fared.

On the other hand, she had not even heard from Lady Easton on the subject of Mrs. Jordan yet and now it seemed Lady Featherstone and Lady Redfield had arrived looking harried. She could not be sure why they had come, but it did not seem likely to put Lady Easton in a very happy frame of mind.

If she were to be caught going to the exhibition, Lady Easton might very well pack her up and send her home. She suspected her father would not be pleased either. He might not be as tightly wound as Lady Easton, but he still had limits.

But then, how could she bear to miss it? Why was it so wrong for a lady to view a match? She'd already viewed all the practices and seen all the men shirtless. Anyway, was a lady not to know what a man looked like without his shirt?

Of course, she knew perfectly well why society did not think a lady should view men shirtless or cheer on what was a violent sport. She was just not certain society was right.

And after all, there was no reason anybody would note her if she were dressed as a servant of some sort. She had noticed that people often looked through or past a servant, but not directly at them. Surely, she would not be recognized.

As she mulled over the idea, or rather talked herself into the idea, she heard Lady Easton bellow her husband's name such as she'd never heard before.

Bemmy folded her arms and said, "I'm surprised that didn't shake the house. I wouldn't be in the master's shoes just now for anything in the world."

"I wonder what has happened?" Caroline said. "It must be to do with whatever Lady Featherstone and Lady Redfield have come for. Goodness, I'll never get tea now."

"Don't you worry 'bout that," Bemmy said. "I'll nip down to the kitchens and tell cook you need a tray on account of a headache and while he's at it he can add a cup for me too."

Caroline nodded, always admiring of Bemmy's practicality and ability to get a thing done. As her maid left the room, she saw Lord Easton sauntering down the hall, looking entirely uncon- cerned over the alarming summons from his wife that had just echoed throughout the house.

As the minutes ticked by, Caroline did not hear anything further from the drawing room. Lord Easton, regardless of why he'd been called to his wife's side, did not stay by her side long, as she heard him in the front hall telling Bramley he was off to the pavilion to see the Prince.

Bemmy came back as good as her word, with a tea tray and a mountain of biscuits. Caroline poured and Bemmy said, "Lord knows what's gone on in the drawing room, but Mr. Bramley is wound tighter than a cat with a bell tied to its tail."

"As long as it doesn't have to do with me, I will just hide up here until dinner. In any case, you've brought enough food that I could probably forgo dinner too if things seem dire."

Bemmy chewed on a biscuit and said, "I never did see the likes of this house. Not a day goes by where somebody isn't up in arms 'bout something. It's a miracle they all don't fall over from the apoplexy."

Caroline giggled and admitted her thoughts were not dissimilar. It was a good reminder that not all the world was forever outraged.

They drank their tea in companionable silence, only occasionally broken by Bemmy as she related some interesting thing about her family or the townspeople or the town itself.

It turned out her father was skilled with a knife and was forever carving forest animals and sea creatures from bits of wood. He'd hide them round the house and whoever found one could keep it. Bemmy had an extensive collection of them, her favorites being a delicate little octopus and a pod of whales.

Somehow, from there, Bemmy explained the ins and outs of buying flour from Mr. Smith's shop. The fellow always put the new flour he'd brought in on top of what he already had so everybody knew if the bin was getting too low they were getting close to flour that had been there for years and so they went further afield for their purchase. Poor Mr. Smith could not work out why he could never move more than half a bin in a month.

Though Caroline could not have said how, Mr. Smith's poor inventory management led Bemmy to think of The Ship Inn, the place they might go on the morrow to see the exhibition.

"That's where the Prince will hold his ball," she said. "In the winter months, we have our own dances in the hall there, but in the summer it's taken over by the swells."

Just before Caroline wondered aloud if the Prince's invitations had been sent and whether there was any chance at all of her going, there was a soft knock on the door. It opened and Lady Easton took in the scene.

Caroline supposed she would be surprised to see her lady's maid having tea with her.

Bemmy stood and said, "Lady Easton, I did take it upon myself to have my tea here on account of Miss Upton's headache. One never knows if a headache will develop into something more serious and I was determined to have my eyes upon her at all times. I once saved a charge in similar circumstances who started with a headache and ended with a high fever. Had I not been there, well…"

Caroline was vastly entertained to watch the flashes of emotion cross Lady Easton's features. Shock when she came upon the scene, alarm at the mention of serious illness, and finally gratefulness over Bemmy's thorough attentions.

"You are very good to do it, Bemmy. I would have a word with Caroline alone for a few minutes and then you may continue your vigil. You will alert me to the smallest change."

"Oh, Lady Easton, my headache has begun to fade already," Caroline said hurriedly, lest she be trapped in the room for days with an illness she did not have.

"I wondered if it were a general weakness, my lady," Bemmy said gravely, "brought on by lack of nourishment, as sometimes happens in the young. It's been my experience that anything sweet often does the trick and so tea and biscuits were the remedy."

Bemmy made a pretty curtsy and as she departed the room, Lady Easton said, "You are a treasure trove of information, Bemmy, you really are."

Caroline pressed her lips together to avoid collapsing in a heap of laughter. Bemmy had the good grace to blush, knowing full well she was a treasure trove of nonsense and fabrications.

"Now," Lady Easton said sitting down, "I do not like to bother you when you have a headache but as it is fading, I will venture it. It seems the dinner at Alvanley's is being talked about in an unflattering and false manner. All sorts of lies have been spread about."

Lady Easton went on to inform Caroline of the outrageous stories of dancing on tables and a scavenger hunt in the dark. She hardly knew what to make of it. Certainly, nobody would believe it, it was too ridiculous.

"I know perfectly well that none of it is true and Richard is convinced it was some young gentleman who only wished to tell a wild story to impress his juvenile friends."

"I am very sorry to have involved you in such a thing, no matter how it came about."

"It is not your fault," Lady Easton said. "The blame is firmly laid at my husband's door. I did tell him it was not suitable and then, as soon as he saw Mrs. Jordan and Mrs. Fitzherbert, he should have whisked you away."

Lady Easton was silent for what felt like a full minute. Then she said, "I do not know what has happened to him. I really do not."

Caroline was indeed sorry that such a story had made the rounds. Not really for herself, as the tale seemed too silly for any rational person to countenance, but for Lady Easton. The poor woman worked so hard to maintain a strict decorum, this was precisely the sort of thing that would affect her deeply.

As for Lord Easton, Caroline suspected he'd laughed off the tale as being the ridiculous story that it was.

"In any case," Lady Easton said, "letters are going out to my friends. I will have all the ladies of the society by our side. Further, our dinner on Thursday will cement the idea that we have formed a new set. A set characterized by dignity and restraint. We will do things with solemnity of purpose—I'm thinking of card parties and musical evenings to begin. Alvanley and his cronies may host their unseemly parties and toy with the reputations of others, but they will no longer toy with us. And that reminds me, whenever you are walking out of the house, always direct your gaze to the right."

"To the right?" Caroline asked, entirely mystified as to how the direction of one's eyes indicated a solemnity of purpose or showed dignity and restraint.

"Mrs. Fitzherbert lives to the left," Lady Easton said. "We should not like any unfortunate encounters."

Poor Mrs. Fitzherbert. Caroline hoped the lady was not aware that others would take such steps to avoid her.

"I suppose that means we do not attend the Prince's ball on Tuesday next?" she asked, half hoping her assumption was wrong.

"Certainly not," Lady Easton said with a sniff. "I will not have you in harm's way again. He may be the regent, but his judgment in friends is deplorable. One had hopes that he might grow out of it, but really, how much more can he grow? From now on, you will be accompanied everywhere you go by at least one of the ladies. Lady Redfield will walk out with you and Bemmy on the morrow—of course I would be happy to do it, but I must manage the preparations for the dinner."

As Caroline took in what Lady Easton was saying, she found herself looking for a way out of the plan.

"But surely, Lady Redfield needn't be bothered. Bemmy is very careful, after all."

"Bemmy is a wonder," Lady Easton said. "I do not deny it. However, I wish all in this wretched town to view Miss Upton in the care of the most eminent ladies in society. *That* will teach them what to think."

Caroline's heart sank. With a friend of Lady Easton's always by her side, there would certainly be no exhibition. There would be no jolly parties or Lord Alvanley's wit to entertain. There would be no Regent's ball. There would be no chance encounters with Mr. Landon. There would be no entertainments at all, for what entertainment could be hoped for when it was accompanied by solemnity of purpose?

"Never fear, Caroline," Lady Easton said, "we will repair this situation and we will persevere. Now, I wonder if you will be well enough to dine with us this evening? We meet in the drawing room at seven forty-five. I do hope you make every effort as it *is* Tuesday and we will have fish. Bramley says it's come straight off the boat this morning."

Caroline nodded absently. She might as well go down at seven forty-five. Fish for dinner was likely to be the most exciting thing that would happen all week.

IF LADY EASTON had been shaken by the talk going round about Miss Upton, Bramley was not less so. Who was this young lady? She was like a violent storm come in to blow them about in all directions. And then Lord Easton had been part of the upset too.

That was on top of dealing with *Bemmy*, as she insisted she was called. Lady Easton was so approving of the woman, but Lady Easton did not hear the maid's effronteries at the servants' table. How was he even to respond upon being informed that Lady Easton and Lord Bertridge *did not laugh enough*. Who did she think the lord and lady were? Punch and Judy?

It felt as if all he had worked toward with Lady Easton as his stalwart ally, all the regularity and timetables and calm proceeding forward, was going down a drainpipe with alarming speed.

He surveyed the dining table and reviewed the menu in his mind as the family came in. At least he could take comfort in the knowledge that whatever disasters were to befall the house next, he could still ensure a very good dinner.

As it was Tuesday, fish would swim to the forefront as it always did on Tuesdays. Even in the dead of winter, when they were down to salted fish made into a chowder, Lady Easton would brook no substitutions. Though, that particular dish was inevitably passed off to the servants' table where it would be glared at.

Fortunately, it was not winter and if there were one positive about residing in this town it was the proximity of fresh fish.

They would dine on clear consommé made from the chicken bones from the evening before, which could not be helped as Cook refused to throw out perfectly good chicken carcasses. But once that anomaly was cleared, in would march the stars of the repast: mackerel with fennel and mint, roasted cod with thyme, and smoked herrings with onion and crème fraiche.

Along with those standouts, he would serve baked aubergine, new potatoes in a parsley sauce, salad with radishes and cucumber, and finally, a cheese board and a strawberry tart. It was a very fine spread.

That, and Lady Easton's clocks ticking reliably throughout the house, were the only shreds of sanity he had left to hold onto.

RICHARD HAD BEEN somewhat soothed that Miss Upton had arrived to the drawing room promptly. She was dressed in a simple white muslin, one she had brought from home, he thought. She looked exceptionally charming and he could almost forget what chaos she had managed to introduce to the house.

He did notice, as she made pleasant conversation, that his opinions on the matter had begun to shift. He began to think that, aside from the strange habits whose fault must be laid at her father's door, she had not really done anything so untoward. It was his uncle who must take the blame for the rumors going round about Miss Upton dancing on a table and participating in some bizarre scavenger hunt with candles blown out. She had not been guilty of any of it and should have relied on the judgment of her elders. Lord Easton should never have taken her there. How was a young lady to know how to proceed if those who were meant to guide her were so inept?

He supposed he'd been rather inept in the effort himself. He certainly had not seemed to have made much of an impression. Perhaps it had been his tone. He might have been guilty of addressing her in a manner more befitting directives to a child. He could not excuse her calling him Bertie, but perhaps he owned part of the fault. Perhaps he'd goaded her into it.

Beyond that, he could not help but to admire how she held up against the rumors that swirled round her. Another lady might have been still weeping in her room and railing against fate and looking for who to blame. Miss Upton had calmly descended to dinner. If one did not know there was something amiss, one would never have guessed. She had greeted his uncle warmly, though he did not deserve such courtesy.

All of her mistakes really could be attributed to another. Now, when she was left to compose herself as best as she could, it seemed she had the instincts of a real lady. A fine lady knew how to carry on unruffled and that was exactly what she was doing.

He could not help but admire it and felt a touch of shame that he had condemned her so early without giving careful examination to the facts. He felt he had almost been rash, which was not at all in his nature.

And then, she was so very lovely. Nobody could deny it.

As they were seated, Lord Easton said, "Caroline, you will be happy to know that the Regent is outraged by the talk that has gone round and he has made his opinion widely known. As he said very publicly this afternoon, "Let the man who invented such tales quake in his boots, for if I discover him he will not be welcome anywhere I frequent and doors will slam against him from here to London."

"That was very kind of the Prince," Miss Upton said.

"I expect word of it has reached the culprit and he is indeed quaking in his boots," Lord Easton said. "He will be discovered."

"How can you be so certain?" Lady Easton asked.

"It was a small party, my dear. Those who were first told by someone in attendance will think carefully if they wish to join the villain in having doors shut against them. One of those persons will go to the Prince. Nobody will wish to ruin their place in society over a story."

Lady Easton nodded thoughtfully. "Excellent," she said. "In the meantime, we have taken our own steps. Caroline is to be escorted everywhere by my friends. Let the talkers dare to impugn the judgement of the ladies Redfield, Featherstone, Mendleton, Heathway, and the duchess."

"Hah!" Lord Easton said, with a laugh. "You bring your forces, very good, yes, that will do very well."

Richard was surprised that Miss Upton did not look as interested in the scheme as he would have thought. It would be an honor to be always in the company of those ladies and therefore endorsed by them.

"Miss Upton will be very well cared for under those matrons' watchful eyes," Richard said.

"It is, of course, very kind. But I really do not require it," Miss Upton said. "Bemmy is quite capable of walking with me when I go out."

"Bemmy is a rare gem in this basket of stones called Brighton, I do not dispute it for a moment," Lady Easton said.

Richard could not help but notice that Bramley's face wrinkled in marked distaste over hearing that Miss Upton's maid was to be a rare gem. He supposed the servants' hall was unsettled over the move to the seaside, which the butler assuredly would not like.

"However," Lady Easton said, "a young lady being escorted by her maid says nothing to passerby. A young lady being escorted by a highly placed matron says everything. Lady Redfield has kindly offered to come tomorrow morning. She's quite looking forward to it, actually, as none of her boys ever seem to have time to go along with her to the shops."

Miss Upton looked resigned to the idea and Richard thought

he might be able to understand part of it. It was likely not that she was opposed to being escorted, but perhaps Lady Redfield's chatter and indecisiveness were found to be wearing. He could not claim he had a different opinion of the lady—if one were to come in wet from the rain, Lady Redfield would invent a compliment on the charm of being damp.

"Well, then," Lord Easton said, "it's all settled and no harm done, eh?"

Only Miss Upton managed to smile at that bizarre statement.

Richard seriously wondered what his uncle was thinking these days. Or perhaps it was just that he *was* thinking these days, and his thoughts were exceedingly odd. Lord Easton would be far better served to go back to his old unthinking days and allow his wife to do the thinking for him.

CHAPTER ELEVEN

LADY REDFIELD HAD agreed to escort Caroline about the town and the lady was as good as her word. She arrived to the house at eleven. Caroline had resigned herself to the idea that she'd be looking at ribbons or buying paper for letters or scanning a shelf of books while the rest of the town was down at the beach to see the boxing exhibition.

She so wished to be there! She was so eager to see how it would unfold. Caroline was certain that Lord Bertridge would do very well and had a yearning to view him boxing in earnest. Then of course, she reminded herself that she must also be interested to see how Mr. Landon would fare.

In truth, her attention felt torn between the two gentlemen. Lord Bertridge was so devilishly handsome that no matter how many times she attempted to dismiss him from her thoughts, her thoughts would rebel and bring him right back up for consideration.

Her thoughts, as unruly as they were, could not be convinced that the lord's nature was not at all suited to her. He was, she was afraid she must finally admit, the stickiest-sticky-stick-stick. Still, for all his stickiness, there was something in his manner, his confidence, the way he carried himself.

And then, she did have the strangest shivery feeling when it seemed he approved of her, right along with the intense irritation of when he did not. He had been unusually kind to her at dinner the night before, at least unusually kind for *him*. It had been in some way touching. Then, might not a stick unstick himself over time? Just because he was a stick now did not mean he would be forevermore.

Her thoughts were very stupid, as she well knew Lord Bertridge, stick or not, did not give a toss for her.

Mr. Landon was of quite a different nature. He was lively and fun and did not take himself too seriously. His interests were closely aligned with her own and he did not think a wife should be kept away from his horses. They were suited, she was sure.

But, though he was a pleasant-looking gentleman, her rambling thoughts did not see him in the same light as Lord Bertridge. Her logic understood the matter very well, but whatever guided her thoughts had seemed to drift into the camp of Lord Bertridge.

It was all ridiculous, in any case. It was not as if either gentleman was pressing a suit. She might look at both men from every angle, but that did not mean either of them were seriously looking at *her*.

Except, she did feel Mr. Landon had an interest. She could feel it in her bones. From Lord Bertridge, though, she could sense nothing.

So why was she being such a fool as to compare them? As Bemmy very rationally said, a bird in the hand was worth two in the bush. If there were a gentleman anywhere near her hand, it was Mr. Landon. It might be early days, but she sensed it.

All of these thoughts passed through her mind as Bemmy was pointing out various establishments to Lady Redfield. Though the lady had a house in town, it appeared she did not get to the shops often. She generally found that her carriage had gone off with one of her sons, or the carriage was there but the horses were gone.

"That one, there, Lady Redfield," Bemmy said, "is Jennings. Mr. Jennings has the finest in everything a proper lady might require by way of ribbons, fans, bonnets, parasols, and reticules. You did say you'd been huntin' for a new reticule? If Mr. Jennings don't have it, it ain't worth having."

At this rather ringing endorsement, Lady Redfield said, "Well of course I have heard of Jennings, at least I think I have. Did I say I required a new reticule? Well, I suppose I might have, one does say things in passing that do not commit to memory. In any case, as it seems I am looking for a reticule and Mr. Jennings does have what's worth having, we ought to go in."

And so they did proceed in, with Bemmy taking the lead. "Mr. Jennings," she said to the proprietor, "I brought two fine ladies to examine your wares. I told 'em, if you don't have it, it ain't worth having. Lady Redfield, in particular, is looking for a new reticule."

Mr. Jennings, a middle-aged man with a shiny bald head, bowed very low and said, "Lady Redfield, just this way to the counter. I am sure you will find something to your liking."

Bemmy said, "Right you are, Mr. Jennings. While you're showin' off your things, I'll take Miss Upton here to the back of the shop to have a look at them new ribbons you talked about."

There was a flicker of confusion on Mr. Jennings' features, as if he had no notion of new ribbons.

Bemmy took Caroline by the arm and firmly directed her down the rather crowded rows in Mr. Jennings' shop. There were twists and turns and boxes stacked to the rafters. It was a veritable maze.

"I do not see any ribbons here, Bemmy," Caroline said.

"No, you don't," Bemmy said merrily. "What you see in front of you is a back door out of this place."

"But you do not mean we should…"

"A course I do," Bemmy said. "Poor Lady Redfield will get so turned round in this place she'll never figure out how she lost us."

Caroline was torn. She would not wish to cause Lady Redfield any trouble. On the other hand, she desperately wished to see the exhibition and she and Bemmy had so carefully worked out how it could be done safely.

"If you want to go, we ought to get going. We don't got

much time," Bemmy said.

"I suppose it would not be too unusual for parties to become separated while shopping," Caroline said.

"Commonest thing in the world."

"And, after all, Lady Easton cannot hold it against Lady Redfield. The point was to be seen and we have been seen by quite a few people already. No mention was made of Lady Redfield accompanying us every minute as if she were a jailor."

"Should we set off while you're talkin' yourself round to it?" Bemmy asked.

"Yes," Caroline said firmly. "Let us go. There is no sense in missing a once in a lifetime opportunity by dithering here all day. We do no real harm."

With that, Bemmy opened the bolt on the door and they slipped out into an alley behind the shop. They would have wished to run, as they still must visit Bemmy's household to retrieve the hat and cloak that would be Caroline's disguise, but that would have called attention to them. The streets were crowded with people heading toward the exhibition. They settled for a very fast walk and were there in under ten minutes.

Bemmy's mother was a comfortable-looking woman whose only real concern of the day was how much her husband might drink at the exhibition. Bemmy was directed to slow him down if she could, as he got very maudlin when he drank. Apparently, the last time he'd over-imbibed, he'd wept for the dozen eggs in their kitchen, as they would never be chickens. There had been no use trying to convince him that the eggs had not had an encounter with a rooster and would never have been chickens anyway.

All Caroline had needed to do was switch her bonnet and don the old cloak in place of her pelisse. That done, they were on their way in a trice.

As they neared the place, the crowds swelled. Caroline and Bemmy joined in the stream of people, just two inconsequential people amongst dozens.

RICHARD SAT IN his stall with his knee man, who happened to be his valet Kingston. His bottle man, Lord Easton, had wandered off somewhere, greeting no end of people he knew. It hardly mattered, he had no intention of allowing any of his matches to go on long enough to require a bottle or sitting on Kingston's knee.

In truth, he thought his stamina would be one of his advantages, he could box all day long if necessary. He was determined to keep his opponent moving as much as possible, as he suspected many of them had been out late, indulging in drink, and would not be at their peak physical shape. Stupid that they would have done so, but he knew enough about gentlemen to know that they'd likely met to toast with one glass, which led to another and another. The key to preparing for anything physical was to forgo the one glass that leads on to too many.

The Prince had taken great care to see to the boxers' comfort. He'd built stalls in a long line, connected to one another and made of rather flimsy wood as they were only meant to last through the exhibition. The front of each stall was only comprised of a curtain, still, it provided some privacy from the hundreds of eyes who had gathered at the seaside to lay their bets and watch the fighting unfold.

The matches would begin with random pairs, each victor advancing to the next round, until the final round and only one victor remained. Richard knew he was favored to be that final man, and as well he should be. He had every intention of it.

He had been doing his best to ignore the cacophony of voices swirling round him, not the least of which was from the neighboring stall housing Mr. Landon. If that fellow could box with his volubility he might get somewhere. As it was, Landon was Richard's first match-up and he intended to make quick work of him.

The sudden intrusion of a female voice coming from Mr. Landon's stall caught his attention.

"There you are, you beggar," the woman said. "I done crossed half of England to track you down."

"Good Lord, Annie," Landon said, "what do you do here?"

"You know what I do here, I done told you of my condition and then you're up sticks and gone in the night."

"As I mentioned when you informed me of the happy news," Landon said smoothly, "it could be anybody's. In any case, I am certain it is not mine."

"You know it's yours!" Annie shrieked. "You're the only man I've lain with. You're the one who seduced me in that house! Now, the butler's seen me growin' and chucked me out."

Richard glanced at Kingston, who stared with a certain fascination at the thin wall that divided the two stalls. He'd known Landon was no good, but seducing a maid? That was beyond the pale.

"Now you listen," Annie said, "I got no intents on being left penniless and alone. You do the right thing."

"What right thing?" Landon asked. "I haven't any money."

"You got to marry me and raise this child."

"Have you lost your wits?" Landon asked with incredulity. "I cannot marry a scullery maid! Really now, you are being too ridiculous."

"If you don't," Annie said, her voice full of fury, "I'll tell all and sundry what you done."

"You can go dance on a table and shout it to the world, but you won't pin it on me. Now go on, get out of here. Bakewell, see this harridan out."

As Bakewell apparently manhandled the woman out of the stall, the last that was heard from Annie was, "Just see if I don't. Just see."

The last Richard heard from Landon was a muttered, "Deuced inconvenient."

Kingston appeared ready to speak but Richard laid his forefinger over his lips to indicate that they should not. If he could hear so well what went on in Landon's stall, then Landon would just as clearly hear anything said by him. He did not know what he would do with the information he'd heard, but for now he'd rather that Landon did not know he'd been overheard.

Actually, he did know one thing he would do as a first step. He would pound Landon to pieces in the ring. That must be a start.

⟫⟩✳⟨⟪

"BEMMY," CAROLINE SAID as they were swept along with the crowd, "there are so many people I doubt we will be able to see anything."

"Never you mind, miss," Bemmy said, "I've got an idea." The maid pulled Caroline to a side street that led away from the seaside rather than toward it.

Caroline was on the verge of questioning why they should go that way, but decided to hold her tongue. Bemmy was overflowing with clever ideas and she supposed this must be one, though she did not yet understand it.

They hurried down the deserted street and came to a halt at the back of a large building.

"That there is The Ship Inn," Bemmy said. "I'm particular friends with a serving girl there what has a room in the attic. She shares it with another girl who won't mind neither, they'll both be run off their feet today and won't care who's peering out their window above stairs."

"Oh I see," Caroline said. "Perhaps, if you are certain they would not mind, we might use the room to view the fight. And then I suppose I could leave them some money for their trouble."

"Now that'd be what's called the sugar on the biscuit, they'd be that happy over it," Bemmy said. "Now we slip in the back door and up the backstairs. It ain't never locked, what with the suppliers coming and going all the time. A man should be at the door, but he won't be—not with the fight getting ready to start."

Bemmy was right, the door was not locked and whoever was meant to be supervising comings and goings had taken himself off somewhere. They slipped in unseen.

Directly to their right, they found the narrow steep stairs leading to the servants' quarters. Bemmy went up as fast as a hare and Caroline was quite breathless by the time they'd reached the attics.

They tiptoed down the dreary hall, its fading wallpaper peeling more than it was intact, and came to a door at the end. Bemmy knocked and, hearing nothing, tried the knob.

"It's latched, just as I thought," Bemmy said.

Caroline could see the small hole in the door, but there was no latch string to pull the latch up. "How do they get in?" she asked.

Bemmy dug through the voluminous pockets of her cloak and pulled out a thin scrap of wood. "You'll see." She slid the sliver of wood in the crack where the door met the casement and slid it up until it hit the inside latch and the door swung open.

Caroline could not help but be alarmed by this operation. "Bemmy," she said, "do you always carry round housebreaking tools?"

Bemmy snorted. "This is how I get in my own house when my ma's gone out. We got some metal on the door, fashioned to look like a sturdy lock and no latch string showing to give away the ruse. We jimmy our way in."

Caroline nodded, as she supposed it made sense. As she gazed round the room, she could not help but notice how dull and dismal it was. Just a square box with two bedsteads with threadbare coverlets. It was not at all like the servants' quarters at home.

Her father's staff lived in bright and cheerful rooms, the women had lively yellow papered walls and the men had manly scenes of riders on the hunt. There were light quilts for summer and heavy for winter and a small carpet next to each bed. Every servant was given their own chest to store their personal items. Each room had a fireplace, and plenty of coal to go with it, though there was no hearth *here*. She could not imagine how cold it must be in winter, with the frigid sea air blowing gales.

She took two shillings out of her reticule and slipped one each under the serving girls' pillows.

"Here we go," Bemmy said, already at the window. "Ain't nobody has a view like this and we don't get jostled around by the crowd."

Caroline hurried over and looked down. The view was ideal. They were above the ring and at just the perfect angle to see everything. Further fortunate, nobody would ever know she was there unless they looked up at the window, and who would look up when the crowd was facing the opposite direction and there was so much to see in the ring?

"I got the lowdown in the servants' hall last night," Bemmy said. "That line of stalls just beyond the ring has got all the men who will fight. The fights are to go by Broughton's Rules, though nobody seemed clear who *he* was. Mr. Bramley did put up a good show of hinting he might know the fella, but I reckon he don't. 'Parently, there's rules about what to do when, but the only one I did understand is if a fella gets knocked down, he's got half a minute to get up again and get back to his side."

"That sounds very reasonable," Caroline said, her mind less taken up by Broughton's Rules and more taken up with wondering which stall Lord Bertridge could be found in. And Mr. Landon too, of course.

"You see on the left," Bemmy said, "there's a raised dais with an awfully big chair. I reckon that's for the Prince to view the proceedings."

Caroline supposed so. She did not know who else would require a chair so large.

"They's to fight in rounds, with the winners going on, until one man is left standing," Bemmy said. "I suppose Lord Bertridge will acquit himself grand."

"Do you think so, Bemmy?" Caroline asked, her heart speeding up. It was all well and good to watch the men practice but now they would fight in earnest. Anything might happen, somebody might be seriously hurt. Lord Bertridge might be seriously hurt. She could not help notice that she had not been equally struck by the idea that Mr. Landon, or any of the rest of them, might be hurt too.

"He'll do fine, if the bettin' on him means anything. The footmen say he's got a threefold advantage—his size, his skill, and his temper."

"His temper?" Caroline asked. "Certainly, Lord Bertridge can be…prickly. But I do not see how being irritable will help him."

"He can be more than prickly and irritable, though he is that," Bemmy said. "Bramley didn't like it one bit but Charlie told us of how he watched the lord's temper erupt a few years ago and it was something to behold. Charlie reckons if somebody hits the lord in the face that temper will come bustin' out again."

Caroline's thoughts were in a bit of a whirl. Buttoned up Bertie had a temper? Was that the wild heart underneath that she'd sensed all along? Is that what he was always covering up?

"What happened, Bemmy? What did Charlie see?"

Bemmy leaned close and confidential. "It seems that one day, there was a ruckus out on the street at Portland Place. A hackney driver was beatin' his horse something terrible, but the poor half-starved thing wouldn't move an inch. The poor creatures give up sometimes, you know. Well, Charlie said the man was so enraged he was set to beatin' the unfortunate animal to death. Lord Bertridge heard the goings on, comes out of his house to see what's unfolding, and takes steps."

"Steps?" Caroline said softly.

"Steps," Bemmy said nodding gleefully. "He takes the whip from the driver and throws it into the bushes, then he pummels the driver 'til he's nearly insensible, then he unhitches the horse and leads him to his own stables. As he's goin' he tells that driver if he sees him again he'll beat him some more. Charlie said the horse went willin' enough, as if he knowed it was his one chance of life. 'Parently, the horse is right as rain now and retired to the lord's estate, gets plenty of oats and is named Icarus, as he rose from the dead."

Caroline felt tears spring to her eyes as she thought of the poor horse. They were sensitive animals and could not hold out against cruelty forever. Beating the man and taking the horse was precisely what her father would have done for the creature. But Lord Bertridge? It was rather hard to imagine. But it must be true, nobody would make up such a story.

Of course it was true. Had she not seen how indulgent the lord was with his dog Edgar? If only he could be so indulgent with people! Or at least, if not all people, then with her. That would be something indeed.

Her attention was pulled as Bemmy grasped her arm and shook it. "It's getting ready to start, there's the Prince with Mr. Jackson."

RICHARD HEARD A horn blow and cheers erupt from the crowd. That was the signal that the first pair of boxers were to come out and take the ring. Richard did not mind being the first pair off, other than he'd have to stand there doing nothing while the Prince made some sort of speech.

Kingston picked up his bottle of water, as his actual bottle man by way of Lord Easton was nowhere to be found. It was no matter, he'd not require a drink for this match—he fully intended to be done with Landon in less than a quarter of an hour. Then, the scoundrel could slink off with his ears ringing and head pounding and decide what to do about the scullery maid who was to make him a father sometime in the near future.

He could at least be grateful that his aunt had put her foot down and Miss Upton would no longer visit the sort of places where Landon could be found. He had found Landon distasteful from the start, but he now knew him to be dangerous.

Landon exited his tent with his man Bakewell, and Richard could not help but notice he looked rather peaked. In truth, they both looked peaked. If Richard had to guess, Bakewell did not carry high hopes that his master would find success in the ring, and Bakewell would be right. The only prize Landon would win this day was a scullery maid named Annie.

Richard strode ahead, his untucked shirt flapping in the breeze. He must soon take it off, which he thought unseemly in front of such a crowd, but there was nothing for it.

He reached the ring and took his corner as the Prince said, "Welcome one and all to what is our first boxing exhibition in the charming town of Brighton."

Cheers went up and Richard thought the townspeople were flattered by the description.

The Prince went on to note that the proceeds from all the food and drink sold in the royal stalls would go to the poor mothers and childrens' fund.

Richard glanced at Landon to see how he would react to the mention of poor mothers and children now that the scullery maid carrying his own child had arrived to town.

Landon was very pale, though Richard could not determine if Annie's arrival was the cause, or a late night doused with gin. Perhaps it was both.

The Prince droned on for some minutes, but finally concluded and sat heavily in his chair. Mr. Jackson came down to the ring and reminded them of the rules. There were to be up to thirteen rounds, unless a boxer reaches seven wins beforehand. Broughton's Rules were in effect, no hitting below the belt, grasping hair and so on. They were to meet at the mark and begin on the horn.

Richard noticed Lord Easton finally arriving and standing by Kingston, looking pleased as punch to be in the ring. He did not suppose his uncle would be of any real use, but he was not opposed to finding him there.

The last instruction from Mr. Jackson was that it was thirty seconds firm to get back to your side after having been knocked down and that knee men and bottle men were not to exchange words with the opponent's men.

Kingston helped him remove his shirt to the apparent delight of the crowd. One particularly crass female shouted, "Take your shirt off in my rooms any day, m'lord." It was a disgrace and Richard forced his ears to shut against the shouting.

Landon looked a deal more amused by the lewd comments being called out. The crowd would shortly see how long that miscreant *stayed* amused.

Richard strode to the mark and raised his fists. Landon met him there, the horn was blown, and the fight began.

CHAPTER TWELVE

CAROLINE PEERED OUT the window of the inn and gripped Bemmy's arm. She had not known the schedule of the fights, nor that Lord Bertridge would match up against Mr. Landon first.

It seemed that poor Mr. Landon was no match for Bertie, as he'd already been knocked to the ground four times and had yet to inflict any damage of his own. She did not think that Mr. Landon had managed even one touch on his opponent.

Lord Bertridge was masterful, he hardly looked as if he were putting in much effort. And then, he was always rather marvelous with his shirt off, muscles flexing, hair mussed and so intent on what he was doing.

What a man he was!

The day had been overcast and Caroline had worried it might rain, but just then, the sun came out from behind the clouds. It must have hit Lord Bertridge directly in his eyes. For a moment, he shaded them and glanced up.

Then for more than a moment. He was staring straight at her. Caroline did not dare move. To jump out of the way and hide would give her away. She was dressed as a servant and must stay looking as if that was just what she was.

Mr. Landon took advantage of Lord Bertridge's momentary inattention. It was the first opportunity that had been given him and he wasted no time. He hit Lord Bertridge squarely in the eye.

The pain of it must have been terrible, as Lord Bertridge's head snapped back from the force of it. The lord staggered, but he did not fall.

The crowd had gasped, and now they grew very quiet. Mr. Landon looked almost frightened at what he'd done. Lord Bertridge raised his fists and, one after the other like lightning, pummeled Mr. Landon.

"And there's the temper, I think," Bemmy said cheerfully.

Caroline was terrified. She'd done it. It had been her fault that he'd been hit. And so hard!

Mr. Landon fell to the ground under the assault and the umpires began the count to thirty. His man shouted at him and tried to help him up, but Mr. Landon waved him off. He would not rise to meet Lord Bertridge again.

Caroline stepped away from the window and sat on one of the beds. "He's seen me, Bemmy. And he's got what I think will turn into an awful black eye on account of it. We really should go."

Bemmy considered it and said, "I reckon you're right. Mostly, I can think of a slip-around for any situation, but this here particular one is layering on the complications. We done ditched Lady Redfield and have to account for that, and now the lord's spotted you, though we can't be sure *he's* sure it was you. I wouldn't like to think of him wanderin' over here between matches to investigate."

"Goodness no!" Caroline said, filling with horror over the idea. "Let us go in all haste."

They left the serving girls' room, Bemmy locking the door behind her by feeding out the latch string and then feeding it back into the room again. They hurried down the stairs and out into the alley and practically ran to Bemmy's house to change out of the clothes that had been meant to disguise her. By the time they reached Lady Easton's house, Caroline's nerves and all the fast walking they'd done felt like they would bring her to her knees.

As they entered the front hall, a plaintive cry came from the opened door of the drawing room. "Is that them!"

It was Lady Redfield, sounding as if she were on the verge of a collapse.

Lady Easton hurried into the hall, with Lady Redfield staggering behind her. "Caroline!" Lady Easton cried. "We have been so worried!"

Bemmy, ever the quick thinker, stepped forward and said, "Now I told the miss that Lady Redfield was a grown woman and could not be in any danger but she insisted that we search the town high and low for the lady. We couldn't think what had happened to her, one minute she was in the shop and the next she weren't."

"But that's precisely what happened to me!" Lady Redfield cried. "One moment you were there and the next you weren't and I too searched high and low."

"Goodness," Bemmy went on smoothly, "I wonder how many times we just missed each other by a minute going from one street to the next."

"That must have been so," Lady Redfield said. "I was forever thinking I'd see you round the next corner."

Bemmy nodded sagely and said, "Well, it's all come out right. Though, Lady Easton, I will admit that I did forcefully march Miss Upton back to the house as she's on the point of falling over from exhaustion. P'raps I shouldn't have been forceful, p'raps it's not my place, but I did see a disaster coming on and thought to nip it lest it go too far."

"Of course you were right to do it, Bemmy. You always do know the correct thing to do."

"I'm very touched, Miss Upton," Lady Redfield said. "You really should not have exhausted yourself searching for me, but I am very touched by it."

"Oh dear, Caroline, you really do not look well," Lady Easton fussed.

"No, I am all right," Caroline said softly, the weight of guilt growing upon her shoulders with each passing minute.

"She ain't all right this minute," Bemmy said, "but she will be. All that's required is a few cups of tea and a heap of biscuits, feet up, and she'll be restored good as new."

Lady Easton nodded. "Yes, certainly, we must do as you advise, Bemmy. You do have rather good instincts about such things. Take Caroline to her room and I'll have Bramley send up a tray. Now Cecilia, you have exhausted yourself too and we will take the same good advice in the drawing room."

Lady Redfield nodded gratefully and consented to be led back while Caroline and Bemmy took the stairs.

Bemmy was exceedingly clever, but just now Caroline wished her maid had not been quite so ingenious. Somehow, she was being hailed as having done something fine. She'd not done anything fine at all. She'd escaped her escort, leaving the poor lady to fret and wander round the town looking for her, she'd gone to a boxing match she ought not have gone to, she'd made Lord Bertridge get hit in the eye, and she'd lied to Lady Easton about all of it. She had not said the words, but she had not contradicted them either. Further, it would all come to light. Lord Bertridge would say that he saw her there, and it would be obvious to anybody that she'd not been searching for Lady Redfield in the attics of The Ship Inn.

What was happening to her? She was turning into an awful person!

As the door shut behind her, Caroline said, "What are we to do, Bemmy? It will all come out when Lord Bertridge announces that he saw me there. Perhaps I ought to go down and tell Lady Easton the truth."

Bemmy looked surprised by the suggestion. She said, "Wait a minute before you do, so as we have a moment to think this through. It was only a bit of a lark after all and nobody told Lady Redfield to make like Captain Cook and circumnavigate the globe in search of you."

"But she would do, she is a kind lady."

"I reckon Lord Bertridge won't say nothing about it. From

that distance he could never be sure it was you and you was dressed as a servant. He'll be too taken up with the matches at any rate. Though, my heart goes to Lady Redfield, as I ponder the matter. She was touched, you see, and I wouldn't like her to think you *weren't* searchin' for her."

"Nor I," Caroline said. "Oh dear, I really do not know what is the right course."

"I'm thinkin' it's always right to protect a person's feelings. If Lord Bertridge was to say anything about it, we could say that somebody told us they'd seen Lady Redfield going toward the exhibition and we thought that a lady of that standing would probably have a private room at the Ship. We searched all the way to the top but didn't find her there. That would account for us being there, and Lady Redfield still gets to be touched."

"But it's just another lie on top of all the others," Caroline said fretfully.

"Aye," Bemmy said, nodding, "sometimes they do pile up."

⇥⟫⟫⟩⟨⟨⟨⇤

LADY EASTON INSISTED that Lady Redfield restore herself with tea, biscuits, and feet up on an ottoman, just as Bemmy had so wisely advised. She did not think Bramley had ever witnessed a person's feet up in her drawing room before, but an exception must be made on account of how valiantly Cecilia had searched the town for Caroline.

Lady Redfield reclined on the sofa as if she posed for an old master painter. Though, the biscuit in her hand somewhat took away from the effect. "Now I suppose," she said, "that this is one of the differences between sons and daughters. I cannot imagine any of my boys exhausting themselves in search of me. Really, were I to go missing, I suppose they'd say, *Silly mama, she'll find her way home eventually.*"

Lady Easton nodded her agreement of the assessment. Cecilia's boys likely would say that. She could only hope it was not an attitude her *own* sons would adopt. Though, she could not be sure.

"Well," she said, "Caroline is a goodhearted girl, after all. Rather two handfuls, but she always means well, I think."

"And now, with this dinner you host this evening, Miss Upton will be exposed to the right people who do and say the right things."

"Just so," Lady Easton said.

Bramley came in with the post on a silver tray, doing his best not to look askance at Lady Redfield's shoes on the ottoman.

Lady Easton took the pile of letters and sorted through them. As she did, the smallest flutter flapped its wings inside her. She recognized one hand—Lady Fanny. Then she recognized another—Sir Matthew. It was a hostess's nightmare to receive notes from guests who were set to arrive that same day.

"Oh bother," she said, ripping open the first. "There had better not be an illness I am to hear of. It will quite upset my seating plan."

My dear Lady Easton,

It pains me to write you this note, but my lord insists. We had thought, considering the recent talk, that the dinner would be called off. You know, let things settle down and all that. I am very sorry to say that we cannot attend. I would be prepared to face it all down, but my lord says our dowager will hear of it somehow and never speak to me again. (She is a terrible dragon so I dare say he's right.) So sorry to have put you out. All the best,

Fanny Brightsmith

"I can hardly believe it," Lady Easton said. "Lady Fanny declines to come to dine. On account of the false gossip spread about Caroline."

"Oh dear," Lady Redfield said, reading the note. "Well, she does say she'd be willing to come. And then, the dowager *is* rather frightening, I believe even her son is terrified of her."

"No need to attempt to soften the blow, Cecilia," Lady Easton said. She tore open Sir Matthew's letter.

He also would not come. Of course he was sorry, but his wife's nerves were delicate and could not hold up against any kind of talk.

Delicate indeed. Lady Hogsworth was the daughter of a naval captain who'd married up in the world to a baronet. There was nothing delicate about her.

Lady Easton ripped through the rest of the letters. All were declines. It seemed the only people who would come to dine were Lord and Lady Maldock, Sir Benjamin and Lady Smithson, and Lord and Lady Reston. They were all older and only ventured out for the occasional dinner or card party.

They had not heard.

She felt rather faint. Such a thing had never befallen her before. Never in her life had Clara Godwin, Countess of Easton, been censured.

Oh, she had watched it happen to other people of course. Occasionally, she'd been forced to do the censuring. But to her! How could it be?

She leaned back on the sofa and fanned herself. "Bramley," she called, "bring the vinaigrette. And laudanum for my tea."

"You do not look well, Clara," Lady Redfield said, she herself leaned back and feet still up.

"Almost everybody has called off from the dinner, Cecilia. How on earth should I look?"

"Almost everybody? Oh dear. But not absolutely everybody, so that's something."

Mr. Bramley hurried in with the vinaigrette and waved it vigorously under his mistress' nose until she waved her hand to make him stop. He placed a small brown glass bottle next to her teacup.

"Do dose my tea, Bramley," Lady Easton murmured. "And make it a strong dose. I am quite in despair."

Mr. Bramley appeared shocked to his shoes to hear of Lady Easton in despair. He carefully poured out the drops and stirred them in.

"Perhaps, my lady," Mr. Bramley said cautiously, "when you feel recovered, we might discuss the final arrangements for dinner this evening."

"The dinner!" Lady Easton wailed.

Mr. Bramley looked further shaken by this reply. He put the cap on the bottle of laudanum and fled the room.

BRAMLEY PACED THE front hall. He did not know what he should do. Lady Easton was drinking laudanum in the drawing room and claimed she was in despair. Lady Redfield was lying back with her feet up like Joan of Arc having returned from battle, though she had only been out walking the town. Some dire communication had arrived in the post and the two ladies appeared overcome by it.

What had happened? Had somebody died? Or was about to die? Was the dinner to be called off on account of it?

What was he to do?

Lady Easton was wailing in a most unseemly fashion, but for all she cried out he could not fathom what had happened. It all ran along the lines of: *How could this happen to me? What are we to do?*

It could not be either of the boys in danger. The bad news, whatever it was, had come by local post. Certainly, if something dreadful had happened to Lord Easton, somebody would have turned up in person to deliver the blow.

Though he did not know what to do to help the situation, he very much doubted Lady Redfield did any more good than he. All she'd managed to say, repeatedly, was: *Now, dear Clara, it cannot be so very bad.*

Whatever it was, it certainly could be so very bad!

Bemmy, that nosy and uncouth lady's maid, snuck up behind him and tapped him on the arm, nearly sending him into a dead faint. Where had she come from? Why must she sneak up on a person like a pickpocket!

"What's the ruckus, Mr. Bramley?" she asked, hooking her thumb toward the drawing room doors.

"We do not have what you would call a *ruckus* in this house," he said sternly.

"All right then," the saucy girl said, "what's the commotion, uproar, hubbub, or clamor?"

Naturally, Bramley would like to appear as if he knew, but would not deign to explain to this cheeky maid.

"Never you mind, Bemmy. Get on with your work."

She marched off as if she were somehow affronted. He paced the hall and it was not a minute before the girl was back again. She'd taken a pair of Miss Upton's shoes downstairs. Certainly she did not polish them in so short a time.

She held them up as she sailed past him. "Wrong pair," she said, walking very slowly up the stairs.

The cries from the drawing room continued, though they did no more to shed light on the situation than they had done. *What am I to do? This is Easton's fault.*

He might have thought that the mention of his lord being at fault was a clue, but he had been in the house long enough to know that if something went amiss, it generally *was* laid at the lord's door. *My God, could he actually be dead?* Lady Easton certainly would blame him for it if he was.

Bemmy came down the stairs again, walking slower than an old woman on her last legs.

She held up a different pair of shoes as she sauntered past him. "Right ones," she said.

As he contemplated taking one of the shoes and hitting her on the head with it, a sharp rap on the door nearly gave him apoplexy. He staggered toward it and threw it open, praying to the heavens it was not more bad news arrived.

The Duchess of Stanbury, Lady Mendleton, and Lady Heathway filled the doorframe.

Bramley stood there, slack jawed, as Lady Easton wailed from the drawing room, *Why me?*

"Great heavens, Bramley," the duchess said, "what on earth is happening?"

"I do not know, Your Grace," Bramley said, staring at the three ladies. "I am very afraid someone has died. You haven't come to say Lord Easton is dead?"

"Certainly not," Lady Heathway said, "Lord Easton would never do something so inconvenient. Now, we do no good standing on the doorstep. Step aside and we will find out what has occurred."

CAROLINE WAS RATHER terrified to go down to the drawing room. Though, as she watched the minutes tick by on the clock that stared at her from the mantle, she was equally terrified to be late. Another quarter hour, and she must descend.

The house had been in chaos all day since she and Bemmy had returned from the boxing exhibition.

Lady Easton had been positively wailing and her cries were clear enough above stairs. Bemmy had grabbed a pair of her shoes so she might descend as if she were taking them to the servants' hall for cleaning. She'd then come back and taken another pair, much to Mr. Bramley's irritation. And then another.

With all the upping and downing with shoes in her hand, Bemmy was able to piece together what went on downstairs.

It seemed quite a few couples had sent their last-minute regrets for this evening's dinner. They could not come, after hearing the gossip spread round about Lord Alvanley's party. None of it was true, she'd certainly not danced on a table or hid in the dark, waiting to be found by a gentleman. The Prince had been outraged and had let all know it. That should have been the end of it.

It was not the end though. It seemed that the Prince's opinion only weighed heavily with his friends and those who wished to curry his favor. It was not well-regarded by those who found his habits unsavory.

Then of course, there were the parts to the story that *were* true. Caroline had been the only young woman present, and the other two women had been Mrs. Fitzherbert and an actress. It appeared the true parts of the gossip were almost as shocking to Lady Easton's friends as the untrue.

The duchess, Lady Heathway, and Lady Mendleton had arrived and, according to Bemmy, the duchess had taken charge. She'd told everybody to pull themselves together and she'd told Lady Redfield to get her feet off the ottoman and back on the floor like a rational person. The end of it was, that those three ladies and their husbands would fill in for some of the guests who would not come.

Caroline suspected the dinner would be very serious, and disapproving.

Lady Easton had been deeply shamed and insulted and it was Caroline's fault. On top of that, the dear lady had not even heard all. Caroline was certain Lord Bertridge would reveal that he'd seen her at the exhibition. Then she would know that Caroline had lied and run away from Lady Redfield and poor Lady Redfield would know that she'd never had a reason to be touched.

With sudden and uncomfortable clarity, as if someone had thrown open the drapes to let in the light, Caroline knew she had acted abominably. Why had she done it? Oh, she supposed she'd bristled at Lady Easton and Lord Bertridge scolding her all the time. Especially Lord Bertridge. He did so disapprove of her! She'd been so stung by it. Having been stung, she'd felt very defiant about it.

Lord Alvanley's dinner could not be laid entirely at her door.

Lord Easton had taken her to that. But other things *could* be laid at her door. Always going to the boxing practices instead of walking along the seaside or peeking in the shops as she was supposed to be doing. Running away from Lady Redfield. Attending the exhibition. Being the cause of Lord Bertridge being hit in the eye. That was all her doing.

Bemmy might have encouraged it, but Bemmy was her maid, not her sponsor. She should have reined in her maid's worst impulses, and reined in her own. It was what her father would have expected her to do.

She had been like a rebellious child. She saw that now. Lady Easton and Lord Bertridge had taken the time to give her hints and if she'd had the sense of a pigeon she would have swallowed her pride and taken them. She had not, though.

Now, there would be a price to pay.

Caroline had nearly gone down to Lady Easton to confess all and take whatever consequences there were, but Bemmy had said she did not think the lady could manage one more upset on this particular day. Though Caroline had vowed not to be led by Bemmy into anymore unseemly situations, she could not deny that her maid was likely right about that.

Bemmy came in with a necklace Lady Easton had sent for her to wear, a delicate braided silver chain that would complement her pale green silk dress. Caroline could hardly bear to put it on, so kind was the lady when she had no cause to be.

"Bemmy," Caroline said firmly, "from now on, I must be very circumspect. I shan't do anything I would mind the entire world hearing about."

Bemmy considered this new idea and said, "It don't sound like much fun, but whatever direction you like to go, I'll be goin' with ya."

"Very good," Caroline said. "No more suggestions of anything we ought to do that we really ought *not* to do. If we don't want people to find it out, then we won't do it."

"Ah, we're goin' on the straight and narrow, are we? Well, I never did try it myself, but where's the adventure if a person don't try something new?"

Caroline rose and shook out her skirt. "Lady Easton may very well send me packing when she discovers all. I can at least ensure that there is nothing further to discover beyond what there already is."

Bemmy nodded sadly. "You poor fancy types got so many rules to follow. I do pity you, I really do."

Caroline thought it was not every maid who would pity the people she served, but then Bemmy was an original. She glanced at the clock and said, "I must go down now. Tonight of all nights, I cannot be late."

Bemmy fussed with Caroline's hair for a last adjustment and said, "Now, keep your head up and don't look like you're a criminal on your way to a hanging. We was just up to some spirited fun, not a murder."

Caroline nodded, though she did not feel much better than a criminal on the way to a hanging.

❦

CHAPTER THIRTEEN

RICHARD HAD HANDILY won the exhibition and he supposed he ought to be pleased about it. The Prince had certainly been pleased. The people who had laid bets in his favor were pleased. His uncle was almost giddy. For himself, he found it hard to be pleased when he saw what sort of battered state he was in.

He'd got out of the cold bath the footmen had filled up and glanced in the glass as they handed him towels. Both of the boys had slipped away from Bramley's clutches late in the day and had witnessed the final match of the exhibition between him and Alvanley.

As they chattered on about this stance or that tactic, Richard examined himself. His left eye was swollen and looked a different size than his right, and the whole was pink and purple. It would only grow darker as the days wore on before it finally began to fade.

He supposed Landon bragged about it just now. That delinquent had lost his match, and if anyone had a right to brag besides himself it was Alvanley, who had given him a far harder time. But Landon was the only fighter to leave a mark on him.

And why did Landon get the opportunity to leave a mark on him? Miss Caroline Upton, that was why.

The sun had made a sudden appearance and he'd shaded his eyes and glanced up to see if it would stay out for long. Had there been no clouds ready to drift over it again, he'd have had to maneuver Landon around so that the sun was in *his* eyes.

But it had not been clouds that had taken his attention. It had been Miss Upton and her maid at a window in The Ship Inn. He might not have been certain it was her, dressed as she was, had her maid not been standing beside her.

She had attempted a disguise to attend the exhibition. That really had been bad enough, but when he returned to the house he discovered that she had been in town with Lady Redfield and then disappeared, that poor lady exhausting herself in search of her charge.

Miss Upton, herself, had been commended for doing the same, searching everywhere for Lady Redfield. Instead, she'd been at the exhibition!

What was wrong with her? Did she feel driven to flout every convention? And then, to use Lady Redfield so poorly!

He'd been further informed that most of the people who were meant to dine in the house this evening had sent their last-minute regrets. Of course, Miss Upton had been the cause of that too. To be fair, he knew that the gossip that had gone round was not true and her attendance at Alvanley's dinner was not her fault, but rather his uncle's. But he could not help thinking that wherever Miss Upton went, trouble was hard on her heels.

Why must she be as she was? When she was not causing trouble, she was…well, it did not matter what she was. It did not matter that she was lovely and so kind to his dog and so cheerful all the time. There were times when she almost made him cheerful too. But then she would go straight into trouble…

He really did not wish to go to this blasted dinner. Not with all that had gone on, not with the rather dull guest list, and not with a black eye.

Kingston came into the room and chased the footmen out of it. His valet had taken on a certain dignity caused by the results of the day. Richard supposed his knee man would regale the servants' hall with everything that had transpired. Kingston did not know everything, though. Kingston did not know that one of the servants he would regale had been there too, accompanying Miss Upton.

His aunt did not yet know either and Richard was of two minds about telling her. Certainly, Lady Easton ought to know the truth. On the other hand, he did not think his aunt could manage one more upset presently. He sympathized, as he would be in the precise same situation if he'd not boxed out so much of his irritation.

He would likely tell his aunt at some point, but tonight was not the time.

Blast this dinner and blast that girl.

CAROLINE ARRIVED TO the drawing room on time and found Lady Easton and Lord Bertridge already there. At the sight of them, she felt an enormous cloak of guilt settling round her. Lady Easton looked at her kindly, and the lady was so kind! As for Lord Bertridge, well, he likely knew that she had run off from Lady Redfield and attended the exhibition. Bemmy had been convinced he would not make it out, but the way he turned away from her just now…she was certain he knew.

As Lady Easton questioned her on whether she was quite recovered from searching the town earlier in the day, Caroline answered that she was very well. Though in truth, she was not at all well. Her thoughts whirled and it made her head ache. She had such a great urge to confess all, though she could hardly do it with guests poised to arrive. She must do it at some point, though.

Lady Easton would pack her up and send her home. She was sure of it. She'd caused far too much trouble and the lady must be exhausted by it. Caroline supposed Lord Easton might argue against it, as he did have a debt to settle with her father. Though, if Lady Easton did not wish her here, she'd rather not stay.

And, oh, her father. What could she say to her father about her conduct? Baron Dunn expected all his children to be rational and kind. She had been neither. She'd been unthinking, flighty, and unkind.

Lord Easton sauntered in a full four minutes late, but he could not be properly reprimanded by his wife as guests had begun to arrive in the front hall.

Caroline breathed in deep. Whatever was to be the consequences of her actions, for now she must hold up her end at dinner. Lady Easton had already been traumatized over having so many guests cancel, it was imperative that she end the night feeling the dinner had been a success after all.

CAROLINE WATCHED BRAMLEY stand at the doors, back straight and chin up, with all the dignity he could bring to bear. He caught Lady Easton's eye and slowly nodded. It was an emphatic sort of nod, meant to communicate something or other.

Lady Easton fanned herself and smiled and appeared flushed. Some sort of information had passed between them, though Caroline could not say what. She *could* say that whatever the message had been, Lady Easton had been fortified by it.

The senior footman led a newly-arrived couple to Bramley's side. In an impressively sonorous voice, he announced, "The Duke and Duchess of Stanbury."

An imperious-looking lady sailed in with her husband leading her by the arm. She was dressed in brocade, which Caroline thought must be very hot, though the lady did not seem to feel it. After a friendly and familiar nod to Lady Easton, the duke left his wife with her hostess and made his way over to Lord Easton.

"Clara," the lady said, "you do look quite recovered from the excitement of the day. That plum color suits you exceedingly."

"Theodosia," Lady Easton said, "you know very well you were instrumental in putting things right this afternoon."

The lady nodded graciously, as if she were quite used to collecting accolades and in fact considered them her due.

"May I present Miss Upton," Lady Easton said. "Caroline, this is the Duchess of Stanbury."

Caroline curtsied low. "Your Grace," she said.

"Let me look at you, yes, very pretty," the duchess said. "Clara, I find there is something noble in the forehead, do you not think so?"

Lady Easton nodded in agreement, seeming well-pleased, though Caroline could not imagine that her forehead said anything at all.

"Miss Upton," the duchess continued, "I presume you have been apprised of our singular interest in your affairs. Going forward, you will always have one of us by your side. Now tell me, do you swim?"

"Indeed yes, ma'am," Caroline said, "though never yet in the sea."

"That will change on the morrow, I will see to it. My butler is a great predictor of weather and he says tomorrow will be particularly fine. I have already sent a note to Mrs. Gunn that we will have need of her. I only trust my person to Mrs. Gunn, you see. I shall arrive at nine o'clock to collect you."

"That is very kind, ma'am," Caroline said. She was at once looking forward to trying out a swim in the sea, a bit taken aback that she was to do so with a duchess, and certain she did not deserve such a courtesy.

Bramley announced, "Lord and Lady Heathway and Lady Redfield."

As those three came in, Bramley stood at the door and another couple appeared. It seemed they had got to the moment of the evening when everybody would arrive at once.

"Lord and Lady Maldock and Sir Benjamin and Lady Smithson."

More people arrived soon after by way of Lord and Lady Reston and Lord and Lady Mendleton.

Caroline was introduced to all and had little time to reflect on her own dampened feelings. She worked hard to smile and show a gracious deference to Lady Easton's guests.

It was rather a relief when Bramley signaled his mistress that her guests could proceed to the dining room. She felt a little unsteady on her feet and thought a dinner would go some way to restore her. She could not ever remember feeling so out of sorts.

Caroline realized this night was not to be got through hour by hour, but minute by minute.

BRAMLEY HAD GIRDED himself to manage this dinner with all the aplomb he was renowned for. Whatever upsets had shaken the rafters of this abode earlier in the day, the finest butler in England did not let down the house.

He had been consulting with Cook for the past week and was well satisfied with the results of their Herculean efforts. Particularly their efforts on this particular day, which had scaled new heights. The dinner would be five courses, beginning with a brown soup as there was no use trying a white soup when Lady Heathway was in attendance. The lady had as strong an aversion to it as Cook did to stewed tomatoes.

Then would come the fish course of turbots à l'Anglaise, trouts poached in white wine and butter, cold crabs dressed in parsley and mayonnaise, steamed courgette medallions with parmesan, roasted and mashed aubergines with lemon and herbs, and thinly sliced radishes tossed in oil, vinegar, sugar and salt.

Following that, the meat course would be roasted beef, broiled capons, baked chicken with an accompanying egg sauce, thinly sliced ham spread with a beaten cream cheese dusted with nutmeg and rolled and cut into roulades, mashed potatoes, broiled onions, and wilted Swiss chard with a vinegar-mustard dressing topped with toasted walnuts.

Once all that was got through successfully, the rest would be like a horse trotting downhill until reaching the inevitable moment of glory. A next course of fennel salad, pickled cucumber, jellies, and strong cheeses would be brought out. The cheese board would feature Bemmy's recommendation of a local blue.

Though Bramley was always reluctant to take any hint from that harridan of a lady's maid, she had brought in a sample from her gentleman friend and he had to admit that it was very good. It would have mattered little what he thought anyway, as the cook was wild for it, and so it had been settled.

Then finally a dessert course of Wensleydale and cheddar cheeses, blancmange, strawberry tarts, a savoy cake with brandied cherry cream, and, very daringly, a sliced pineapple.

Word of the various guests canceling, and the hysterical state of the mistress had, of course, reached below stairs. Cook and Bemmy had conspired in a corner over it and then Cook had convinced Lady Easton that this current habit of renting a pineapple nobody ate was small and undignified. He advised it be purchased, sliced, and served with a syllabub.

Of course, Lady Easton was at first dubious at the suggestion, it had not even been clear whether they could locate a pineapple to *rent*. One had arrived for examination but had been clearly rotten and the merchant had been sent packing.

However, it seemed that Bemmy had her own sources. She knew of an old baron not a half hour outside of town who successfully cultivated them in his hothouse.

By way of Mrs. Gunn, who seemed to know quite a lot about the Marine Pavilion's kitchens, Bemmy had been informed that he regularly sold the kingly fruit to the Regent. This was a hushed affair, as the baron did not care to be bothered by people banging on his door and the Regent *did* care to always have pineapples on hand that had not rotted on a boat on the way to England.

With the help of Mrs. Gunn, who appeared to be a great favorite of the baron, a pineapple might be had for sixty pounds.

It was an enormous sum of money. Lady Easton had trembled over it. It seemed it could not be done. And yet, she so wished it to be done. She had a look of almost vengeance in her eyes and Bramley knew well enough that she desperately wanted a pineapple more for those who would *not* come, rather than those who would.

Finding his aunt in a state over it and agreeing that it might prick some regrets in some who had stung his aunt with their refusal to dine, Lord Bertridge had stepped in and took over the cost. This was comfortable to everybody, as he was the one person in the house who could well afford such a luxury. Everybody knew he was rich beyond measure and as he rarely gambled, he stayed rich. He was not usually careless with his fortune, but he did have rather a soft spot for his aunt. Further, though he was not a gambler by nature, he'd given Lord Easton fifty pounds to bet on himself and taken home eighty pounds for his trouble.

Lord Easton had been informed of the plan to purchase the pineapple, lest he faint dead away to see it cut on his table and imagine that he'd paid for it himself.

In the late afternoon, Cook, an armed coachman, and the two footmen had barreled off in the carriage with Mrs. Gunn to see the baron about his pineapples. When the old gentleman was apprised of the reasons for wanting a pineapple—that it was a matter of vengeance over a snub and that they planned on actually eating it, rather than passing it from house to house as decoration—he was fully invested in the idea.

He was downright enthusiastic about it when he was informed that Sir Matthew had been one of the people claiming they could not come for dinner. According to the baron, the fellow was rather highhanded for a mere baronet and his wife was irritating with her lofty airs. He selected the most flawless pineapple in his hothouse—it was just perfectly ripe and must be served within three days to assure its finest flavor.

This magnificent fruit, which was under secure lock and key and guarded by a watchman, was to be the pièce de résistance of the evening. He and Lady Easton had conspired between them for over an hour on how it might be carried off.

A large round silver platter would form the base, the glorious crown of the fruit placed in the center. The core and tough outer skin would be carefully removed and then the delicate yellow flesh sliced in rings. Each ring would be placed on a vibrant green butterhead lettuce leaf cut to the shape of the ring with just a quarter inch edge showing all round. These would be artfully placed in concentric circles round the crown. Each ring's hollow center would be filled with a syllabub in which a fourth of the sweet wine was replaced with juice from the pineapple. It would be served by himself using a gold-plated spatula with an ebony handle.

The platter would be brought in and served with the rest of the dessert course, as if nothing unusual was being presented. No special mention of it would be made, no fanfare at all. That would give the moment its elegance and savoir faire and it would also teach those who had failed to attend precisely what they had missed. Everybody would know that Lady Easton had served a pineapple as if it were no more trouble than a bowl of blueberries.

Bramley nearly quivered over the triumph of the scheme.

Now, if only he could be assured that neither Miss Upton and her alarming habits nor Lord Easton and his alarming ideas and opinions would ruin what was to be the most talked-off dinner of the summer.

It might just be the most talked of menu of the decade. It might just be the pinnacle of his career. When he encountered some other butlers in London that he was acquainted with, it would be his pleasure to offhandedly say, *Indeed, we served the pineapple. We feel there is something small about having it only as a decoration. But then, our household does keep to its own high standards.*

He would go mad if anybody failed to cooperate. Nobody had better put a foot out of place.

LADY EASTON LOOKED over her dining table. She could not be dissatisfied—there may have been those who had very mistakenly declined to honor her invitation, but she had managed to fill her table with the most illustrious people just now staying in Brighton.

She may have briefly allowed hysteria to overtake her earlier in the day, but with the help of laudanum, the duchess' good sense, and the pineapple that had been acquired, she was very much recovered. Let those fearful fools who had stayed away consider that a duke, a duchess, a marchioness, and a marquess had no such qualms about gracing the table of Clara Godwin, Countess of Easton.

And then, everything was going so well! Though Caroline seemed just a bit pale, she could not look more lovely and it was clear enough that she'd entirely enchanted the party. Even her lord was on his best behavior this night, almost seeming like the old Easton she'd grown so comfortable with. And, of course, there was the pineapple to arrive shortly. She had not even told Theodosia about the pineapple.

The duke was placed on her right and he now said, "Lady Easton, though I suppose you do not follow the boxing sport, you must be exceedingly proud of Lord Bertridge carrying the day today."

Clara nodded, though that had been the last thing on her mind. She only ever remembered it when she looked toward Richard and saw his black eye. She did hope it would go away soon, it was quite disturbing to think of her nephew using his fists. Attempting to hit another person did not seem entirely rational, regardless of people calling it a sport.

"Well," the duke went on, "I suppose with Bertridge's triumph at the exhibition, this dinner, and perhaps further happy news to come, nobody will bother to remember if some nonsensical talk ever went round."

While Clara was assured that the dinner would answer any questions society might have about the lack of veracity in the story that had gone round about Caroline, she had not considered that Richard's boxing success would help at all. And what further news did the duke hint at?

She must have looked very confused, as the duke said, "Of course, I know nothing, I have only presumed."

"May I ask, duke," Clara said, "to what you refer?"

The duke's eyes drifted first to Caroline, who was very prettily entertaining Lord Maldock, and then across the table to Richard. Her nephew was entirely ignoring Lady Smithson, who looked about her with a vague smile. What was he doing? Why was he staring at Caroline rather than talking to Lady Smithson? Certainly, Caroline could not be saying anything untoward, Lord Maldock appeared entirely charmed.

"I imagined an engagement was in the works," the duke said. "My wife tells me I am rather good with those sorts of predictions. She says I am skilled at picking up that which is not said but only lingers in the air. Even so, I would not have mentioned it had there not been such long acquaintance between us."

"An engagement?" Lady Easton said. What did he mean? Did he mean between Caroline and Richard? Why on earth would he think it? There could not be a worse match ever conceived! It was quite absurd.

"Ah," the duke said, quietly laughing, "I see I am not so very good at guessing after all. I expect the duchess only flatters me, just as she does our butler's weather predictions, which are almost always wrong. Sometimes astoundingly so."

"Oh no, duke, I am sure you are very good with your guesses, but in this case…well, in this case you are mistaken. There is nothing at all between them."

"I see," the duke said good-naturedly. "In any event, I expect this dinner will be enough to educate the talkers on their mistakes. As a duke, I may not be skilled at guesses regarding matchmaking, as we've just seen, but it seems wherever I sit down is of some note and I am happy to use that privilege in your service."

"I am most obliged, and obliged to Theodosia too. She is a stalwart friend."

The duke smiled as he looked down the table at his wife at the right hand of Lord Easton. "She is *very* stalwart. Always has been."

Clara nodded. As she had been talking to the duke for some time now and everybody would be waiting for her signal, she turned to Lord Heathway. Hoping to give herself a moment to think, she said, "Lord Heathway, Penelope tells me you have recently visited Barlow Hall. I understand it is very grand, do tell me of it."

Lord Heathway was more than happy to extoll the many wonders of the hall, most of which passed out of Clara's mind as quickly as it went into it.

Why had the duke been certain of a match between Caroline and Richard?

She surreptitiously glanced at her nephew. To her relief, he was finally talking to Lady Smithson, or rather, *she* was talking to him.

He did not look his usual steady self though, and he kept glancing around as the lady chattered on.

It was not at all his usual behavior. Lady Smithson could sometimes be tedious, as she had an unfortunate habit of cataloguing her sewing projects. Or worse, talking about her grandchildren though they were only babies still.

It was hardly very interesting to hear that the youngest had said something that might have been close to mama, or perhaps it was baba. Lord Reston on her other side had probably just heard all about it, based on the eagerness with which he had turned to Lady Heathway. For all that, Richard never allowed his boredom to show to a lady at dinner.

Did his black eye pain him? She could not imagine what else it could be. Certainly, it had nothing to do with Caroline. She had the distinct impression that her nephew regarded Miss Upton as more of a nuisance than anything else.

Perhaps his dog was ill? He did so love that creature.

Clara could not consider the matter further—just as Lord Heathway was relaying how often he'd got lost in the long corridors of Barlow Hall, the footmen filed in with dessert. Bramley brought up the rear, carrying the sliced pineapple himself.

The whole spread was laid quickly and expertly and Clara was sure Bramley had rehearsed the operation with his footmen for it to come off so seamlessly.

She made some inane comment on the alleged charms of Barlow Hall, all the while keeping one ear open to hear the pineapple's reception.

It was just as she hoped. Quiet gasps, whispered appreciation, the duchess was even heard to say, "Brava, Lady Easton."

Clara casually turned to the duke, as if nothing at all unusual had just occurred.

The duke dabbed his napkin to his lips and said, "If *that* doesn't stop the chattering, I do not know what will. Well done, Lady Easton."

Clara nodded graciously. As she had hoped, it was a triumph.

Chapter Fourteen

IT MAY JUST have been the longest dinner of Caroline's life. She had hoped that eating would restore her energy, but it had not. However, she could at least consider how well it had gone. Lady Easton was as pleased as Punch over it. Or perhaps it would be more accurate to say, pleased as pineapple over it.

The pineapple had indeed been a surprise, both welcome and unwelcome. Caroline had never tasted one before and it had been a revelation. She had not, prior to this moment, considered it very sensible to cart fruit across an ocean. Now, she understood why it was done.

Pineapple was both sweet and tangy, it had a certain pleasant bite on the tongue that was refreshing after a heavy meal, its texture was soft and yet not too soft. Examining it on her fork, she saw that the flesh was comprised of triangles and then within those, small ovals, each one a burst of flavor.

The crown of the fruit, which Bramley seemed to regard as a proud father, was spiky and looked as if it might cut a wayward finger. She could not imagine what sort of tree could hold up a fruit of that size, but was very glad she had not wondered it aloud. Lord Maldock informed her that they grew very close to the ground.

If she felt anything at all uncomfortable about the pineapple, it was the cost. She could not know what had been spent on it, but it must have been dear, indeed. Knowing that it was likely part of the effort to tamp down talk about Miss Upton dancing on Lord Alvanley's table, and Miss Upton in a lights-out scavenger hunt, and Miss Upton dining with an actress, and knowing that Lord Easton had recently lost some large bets and was rather thin in the pockets, the guilt that had become her constant companion only grew heavier round her shoulders.

Still, she had done the only thing she could do during the interminable dinner. She'd worked very hard to be pleasing and she thought she'd done a credible job of it. Both Sir Benjamin and Lord Maldock were exceedingly interested in horses, Lord Maldock knew her father well and Sir Benjamin hoped to know him at some time in the future.

It had been no great effort to keep the conversations going in the direction of horses and she could easily speak to the finer points of selecting a stud or managing oats or arranging proper ventilation in a stable. It was not, of course, her own opinions that were sought after but those of her father. Fortunately, she knew his opinions as well as her own.

Caroline could not ignore the looks from Lord Bertridge that came her way across the table. She could not ignore what they meant. He knew she'd run off from Lady Redfield, he knew she'd gone to the exhibition, and he knew she'd pretended to search for Lady Redfield when she'd done no such thing.

He knew what she really was.

How had she become that, though?

She'd never thought of herself as a careless person.

She had, since the ladies had retired to the drawing room, occupied herself with a bit of sewing as the matrons discussed the pineapple in great detail. Nobody had paid much attention to her, other than Lady Easton requesting that she play when the gentlemen came in. She was happy to agree to it, as she was exhausted from talking and she really did not wish to speak to Lord Bertridge. Or worse, there be an opportunity for him to speak to her.

Her thoughts were promptly interrupted by the drawing

room doors opening. The gentlemen were coming in. They had not spent long over their port. Or perhaps they had and she had lost track of time as she fretted.

In any case, she would make all haste to the pianoforte and stay there for the rest of the evening.

She had already chosen music as she did not care to invite any help over to her in a search. She had been pleased to find several of Pleyel's sonatas, they being far easier to master without heavy concentration than most of Lady Easton's collection of music.

Caroline began to play, hoping that the lords and ladies would not stay too long over cards. It was probably a hopeless sort of hope, though, as it appeared the duchess and Lady Heathway and the duke and Lord Heathway were in the long habit of playing against one another and eager to begin. Both of those ladies possessed more vitality than one would expect from a matron, and neither of them appeared to be flagging in the least.

As she played, she glanced round the room from time to time. She noted that Lord Bertridge was paired with Lady Redfield to play Sir Benjamin and Lady Smithson. She suspected he was not happy about it. According to Lady Easton, Lady Smithson was prone to prattle on about her grandchildren as if they were the most interesting people in the world. As for Lady Redfield, she was positively ghastly at cards—her own baron had refused to partner with her when he'd lived.

The time passed, inching along slower than time had ever moved before. Caroline felt the heaviness of her feelings wearing out her strength. In truth, there were moments when she'd felt almost dizzy, and she had to use all her concentration to keep the keys in focus. Her body was tired, but it was her spirit that was entirely exhausted. All she could do was keep playing and pray for her bed.

One hour passed, then two. Caroline's fingers felt shaky on the keys and she had taken to breathing in deep to steady herself.

A commotion of people rising caught her attention and she stopped her playing. It seemed Sir Benjamin and Lady Smithson would depart, as they were to set off for York very early in the morning.

Caroline stood and curtsied from where she was, as the last breathless conversations about the pineapples were had amidst the goodbyes.

She gratefully sank down on the bench again after they'd gone, assuming Lord Bertridge would be left to play piquet with Lady Redfield. Though, if poor Lady Redfield could not manage whist, she had no idea what the lady would do with piquet.

Instead, Lady Redfield picked up a book and Lord Bertridge looked in Caroline's direction.

She prayed he would not come toward her. But her prayers were not answered and he did, stopping at the instrument.

Caroline did not look up, but rather pretended she must concentrate on her playing. She could not bear to look at him and see the condemnation in his eyes.

"Miss Upton," he said in low tones, "though I would not burden my aunt with what I observed this day, I will go so far as to burden *you*. As you are well aware, you were spotted at the exhibition with your maid, somewhere in the attics of The Ship Inn. Do you dare deny it?"

"I do not," Caroline said softly.

Lord Bertridge was silent for a moment and though Caroline did not look up she could feel the heat of anger coming from him.

"I do not understand how you can be so careless of other people," he said. "Of my aunt, and of poor Lady Redfield. Do you have no concern for anybody? Are you so selfish that you would disregard my aunt's feelings after what she has done for you? Are you so thoughtless, that you would cause Lady Redfield hours of worry and exhaustion? Are you so heedless that you would allow the good lady to imagine that you had equally exhausted yourself in search of *her*, all the while viewing an exhibition that was wildly inappropriate for you to attend?"

"It is all true," Caroline said quietly. "I will tell Lady Easton everything on the morrow. I know she will send me away and she will be quite right to do so."

"And there you do it again," Lord Bertridge said. "Whose feelings will *that* assuage but your own? Do you imagine my aunt will rejoice simply because you have decided to confess?"

Caroline did not know what to think of that statement. What else was she to do but tell Lady Easton the facts of the matter? It was true that the lady would be made unhappy, but she owed her a full explanation. She deserved what would be the consequences of her awful behavior.

Or perhaps she might just inflict the consequences on herself, without disturbing the lady's peace any more than she had done.

She rose and said, "I will claim an illness which must force me to go home."

"You will do no such thing," Lord Bertridge said heatedly. "You will work to be a credit to my aunt and give her the satisfaction that she has worked for and deserves. At least do that much for her."

As his words poured over her like boiling water, the room began to sway. Caroline steadied herself with a hand on the pianoforte, but the room would not right itself. She felt herself falling into darkness.

⤞⤚⤚

CAROLINE WOKE TO find herself in her bed, Lady Easton chafing her hand and Bemmy applying a cool compress to her forehead.

"Ah, there you are," Lady Easton said, "you've come round."

"But what—"

"There now, do not speak. You fell in a faint in the drawing room. I was inclined to send for the doctor, but Bemmy insists it is not at all necessary. She is convinced it is only a matter of not having had enough tea to drink. I did not know this myself, but apparently wine depletes the body of tea at an alarming rate. We did have three types of wine at dinner and I do not believe you touched your tea in the drawing room."

Caroline attempted to parse Lady Easton's words. As far as she could make out, she had fainted dead away as she stood by the pianoforte. Somebody had got her up the stairs, and then Bemmy had told some nonsensical story about tea and wine.

"Don't you worry, miss," Bemmy said. "I've already given orders for a tea tray to be made up and I'll stay by your side all the night long."

"You really are too good, Bemmy," Lady Easton said. "You are quite the comfort."

"I would suggest, my lady," Bemmy said, "that you get some rest. No use two of us losing sleep."

"Please do, Lady Easton," Caroline said. "I do not know why I should have fainted, but now I am only tired."

"I suppose getting some rest would be sensible," Lady Easton said. "Now Bemmy, you are to wake me regarding the slightest change. Do not hesitate a moment to do it. I'll send Easton to sleep in his dressing room and so you may knock on my door as loud as necessary. I wish to be kept apprised if there is any change at all."

"Right you are, my lady," Bemmy said.

Lady Easton squeezed Caroline's hand and rose.

Caroline said. "Lady Easton, I am sorry if I caused a scene in the drawing room. It must have been unpleasant, and you had worked so hard to make the evening a success."

Lady Easton smiled. "There is no cause for that sort of talk, Caroline. The party was wholly convinced that you collapsed under the stress of being wrongly accused by gossiping tongues. By the morrow, you will be painted as Claudio's young Hero, horribly wronged and courageously withstanding the onslaught of vicious talk. You have perhaps done what not even a pineapple could do, you will be entirely vindicated."

With that, Lady Easton let herself out of the room.

Caroline looked toward Bemmy. "I did not feel well, dizzy and sick, and then Lord Bertridge came to the pianoforte and gave me a terrible scolding. It was all too much, I suppose."

"A scolding?" Bemmy said. "He didn't look very scolding when he carried you up here. He looked terrified, if you ask me."

Caroline's face flamed at the idea of Lord Bertridge being forced to carry her up the stairs when he'd probably wished to throw her down them. Of course it would be him called upon to do it—the other gentlemen of the party were too old and Bramley, well that would have been ridiculous and he'd never have managed it.

"What on earth was the fellow scolding you about at a party?" Bemmy asked, folding her arms.

Caroline related the awful set down, at least as much as she could bear repeating.

A usual maid might have trembled over the idea that a lord of the house had spotted them at the exhibition and made stern remarks about it. Bemmy chose another direction. She was positively outraged.

"He said *that?*" she huffed. "I see. I suppose we're to know that Lord Starched-Pants never puts a foot wrong, are we? I suppose Lord Stone-Face is as pious as the archbishop! I reckon the Earl of Frowns delights in sharing his dark moods liberally. I imagine the Prince of Miserable can't bear to see anybody otherwise. As far as I'm concerned, Sir Moody wallows in his own perfection like a pig in a pen.

"That is perhaps enough name calling, Bemmy."

Bemmy nodded, though Caroline was certain the maid had a whole host of other derogatory names waiting to be announced.

"I'm only sayin,' I wouldn't mind blacking his other eye."

Caroline decided to ignore the idea that her lady's maid wished to wallop a lord of the house. Rather, she said, "Lord Bertridge urged me to forgo speaking to Lady Easton about any of this, but rather to work very hard to be a credit to her from now on."

"As if you ain't been," Bemmy fumed. "And didn't you already vow to go on the straight and narrow without any talking from him?"

"Indeed I did," Caroline said, "and I am determined to do it."

"Well, all right," Bemmy said. "Never mind Baron Sternfellow's lecture. He's at least right about letting the matter lie quiet. Rest now and I'll go down and see about that tea tray."

Caroline nodded gratefully as Bemmy bustled from the room.

In the stillness that followed the closing of the door, Caroline could hear Lord Bertridge's voice in her ears all over again. He had not been just aggravated, as he had been in the past. This was different. He positively disdained her. He was revolted by her behavior. He may not have come out and said so, but he utterly condemned her.

Why could she not be more like Bemmy? Why could she not find her own outrage at his scolding? Why could she not brush off the opinions of Baron Sternfellow, the Earl of Frowns?

She did not know why, but she could not.

RICHARD WENT QUIETLY into the library to fetch a very large glass of his uncle's brandy. He was shocked at what he'd done.

He'd meant to give Miss Upton a grave assessment of her behavior. He'd meant to extract a promise from her that she would work to be a credit to his aunt going forward. He'd not meant, however, to cause the lady to be taken ill and swoon.

What a beast he was! He'd sounded like his father, he was sure he had. That could not continue, he could not turn into his father—that man had been cruel whenever he was in a temper. The things Richard had overheard him say to his mother…but then, his mother was able to give back as hard as she got. Miss Upton was not like that though. She could not hold up against such an onslaught.

He had let his temper rule him, just as his father had always done. He had indulged it, just like his father.

It was precisely what Richard had worked so hard to control. He was meant to be reasonable, measured, and unflappable. His temper, that awful inheritance, had been ordered into a locked box.

As soon as her eyelashes fluttered and she sank to the ground, he knew he'd gone too far.

Why had he done it? After all, Miss Upton's behavior had not been very good, but it had hardly been criminal.

She was impetuous and he was near certain that had led her to The Ship Inn. It would have been nice if her maid had cautioned her, but that girl had an air of boldness about her he could not quite put his finger on. The maid would have gone along willingly enough. The two of them had likely acted on the spur of the moment, giving little thought to the consequences.

Had Miss Upton been accompanied by the duchess, she would not have escaped her chaperone. But Lady Redfield, well, a toddler just up on its legs could probably outwit that lady.

Richard was certain he'd been white-faced as he'd carried Miss Upton to her bedchamber. She was light in his arms and he had been surprised by it—her presence in the house was so full of upheaval that he'd thought she'd be more substantial. How could one so light create such havoc?

He'd been careful going up the steps, holding her neck steady with one hand and his other arm under her knees. She looked very innocent then, as if she could never do a wrong thing.

He'd left behind the chattering in the drawing room, which appeared to be in Miss Upton's favor and against society's wags, with only his aunt hurrying beside him.

Poor Lady Easton had all sorts of speculations on what could have caused Miss Upton to faint—the heat, too much playing of the pianoforte, the pineapple, the endless search the lady had allegedly made for Lady Redfield that afternoon.

She did not guess the real reason though, and Richard did not inform her of it. What was he to say? *It appears, Aunt, that I am just as beastly as my father and have now had the pleasure of making a lady collapse.*

He must get control of himself.

Now, he walked out of the library with a full tumbler of brandy. He planned to take it to his room, dismiss his valet, and brood out the window with only Edgar for company. At least his dog would still hold a high opinion of him.

As he crossed the hall, he spotted Miss Upton's maid officiously marching toward the stairs that led to the kitchens. As she passed by him, she muttered, "The poor lady is nearly destroyed, and for what?"

Richard stopped walking, finding himself speechless. He turned and watched the maid storm down the stairs, the words to reprimand her utterly failing to appear in his mind.

Perhaps he should just take the punch. She was right, after all. He had been cruel for what? Further, he had no wish to reprimand the maid's loyalty to her mistress.

He trudged up the stairs. Even a lady's maid could see he'd been a beast and was surprisingly unafraid to say so.

He was completely unraveling.

CAROLINE HAD BEEN confined to bed for a full day, though she felt perfectly able to rise. Once she had understood that there was no getting up, she resigned herself to it.

Bemmy was enthusiastic over the confinement and looked upon it as a day off. Her maid had convinced Lady Easton that Miss Upton must be watched all day and who else to do it but Bemmy? Between tea trays filled with assortments of sweets and savories, they played Casino under Bemmy's unusual directions— it seemed her family regularly changed the rules of card games to suit themselves.

Caroline found her equanimity slowly returning under Bemmy's cheerful rationality. As her maid had pointed out, no real harm had been done to anybody, except for Lord Bertridge's black eye, which she felt the Baronet of Bluster richly deserved.

Caroline did not think he deserved it, but she also reminded herself that she was not exactly Moll Cutpurse. She'd done wrong, she'd made stupid mistakes and had been careless of other people, but she'd vowed to correct herself going forward.

There was no getting back into Lord Bertridge's good graces, but then she supposed she'd never been in them in the first place. He had not liked her right from the outset. She was convinced that his approval had only begun to mean more and more to her simply because it was impossible to get.

She would be rational from now on. Miss Upton would be a credit to Lady Easton and her friends, and she would start seriously thinking about her future. She was not here for frivolity, after all! She was supposed to be getting herself married.

So far, the only likely candidate was Mr. Landon. He *was* likely though, with his keen interest in horses. He did not set her heart ablaze, but they might get on well together.

Bemmy had been down to the kitchens to fetch yet another tray of sandwiches and cakes. Now, she pushed the door open with her foot, crossed the room, and set it down on the table beside the bed. Hurrying back to close the door, she turned and said, "You'll be happy to know he is moping."

"Bramley is moping?" Caroline asked.

"Not Mr. Bramley. Him. Lord Bertridge. Moping like a schoolboy on account of his wretched behavior toward you."

"I see," Caroline said, delighted with Bemmy's unwavering loyalty, though it be exceedingly farfetched. "I suppose he stopped you in the corridor and said Bemmy, I am just now moping over what I said to Miss Upton."

"He did not, though I heard it loud and clear anyway. I can spot moping a mile away. My youngest brother is king of the mopers, crowned on the day he was born. Not a thing happens to that fellow without a full week of staring out windows and long and heavy sighs. The lord shows all the signs."

Seeing that Caroline did not look particularly convinced,

Bemmy said, "The great lord is in the drawing room pretending to read. They left the door open for some reason. There he is, book in hand, staring at the wall and not the book. Classic moping."

"Well, if he is moping, it's likely about his black eye."

"That's not what comes to *my* mind. I reckon he's moping for being a cruel creature and sending a lady to her bed." Bemmy paused and said, "Are you sure you won't have him? P'raps he's learned his lesson on the cruelty front and he's devilish handsome even when he's moping."

"Bemmy, I am not the queen. I cannot point at people and tell them how to feel. Lord Bertridge may be handsome but he highly disapproves of me. And so that's that."

"Shame," Bemmy said. "Oh, and this came for you." Bemmy pulled a letter from the pocket of her apron.

Caroline took the letter. It was locally sent, and in a flourishing hand. She tore it open.

My dear Miss Upton,

On account of Clara swearing that you needed to rest today, our sea bathing adventure has been put off. I, myself, think it would have done you good, but Lady Easton currently relies on the opinion of some person named Bemmy.

Do not be downhearted! I have sent word to Mrs. Gunn and I will collect you on the morrow at nine and we will go forward with our plan.

In the meantime, I am delighted to tell you that word of your dramatic fall to the floor due to the stress of untrue gossip has reached the Prince's ears. He is outraged on your behalf and has issued a warning to all of society—let Miss Upton's name be on their lips for anything less than high praise and they can pack their bags and go. Lord Alvanley was heard to say he would skewer anybody who dares impugn Miss Upton, and we all know how terrified of his wit society is so that might be even more of a warning than the Regent's.

My butler, who is a great predictor of the weather, tells me tomorrow will be particularly fine and warm.

Theodosia Whitby

"It seems I am to go sea bathing on the morrow," Caroline said. "The duchess' butler claims the day will be lovely."

Bemmy glanced out the window at the overcast sky and snorted. "Her Grace's butler is as mad as March hare. Anybody can see that weather is set to come in.

⚜

CHAPTER FIFTEEN

"A BSOLUTELY EVERYTHING HAS righted itself," Lady Easton said.

Richard had been in the drawing room most of the day, pretending to read a book. He'd left the door open so he might spot Miss Upton if she ventured down the stairs. He wished to get an apology done as soon as possible.

He never did see her, but now his aunt had come in for tea.

"Caroline is on the mend from her faint," Lady Easton went on, "and it seems the circumstance was fortuitous. Everybody is talking about how cruel and unfair society can be as if they were talking of somebody other than themselves. Lady Myrtle just stopped me in the street and claimed that anybody in her circle daring to spread false accusations would be shown the door. And, of course, she's heard about the triumph of our pineapple."

Richard felt there was some irony in the idea that society should be blamed for Miss Upton's faint, when it had been himself, the gentleman so well known for being a stickler for propriety. He was the gentleman never involving himself in duels or foolish bets, and certainly never losing his temper. Now *he* was the person everybody wished to show to the door on account of Miss Upton's faint, though they did not know it.

"You do seem out of sorts, Nephew. I suppose it's the black eye."

"My eye will heal," he said.

"And thank goodness for that. You look like a highwayman or a pirate or some other person prone to brawling. It really doesn't suit you."

Bramley came in with the tea. Richard thought the butler carried himself with some new sort of aplomb. It was due to the pineapple's recent success no doubt.

The butler set the tray down and motioned for the footmen at the door. Charles walked sedately into the room with a silver salver holding a letter. Even the footmen had taken to walking round like they served in the palace.

Lady Easton took the letter. Before she could open it, Bramley said, "Delivered by hand from the Marine Pavilion, my lady. One prays that a certain Prince does not experience envy over a certain fruit originating in the tropics that was served at a certain dinner in a certain house."

With that, Bramley turned on his heel and serenely departed the room.

After the door shut, Richard said, "I had no idea a pineapple would invite bold speculations from Bramley."

"Oh dear, it *is* from the Regent. What does he want? You don't suppose it could be about the pineapple? Perhaps he does not like that we went to the baron for it?

"You'd best open it and find out, though if the Prince thinks he can start telling people where they can buy things, he'll find he's made a fool of himself."

Richard watched with interest as his aunt perused the letter. She sighed a great deal and then her lip positively quivered, so perhaps it was some condemnation over the pineapple after all. Quite ridiculous if it was.

"Well," he asked, as she laid the letter down.

"I'm too distraught. You'd better read it for yourself," Lady Easton said, wringing her hands.

Richard picked it up, preparing himself to be aggravated and reminding himself that his temper, so recently having escaped from its box, had been securely locked up again. It must stay locked regardless of whatever nonsense the Regent had written to his aunt that had upset her.

Lady Easton,

I had previously sent an invitation to your household to my ball on Tuesday next and find myself aggrieved that I have not yet received a favorable reply.

I firmly believe that were you, Lord Easton, and Miss Upton to fail to attend, it will give fuel to the talkers. As those flames have recently been tamped down on account of Miss Upton's regrettable illness, that would be unfortunate. In fact, I cannot allow it. I am determined to show the world that Miss Upton is highly approved of by their Regent and future king.

I look forward to seeing you all on Tuesday. And Bertridge too, if he likes to come.

George P R

Richard's temper tapped on the sides of his box, trying to get his attention.

And Bertridge too, if he likes to come. It was written as if he were some poor relation that must be reluctantly accommodated. The Prince would be well-advised to know that Bertridge did not, in fact, like to come.

"Do you see?" Lady Easton said. "He commands us to go."

"Apparently though," Richard said drily, "he does not command *me.*"

"It is the most nonsensical thing in the world," Lady Easton said fretfully. "To reestablish Caroline, we must avoid the Prince's set, not go to his ball."

"Well, it won't be just his set, will it?" Richard said. "I suppose everybody in town was invited. Or at least off-handedly asked if they'd like to come too."

"Perhaps," Lady Easton said, not quite catching his irritation upon discovering himself an afterthought in the prince's letter. "Though I will wish to keep Caroline well clear of Alvanley and his friends."

"Especially Mr. Landon," Richard said. "Keep her well away from that fellow."

"I do not know him, is he unseemly in some way, or just poor?"

"Worse than unseemly, though I won't go into detail. And a poor second son, though he has his own unique hopes on the subject."

"But you will be there to help, will you not?"

"Certainly not. The Prince has practically said he does not wish it and with the state of my eye, I do not wish it. Nor do you need me. You and your friends will be well able to manage one young lady at a ball."

Though he said he would not go because the Prince would not prefer it, that was only part of the reason. Being such an afterthought on the invitation did have its sting, but mostly he did not wish to go on account of Miss Upton.

He found he did not wish to view her dancing with other gentlemen or being as gay and happy as he was certain she would be at a ball. She would be surrounded by those who approved of her and she would have no interest in being watched by her scolder. He would be, he knew, a wet blanket on the whole proceeding. A ridiculous wet blanket, as he was certain would be made use of by Alvanley.

Further, every time he glanced into a looking glass and noted his black eye, he wanted to pound Landon into the ground. He could not allow his temper to make a reappearance.

He'd be far better off at home with a book and a brandy. Perhaps he might actually read the book that had been in his hands all day long.

"Yes, of course, the ladies will come if I ask. It is most upsetting, though!" Lady Easton said, just now wringing her hands with more vigor than Richard had ever remembered witnessing.

The door was opened and Lord Easton strolled in. "My dear, how do you do this day? Still reeling from last night, I suppose. Richard, I'm sure your eye looks better than yesterday. How is

Caroline?" he asked.

"She is fine," Lady Easton said. "Oh, Easton, you'll never believe. The Regent has sent me what amounts to an order to bring Caroline to his wretched ball!"

"I see," Lord Easton said with equanimity. "Yes, I did say you did not plan on going. How funny that he would have written you about it."

Lady Easton looked at her lord as if he had just dropped from the sky. "Funny? Easton, I do not know what has happened to you recently, but I do not like it. I do not find it altogether fair to be married to one gentleman and then suddenly another takes his place. What next? Will you dye your hair black like Lady Redfield's dead baron?"

Lord Easton laughed heartily. "Considering how little I have of it, that would really be amusing. It really would. Alvanley would be delighted to joke about it. What might he say? I'll think of it. Perhaps…no, I never can think of something. Alvanley would though, I'm sure of it! He'd find wit in my wisps! Wait, now that was almost witty, I think."

With that, Lord Easton helped himself to a biscuit and looked entirely pleased with the world.

His wife and his nephew seemed a bit less so.

THOUGH DAWN HAD certainly come, it would not be apparent from the window. It was a dark and grey blustery day with intermittent downpours. Caroline was very afraid the duchess' butler would rue his prediction of fine and warm weather. Whatever was the case, the sea bathing would need to be put off once more.

Though Caroline was fit as a fiddle, she'd had breakfast sent to her room. She must face Lord Bertridge eventually, but she did not feel up to seeing him in the breakfast room this morning.

Despite the fact that she would not go sea bathing this morning, she was beginning to feel more cheerful. It seemed that she would go to the Regent's ball after all. She was certain Lord Bertridge would disapprove and she did not want whatever burgeoning equanimity she was developing to be shaken.

She was hoping that Bemmy would come to tell her he'd left the house, as her maid did keep a rather sharp eye on him these days.

The night before, Lady Easton had come into her room to tell her of the Regent's invitation, seeming more like she announced a funeral than anything else. Of course, Caroline realized that the lady had not wished to attend, but apparently the Regent had insisted.

In any case, she would go!

The door flew open and Bemmy barreled through it. "You'll never believe it, but the duchess is downstairs and she won't be put off. Lady Easton says it's ridiculous weather to attempt the sea but the duchess says it doesn't matter that it's raining as you'll both get wet anyway and her butler says the weather will clear in no time at all. That butler's got feathers for brains, if you ask me."

"Goodness," Caroline said. "We are really to attempt it?"

"So says the duchess and it seems Lady E has been run over by the woman's determination."

"I'd better change then. I expect she will not like waiting."

"I expect you're right. She strikes me as the toe-tapping kind," Bemmy said, hurrying to the wardrobe. She pulled out what she was looking for and said, "I'm to accompany you, but don't expect me to get in that water. Mrs. Gunn or no, I wouldn't like to be swept out to sea."

"Nor would I," Caroline said, feeling the smallest bit of trepidation.

Bemmy was tearing through clothes to find what she was looking for and throwing things on the bed.

"Oh Bemmy!" Caroline cried. "I just realized I do not know the proper operation. Do I wear my regular clothes and then change in the bathing machine, or do I prepare myself here?"

"It's done both ways, but the duchess ain't going in for changing outfits, she's got an oil skin cap on, she's in her bathing pelisse, and I saw the sight of a shift peeking out at the bottom. That's what you'll be wanting to do. I'll pack a dry shift in a bag and then when you come out, that's when you change."

Caroline nodded as Bemmy helped her into one of the shifts that Mrs. Bell had specifically made for bathing. It was a plain brown cotton and, like her walking dresses, it had light weights sewn into the bottom of the garment. These weights were smaller and fewer—just heavy enough to counteract the seawater. This would prevent the material from floating up around her.

Its corset was lightweight and not at all binding. The pelisse that would go over top of all was a light silk, long and voluminous, covering everything from her neck to her ankles. Special shoes had been made—very light but with a hard sole and firmly buckled round the ankle and instep so that they could not be swept off.

"Have I got everything?" Caroline said, as Bemmy buckled her shoes.

"Everything but a cap, which you don't need anyway. I've pinned your hair up tight enough and the salt water does wonders for a lady's hair. I'm surprised the duchess don't know it."

"We'd better go down," Caroline said.

"Right you are."

They hurried down the stairs, Bemmy carrying Caroline's bag and struggling into her coat. The duchess waited in the hall, and she was indeed toe-tapping.

"I am sorry to have kept you waiting, Your Grace," Caroline said. "I just thought, with the weather…"

"You thought we'd call it off," the duchess said. "You will find that a duchess is made of sterner stuff than that! In any case, my butler says this is what is called an Ephemeral Storm—here one moment and gone the next. I expect this will be fortuitous, the sun will come out and we will have the sea to ourselves while the timid huddle in their houses and regret having cancelled their plans."

Lady Easton hurried from the drawing room. "But Theodosia, are you certain it is all right? Caroline is so recently recovered and, in truth, I've never heard of an ephemeral storm. It always seems to me that when it storms, it does so for some hours. At least, from what I can see out a window."

"Clara," the duchess said kindly, "nor have I heard of these ephemeral storms until this morning. However, you and I are not great students of the weather. Carlson regularly corresponds with the renowned Lord Ingraham and has studied all the angles of his meteorological archives. Between them, they have developed their own theories."

Caroline was rather dubious about this idea, and she could see very well that Lady Easton was too. As for Bemmy, her maid had prior informed her that if she wanted a prediction on the weather in Brighton, she ought to ask a fisherman, not a barmy butler.

"Well? Shall we be off?" the duchess asked.

Though the duchess had posed it as a question, Caroline well knew it was an order.

They were off.

RICHARD HAD SLEPT in later than his usual habit, as he was prone to do when it stormed out of doors. He found storms strangely restful, as if nobody could encounter trouble when all were safely indoors. He had perhaps also slept late as he was late to get to sleep—his mind had been restless and loath to settle.

Kingston brought him up a tray of coffee, toast, and eggs, and heated water for his shave. His valet, nearly always anticipating his thoughts, had also brought a plate of sausages and bowl of water for Edgar. His dog might be in the usual habit of itching to go out first thing in the morning, but if it was raining he barely lifted his head and hoped not to be noticed.

He could hear the outer doors to the house opening and closing and could not imagine who had arrived just after nine in the morning. Not only was it early for a call, but what could be so important as to venture out when the rain came down in buckets?

It was probably one of his aunt's friends, they barged into one another's houses whenever they liked, always with some emergency or interesting news in their reticules, and he supposed rain would hardly put them off. Except Lady Heathway of course, who sent alarming letters at all hours of the day and night.

"Who is it coming in at such an early hour?" he asked Kingston.

"The duchess, my lord," his valet said.

"I suppose she's huddled in the drawing room with my aunt, discussing some vital piece of information." Richard paused. In what he hoped was an offhand manner, he said, "Has Miss Upton joined them?"

Kingston folded his shaving towel and said, "The duchess and Miss Upton have left. They are to go sea bathing this morning."

Richard sat up and peered at the window. "Sea bathing? In a storm?"

Kingston nodded. "That's about what everybody else thought, my lord, but the duchess says it's an ephemeral storm and should dissipate soon."

"What in the world is an ephemeral storm?" Richard asked.

Kingston looked down his nose, as he was wont to do when he wished to indicate disdain. "Nobody seems to know except the duchess' butler."

"This is madness," Richard muttered. He leapt out of bed and said, "Never mind the shave, I must get dressed before that lunatic duchess drowns Miss Upton!"

THOUGH THE DUCHESS' butler had thought the storm ephemeral, Caroline thought it looked rather permanent. The rain had poured down the coach's windows and she had some pity for the poor coachman and grooms who were out in it. The duchess had not forgotten their comfort, as they wore oil skin coats with hoods, but for all that they could not be comfortable.

The rain did begin to lighten though it still came down steady. Caroline could at least see something out her window now.

Though, having viewed it, she was not certain she liked it.

The waves were larger than Caroline had ever seen, they must be nearing two feet. They broke close to shore, and then beyond that the sea bobbed up and down rhythmically.

"Now you see, Miss Upton," the duchess said cheerfully, "the trick will be to get past the breaking water and then we can float up and down on the waves. Mrs. Gunn will get you through it."

Caroline looked at the white water crashing in rhythmically and thought that would indeed be a trick. Or a miracle. Bemmy was only wide-eyed.

"Ah, there is the good lady now," the duchess said.

Having seen Mrs. Gunn prior, Caroline well knew it was she that stood next to a bathing machine. While she looked stoic in the weather, the fellow who held the horses looked rather less so.

The footmen had opened umbrellas ready for them to come out, which did strike Caroline as rather ridiculous. Whatever was to happen, they would be soaked to the skin in the very near future.

Bemmy had been left in the carriage and would meet them in the sea bathing machine with the dry clothes once they came out of the sea. Caroline was very much hoping they *would* come out.

She and the duchess had been hustled into the bathing machine by Mrs. Gunn, who climbed in after them. "We'll want to know how we're goin' on in this kind of sea," the matron said. She turned a critical eye on Caroline. "Do you swim well, girl? I won't be takin' no delicate flowers in there today, so if you is the screamin' and flailing type, come out with it."

"I can swim the distance of my father's lake," Caroline said slowly, "two hundred yards, I think. But of course, I have no experience with waves."

"Can you hold your breath underwater?"

"Yes," Caroline said, though she'd never tried out exactly how long she could do so.

"Right," Mrs. Gunn said, "I'll take the duchess out first as she's got experience and I know I can leave her bobbing on the swells while I come back for you. Then, we'll get close to the breakers and duck under them quick as you like. Push yourself forward underwater and I'll pull you. Then, it's all easy as you please."

Caroline did not know if anything about this venture would be easy, but it seemed it was going to happen, nonetheless.

Mrs. Gunn signaled out the door and the horses went forward with a lurch. Caroline held on to a hook meant for hanging clothes to steady herself. The machine stopped and Caroline could feel the water washing up against the floor of the compartment.

They waited while the man unhitched the horses, who were no doubt eager to get out of the sea on such a day. Caroline could not imagine convincing one of her father's horses to perform such a feat.

The man and the horses were gone and out of sight. The duchess threw off her pelisse, which Caroline caught and hung up.

"Let us proceed, Mrs. Gunn," the duchess said, as if she were ordering a battalion forward into battle.

She watched with trepidation as Mrs. Gunn and the duchess made their way into the water. Though Mrs. Gunn had said she would hold Caroline's hand, she did not do so with the duchess.

Surprisingly, the duchess dove under a breaker of her own accord and swam out of reach and into the swells. She looked positively delighted with herself.

Mrs. Gunn came back for her with alarming speed. Caroline had little time to think, which was perhaps best. They were down the steps of the bathing machine and into the water in a trice.

"Here we go, duck down and push forward!" Mrs. Gunn shouted.

Caroline did as she was told and found herself in a maelstrom in which there was no up or down or forward or backward. The water was icy and sent prickles all over her body. Mrs. Gunn pulled her arm.

And then suddenly, the maelstrom dissipated, and she popped up into the swells.

"Well done, Miss Upton," the duchess called from a dozen feet away.

She had done it. Or rather, Mrs. Gunn had done it.

The swells rose up and then dropped down and then up again as if she were rolling up and down hills. The rain splattered down around them and the water began to feel less cold. The salt in the water buoyed her up and she barely had to tread—so different from her father's lake of fresh water. It was glorious.

As she floated up and down, she spotted Bemmy hanging out the coach window. Her poor maid had clutched her hand in the carriage and whispered, "Don't do it. Don't go."

To assure Bemmy of her safety, Caroline kicked herself up and waved to her vigorously with both arms. Then she squinted. Why was Lord Bertridge there?

CHAPTER SIXTEEN

RICHARD HAD NOT bothered to wait for the carriage to be called, nor had he told anybody where he was going. He stormed out of the house and headed toward the sea.

If that eccentric duchess and her nonsensical butler with his ephemeral storms caused any harm to Miss Upton…well, he could not say what he would do.

The beach was empty but for one bathing machine at water's edge. Of course it was, any rational person had called off their plans for sea bathing in this weather. In the distance, beyond the breaking waves, he saw three heads bobbing. They would appear, and then disappear. What were they doing out there?

What was *he* doing *here*?

He had not had much of a plan when he left the house, other than to urge the duchess to call off the expedition.

He was too late for that, they were already in the water.

So now what?

He spotted the duchess' carriage. And that infernal lady's maid, Bemmy, hanging out a window.

He strode over to her. "How long have they been in the water?" he asked abruptly, though he had no idea what he would do with the information.

Bemmy looked him over with that saucy air she had and said, "Just a quarter hour now. Was you worried?"

"Any rational person would be and I'll thank you not to question me," Richard said sternly. She really was the most confound-ed creature.

He looked back to sea. Miss Upton was waving at them with both arms. She was waving for help. Did not Mrs. Gunn see that she was in distress? No, she did not, she was gabbing away with the duchess while Miss Upton was yards away and seemed to be drifting further out.

Bemmy leaned further out the coach window and waved back to Miss Upton.

"For God's sake," Richard said, "she is not waving hello, a person waving in the water is in distress!"

"What?" Bemmy cried, throwing the carriage door open and almost knocking him over with it.

The coachman stood up on his perch and shaded his eyes from the rain. The footmen stood on the side rails to get a better view.

Richard threw off his coat. If Mrs. Gunn was not prepared to assist, he'd do it himself. If Miss Upton went under in those high seas she would never be seen again.

How careless of them all! Miss Upton would be weakened from her recent illness, an illness he had himself caused. She'd likely never been in the sea. What a day to tax her with it. It was too much for her constitution. They all should have known it.

He raced down the beach and into the water, throwing him-self under a breaking wave. Coming up on the other side, he swam toward Miss Upton.

She lay on her back, no doubt trying to regain her strength though she was surely exhausted. He would have to keep her on her back and tow her in until he could stand and carry her out.

Mrs. Gunn was the first to spot him as he approached closer. "What in the Lord's good name are you about, swimmin' out here in your clothes? Young gentleman, you ain't thinking of doin' away with yourself now, are you?"

"Do not be ridiculous!" Richard shouted. "Can you not see that Miss Upton is in distress?"

Miss Upton herself was no longer lying on her back but tread-ing water. "My lord?" she said.

Suddenly, she did not look in distress. She *did* look decidedly confused.

"You were waving both your arms," Richard said accusingly. "Any sailor knows that a person needing assistance waves both their arms."

"No they don't," Mrs. Gunn said, riding up a swell with a look of supreme authority, "they don't got the strength for it. The drowning generally go down all quiet-like."

"Thank you, Mrs. Gunn," Richard said heatedly, kicking hard underwater to keep himself afloat as his clothes worked to drag him down, "but while you were talking to the duchess you had not Miss Upton in view and she was signaling distress to the shore."

"I waved hello to Bemmy," Miss Upton said. It was said quiet-ly and barely heard above the waves and the rain drops. She disappeared down a swell and then reappeared on the top of another.

She waved hello? She waved her arms like a drowning per-son…to say hello? Of all the—Richard felt his box unlock of its own accord and his temper burst out like the scudding grey clouds overhead.

"That is it! Absolutely *it*," Richard shouted, pounding the water with a fist. "All of you, out of the water right now. This insane scheme has ended!"

"Goodness, Lord Bertridge," the duchess said soothingly as she crested a swell, "if you feel that strongly about it, I dare say we will. I am beginning to get chilled, in any event."

"Proceed then," Richard said. "I will follow and make sure everyone has safely exited."

To his relief, they all did as they were told. Though, Mrs. Gunn just barely contained her laughter.

Miss Upton was waving hello to her maid. Who waved to their maid while swimming? How was he to know she was waving to her maid and not drowning?

He watched carefully as Mrs. Gunn took Miss Upton under the breaking water and they stumbled out of it. Her fine-boned ankles showed from under her sea bathing costume, which he should not be looking at but was looking at.

The duchess went under the break herself and Mrs. Gunn helped her up the stony beach.

He began to feel ridiculous, swimming in his clothes and noticing ankles. He also began to feel exhausted.

At least the beach was empty and nobody would have witnessed this debacle. He was both furious and relieved. He really had thought Miss Upton was on the verge of drowning. In that moment, he was seized by the idea that she could not be allowed to drown.

She was vexing and impulsive and trouble wafted round her like an ill-omened shawl. But she could not be allowed to drown.

BEMMY HAD RUSHED into the bathing machine looking white-faced. "Was you drowning?" she whispered into Caroline's ear.

"Do not bother attempting a whisper in a bathing machine, Bemmy," the duchess said. "We can hear you quite clearly and Miss Upton was certainly not drowning."

Bemmy breathed a long sigh and said, "I thought Miss Upton waved to me and I waved back but then Lord Bertridge said I was wrong and she was in distress. My heart nearly pounded out of my chest."

Caroline did not answer, but her heart had nearly pounded out of her chest too. What a shock to hear his voice out there, and then there he was.

What had he been doing at the beach? Had he come to be certain they were all right?

And then to attempt such a daring rescue! It would take

enormous strength to swim while being weighed down so heavily by a full set of clothes.

It was very touching that he'd tried it, though she had not in fact needed rescuing.

Of course, she must not flatter herself. He might just as well have wished to save her from drowning to prevent any trouble to his aunt.

He'd been so forceful, ordering them all out of the water as he did. While swimming in high swells had been exhilarating, it had perhaps not been the most sensible thing in the world.

She peeked out the small window of the bathing machine and saw him storming toward the road. She could not imagine what he would say upon entering the house soaked in seawater.

"I fear Lord Bertridge was not approving of our plan," the duchess said. "Poor fellow, he is so little approving of anything."

While that was true, Caroline had a great wish to defend the lord. "It was very gallant though," she said, "to rush to the rescue as he did."

"Oh yes, Bertridge is no physical coward," the duchess said. "It's his mind, you see. He's wound tighter than the clocks he and Clara are so fond of. I suppose he'll mellow with age. At least, one hopes."

Caroline had often thought the same, though she found it somehow uncomfortable to hear the duchess say it.

"He was a right Sir Galahad, coming to a lady's rescue," Bemmy said boldly. "P'raps it softens some opinions I might'a formed."

The duchess looked askance at Bemmy, clearly unused to hearing that a lady's maid went about forming opinions.

"And here I was," Mrs. Gunn said chuckling, "thinking he was doing away with himself. It would be the day for it—a man gambles away his fortune and wakes to a storm, it's been done like that before."

Caroline shivered at the notion.

"If one thing can be said for Lord Bertridge," the duchess said, "it is that he will never find himself in such dire financial straits. He is careful with his estate and the people who work on it. His wife, whoever she may turn out to be, may not wake to jokes and hilarity every morning, but she will wake secure."

Caroline, though she knew that fact perfectly well about Lord Bertridge, suddenly felt the full force of it. The duchess was right. He might steam and bluster about this or that thing, but he was careful and anybody dependent on him would be safe.

He was very like her father in that way. Baron Dunn did not have the same means, or in any way a like temperament, but he always ensured that his wife and children never felt the pinch when a horse race did not go his way. He would take the pinch himself and he would protect the family always.

She could not say why, but she very much felt like crying at that moment.

RICHARD HAD NOT been able to slip into the house unnoticed. Bramley, as always, was lurking within range. The butler appeared startled to find him dripping wet and Richard had muttered something about taking a walk. Let Bramley believe he dripped with rainwater, though he'd told the truth to Kingston as he had no idea what saltwater would do to his clothes or what the remedy might be.

Kingston, the consummate valet, had only nodded when he was informed that the clothes, and the person in them, had recently been in the sea. He would tell nobody, Richard knew well enough. As for that confounded Bemmy, he supposed she'd make it her business to tell everybody below stairs.

Well, if the story were to come out, he'd face it down. It was preferable to have made the attempt than to have seen a person waving for help and done nothing by assuming it was a joke.

He'd since dried off and made his way to the drawing room.

Miss Upton would return to the house soon and she must take tea eventually. She could not forever have it sent to her room.

He was determined to get his apology out and done for his harsh words on the night of the dinner. He was not often in the wrong, at least he did not think so, and he found it preyed heavy on his mind, always prowling round and presenting itself for consideration.

As he absentmindedly rubbed Edgar's head, he wondered how those in the habit of doing harm could bear it. How did Landon carry on, having wronged a woman in the gravest fashion and left her with child? Did it keep him up at night? He doubted that it did, though he could not fathom how the fellow got on with things. Whatever the case, he himself could not carry such a burden round with him for long.

He heard Miss Upton come in the front doors and Lady Easton fluttering round her in the hall. Edgar's ears pricked up as Miss Upton assured his aunt that they'd had a lovely time, despite the storm not being as ephemeral as had been hoped. Fortunately, he heard no mention of himself flinging his person into the sea on a doomed rescue mission, so that was at least something.

His aunt bustled into the room. "That is Caroline just come back. I've sent her above stairs to thoroughly dry off. I do wonder about Theodosia going forward with the scheme."

"You've said yourself she takes great pride in her swimming," Richard said. Though if he had the luxury of always being honest, he might have said, *The duchess is a one-woman Mongol Horde who is entirely too dependent on her own opinions and the absurd weather predictions of her butler.*

"It's that butler of hers, Carlson," Lady Easton said. "I am not at all confident that he knows as much about the weather as he thinks he does."

Based on what he had witnessed just an hour ago, Richard was entirely confident that Carlson knew no more about the weather than a piece of furniture, though he did not say so.

He had thought Miss Upton would be above stairs for quite

some time, warming herself, but she came into the drawing room not ten minutes after she'd arrived back to the house.

Richard rose and issued a slight bow and then seated himself after she took the chair next to his aunt. Edgar trotted over to her and waited to be petted. All but her hair appeared dry, *that* had been surely re-pinned after the exertions of her adventure, but it was still quite clearly wet.

"Dear Caroline," Lady Easton said, ringing the bell, "we must have a fire to take out the damp in the room. You may sit by it and dry your hair."

"That is very kind, Lady Easton," Miss Upton said.

"Was it quite dreadful?" Lady Easton asked. "I feel it must have been, though you claimed it was pleasant when you came in. Theodosia would have told you to say that, she so little likes to be wrong."

"Oh, no, my lady," Caroline said, avoiding Richard's eye and looking at Edgar instead, "it was an adventure like no other. I did really enjoy it." Miss Upton paused under Lady Easton's frown. Softly, she said, "There was so much to appreciate about it."

Lady Easton shrugged and said, "I wonder where can Bramley be? I'll just step out, I imagine he's arranging things in the breakfast room. I really do not want you to take a chill, my dear."

After Lady Easton departed, Richard dove in. "Miss Upton, please do allow me to apologize for my words in the drawing room the other evening. I allowed myself to indulge in temper and it was entirely misguided. You, unfortunately, paid the bill for that indulgence."

Miss Upton blushed prettily and said, "It was a bill I ran up with my own actions, my lord."

"It was not the crime of the century, however," Richard said, "though I am afraid I made it seem so."

"I must thank you for your daring rescue this morning, though," Miss Upton said.

"You did not need rescuing, as it turned out."

"But had I…"

"Yes, had you…"

Edgar looked back and forth between them, probably wondering if they were discussing his dinner.

"It was very brave, in a full set of clothes."

"I'm glad you think so, I suspect my valet would call it something else."

"But you might have been pulled under from the weight of it."

"I am strong enough."

"Yes, I know."

"I suppose your maid will spread the tale far and wide."

"Oh no," Miss Upton said, "I have spoken to her about it and she shan't say a word. She really will not, her opinions were vastly modified upon witnessing it."

"Her opinions were modified? I had not known she had any." Though he said it, the truth was he knew full well that Bemmy had opinions about him.

"Perhaps she was mistaken in having them. That does sometimes happen, I think. A person develops an opinion and then they discover they were mistaken."

"Yes," Richard said thoughtfully, "that does happen. Probably more often than one might imagine."

"Yes, I think so too."

They were silent for some moments, the only sound the footfalls of a footman hurrying across the marble floor of the front hall and a rather loud yawn from Edgar.

"I understand we will attend the Regent's ball after all," Miss Upton said.

"*You* will attend, I will go nowhere near it in my current condition."

"Your eye. That was my fault."

"Looking away from my opponent, clumsy as he was, was *my* fault."

"Still, the fault was mine for having been there."

"Perhaps we should dispense with faults, as it seems we could go on all day."

"I have determined to rectify my own," Miss Upton said. "Going forward, I will never give Lady Easton even a moment of worry."

Lady Easton came back to the room with Bramley and the footmen close on her heels.

The footmen built the fire and the lady said, "What do you think, Bramley? If we move that chair just there, Caroline will be close to the fire.

It was all arranged neatly and with little fuss. Richard took up his book and Miss Upton took up her sewing and Lady Easton wrote letters. Edgar, seeing there was no food on offer for him, took up his second favored activity—sleeping as close to the fire as he could manage.

It was quiet in the drawing room, the only interruptions being Bramley with a tea tray and Lady Easton insisting on Caroline taking a sandwich to strengthen herself after her frigid dip in the sea. Edgar had lifted his head hopefully at the arrival of sandwiches, but as Lady Easton's eyes were upon him, he yawned and went back to sleep.

Though the room was quiet, Richard's thoughts were not. He ought to feel very relieved that he'd made his apology to Miss Upton, but somehow he felt worse. She'd taken his condemnations on the chin and vowed to do better.

Who was he to direct the actions of a young lady and make her feel so badly for being...what? Young and impetuous. That was what she was.

What else should she be? Oh, he and his aunt had lauded the idea of a lady being demure. That quality was held up to be the highest accolade. He was afraid he'd been so enthusiastic about the idea because it would be very convenient to never be challenged or worry that the lady had her own ideas about things.

Of course that was it. Was not Lady Cecilia Gentian considered exceedingly demure? And yet, he found sitting next to her at a dinner a positively painful operation. She was more batting eyelashes and staring at her plate than she was conversation. The most notable thing he'd ever heard her say was *Heavens*.

Now here was Miss Upton—intelligent and full of life—and he'd found that unsettling.

All along he prided himself that he was full of good sense. But had he been too regimented in his opinions, expecting anybody in his sphere to fall in line? Had he been too condemning of anything he would not do or think himself? It was beginning to seem as if he were turning into a bit of a stick.

THE DUCHESS, HAVING already dragged Caroline into the sea, was determined to drag her all over Brighton. Three days in a row she arrived to escort Miss Upton to the shops and the seaside. It had been decided between Lady Easton's friends that Caroline would always have an escort among them, but it was then further decided by the duchess that she was the only one suitable.

Lady Redfield was ruled out as she'd already lost track of Miss Upton once.

Lady Featherstone, fashioning herself as a keen crime solving mind since having won Lord Ryland's mystery ball the season before, was far too busy attempting to discover who made off with several nets belonging to a local fisherman. Or, as the duchess put it—*Anne was last seen examining a patch of grass with a quizzing glass. One presumes this is where the nets were last located and that she hopes a passing ant or beetle will stop and reveal where they have gone.*

Lady Mendleton was not a very good walker, preferring her carriage to her legs on account of her penchant for marzipan.

Lady Heathway was too good a walker. She had grown up a vicar's daughter and had spent her childhood walking over hill and dale to visit parishioners. Lady Heathway's walk was everybody else's sprint.

Lady Easton herself had her calendar quite full now that word had got round about her very casually having served a sliced pineapple.

That left the duchess. Caroline was not at all convinced that these various ladies understood how or why they'd been ruled out, but the duchess had ruled herself in.

As she *was* a duchess, poor Bemmy found she must walk three steps behind and carry any packages that had been purchased.

The traipsing this way and that way had been exhausting, but it had not been a wasted effort. Every lady on the street wished to be acknowledged by the duchess. Those same ladies also wished to know Caroline, since the duchess chose to know her.

The duchess was rather marvelous about the whole procedure. Lady So-And-So would make an approach, the duchess would introduce Caroline, and then she would say something along the lines of: *Lady So-And-So, I cannot tell you how much I enjoy Miss Upton's company—she is so intelligent and full of good sense.*

Whatever talk and gossip had gone round about her, Caroline was certain her reputation had been fully restored. It was up to her to keep it that way.

Now, it was the evening of the Regent's ball, and though Lady Easton was not very enthusiastic about going, since they *would* go she was determined that Caroline take the revelers' breaths away.

Mrs. Belle had sent a spectacular ballgown, unique and yet so suited to the seaside. The fabric was an indigo silk, the bodice very simple and unadorned. The skirt was embroidered with indigo sequins and then overlayed with netting of the same color in which larger dark blue stones had been sewn. The whole effect was that of a night sky—as the candlelight caught the stones and sequins, it gave the effect of stars both near and far, winking and blinking.

All was well and Caroline was indeed excited to attend the Regent's ball, but she could not be entirely sanguine.

She really did wish that Lord Bertridge would go.

How different he seemed to her now. He'd boldly charged into the sea to rescue her and then he'd apologized for his scolding in the drawing room. And mostly, what the duchess had said about him was true. He might not be as amusing as Lord Alvanley. Or amusing at all, really. But he was a gentleman in the finest sense of the word. A man who took his responsibilities seriously and was careful of the people dependent upon him. A man who would risk his own person for another. A man who would admit when he'd been wrong.

As she knew from her father, that was a quality to be valued. He'd often said, *A man who can admit error is a man confident in his own abilities. A man who defends a mistake is a man who secretly knows he's an impostor.*

She was beginning to think that the likes of Lord Alvanley were not as interesting as she had at first considered them. After all, what did they care for really? It seemed they only cared for displaying their wit and making jokes. Would Lord Alvanley or Mr. Landon have leapt into the sea to save her? She had her doubts about that. If they had observed her being saved, would they invent jokes about it? Possibly.

For all her wishing though, Lord Bertridge would not go to the ball. At tea, he had confirmed it to his aunt. He would stay at home with a book and would be delighted to miss the regent's ball.

Prior to the duchess dragging her into the sea and Lord Bertridge ordering her out of it, she had been determined to like Mr. Landon. It was very much harder now!

She told herself she must be sensible and accept any reasonable offer that came her way, but she did not want to do it.

She glanced at the clock as Bemmy fussed with her hair.

"There now," Bemmy said, "you're all set to slay the gentlemen and put a few more fellows in your pocket."

"There are still no gentlemen in my pocket," Caroline said laughing.

"Oh I expect there are at least two," Bemmy said. "Though, I did some inquirin' about Mr. Landon with some of my acquaint-ance in the know. Steer well clear of him, I think."

"Goodness, what has Mr. Landon done to fall out of your good graces?"

"He's got unpaid bills round the town and then there's some-thing else, though I don't rightly know what. Mr. Berry, an old gent I've known since I was a babe, told me he's a rotter through and through. Then he was all mysterious when I pressed him on why."

"Well, I suppose every young gentleman in town has unpaid bills," Caroline said. "My father told me they always gamble too much, get in debt, and then have to write their fathers to get them out of it."

Bemmy snorted. "I'd like to see one of my brothers write a letter like that to my da. He'd get a wallop on the head for his trouble."

"I wouldn't wonder if my own father might react similar. He may bet on his own horses, but he would never bet on another's as nobody knows the real potential of a horse but the one who owns it. As for cards, he finds losing money at a gambling table positively idiotic."

"I expect there's another in this house who'd think the same. That other that I've revised my opinion about. You ought to keep that one in your pocket."

"Bemmy," Caroline said, "you must stop imagining that which is not there." As she said it, she thought she would do very well to take her own advice.

"I'm not the imaginin' type, if you get my meaning. Now, you best get yourself off with two minutes to spare. You don't want Lady Easton in a tizzy afore you're even out the door."

CHAPTER SEVENTEEN

Caroline descended the stairs and, for a moment, wondered if Lord Bertridge had changed his mind and would come after all. She could not ignore that the idea sent a burst of butterflies through her, but the feeling quickly dissipated as she noted his attire. He wore the dark silk banyan he was in the habit of wearing at home. He had only come into the hall to see them off.

"Well, Caroline," Lord Easton said cheerfully, "you are a veritable vision. Too bad you don't come, Richard, as I imagine we will have our hands full beating the gentlemen back."

Lord Bertridge never did seem too amused by Lord Easton's jokes, but he looked rather thunderous at that one.

"If there are such ill-mannered gentlemen," Lord Bertridge said curtly, "I suggest you depart the place at once."

"Nobody will dare it while I stand by," Lady Easton said. "In any case, we purposefully arrive late and so I think the likes of Lord Alvanley will have already committed themselves for the evening."

Caroline had not known that they were going late. She felt the slightest twinge of nervousness at the idea that she might sit out for more than one set on account of the available gentlemen having already engaged themselves.

"Now my dear, we do not go that late," Lord Easton said to his wife. "You know you could not bear to be *too* very tardy, it is not in your nature. Do not make Caroline fear that she will sit out, as I doubt that will be the case."

Lord Easton's carriage had rolled to a stop outside of the doors and Bramley opened them.

Late or not, they were on their way.

BRAMLEY WATCHED THE family depart, with the exception of Lord Bertridge, who would not dignify the profligate Regent with his presence. He silently commended Lord Bertridge, as he himself would have refused such an invitation. If he had been in a position to receive one.

However, if good Queen Charlotte were to require his presence some time in the future, he would swim the channel to attend her. He would make the same heroic efforts for the king, though that noble person was currently indisposed.

Bramley had thought a great deal on how he would conduct himself, were he a great gentleman. He was nearly so, as he was a member of an exclusive social club in London, only admitting butlers and valets of fine houses and the occasional renowned chef. He was in the habit of displaying a certain gravitas he had practiced in his looking glass when he attended a dinner there. Lady Easton was highly approving of the look, as she had asked to view it and he had obliged—severe expression, chin slightly raised and presenting a profile, and the slightest furrowing of his eyebrows to indicate sober thoughts.

Lady Easton was in full agreement with him that it must elevate the demeanor of anyone exposed to it.

He had every reason to feel exceedingly dignified at the moment. He had perhaps made it a new habit to take the air in the afternoons before the tea service. He had perhaps, while strolling down the street at a dignified pace, passed by others who served as butlers in the town. He had perhaps noticed their glances and easily imagined their thoughts. *That's Mr. Bramley who served the pineapple at Lady Easton's dinner.*

They were correct. He *was* Mr. Bramley and he *had* served a pineapple. He'd done it with casual aplomb.

Further, the duchess had seemed to take the problematic Miss Upton in hand and he did not expect any further trouble from that quarter. Lady Redfield might lose her charge in the shops, but the duchess would not lose a farthing to a pickpocket. And so, the clocks ticked along and all was right with the house.

He would assure himself that Lord Bertridge had everything he required and then spend most of his evening in quiet recollection of the pineapple.

THE SHIP INN'S assembly rooms were far grander than Caroline had imagined. The ballroom was at least ninety feet long and designed in the neoclassical Adam style with a vaulted plastered ceiling, and there was both a viewing gallery and a gallery for the musicians, as well as a separate room for refreshments and a card room. She supposed she expected something more modest, as her prior visit had been made through the tradesmen's door and into the serving girls' bedchamber.

They had entered the ballroom and stood at the edges, searching for acquaintance. Those acquaintances had presumedly been on the lookout for them too. As if they were great ships coming into port, Lady Easton's friends sailed to her side. Lord Easton, seeing them coming, charted his own course away from this female armada.

The ladies excitedly exchanged information on who was there and who they wished was not there and something about an ear trumpet as Caroline stood on the edges of the gathering.

"Miss Upton," a voice sounded behind her. She knew it well enough, it was Mr. Landon.

He held out his hand for her card, which she gave him,

though she thought Lady Easton would not particularly favor it. While they'd been in the carriage, the lady had been definite in her opinion that they ought to avoid Lord Alvanley's set, though Lord Easton had thought it all nonsense.

Still, what could she do, and while she felt nothing in particular while looking at him, he was a friendly enough gentleman. What more could she ask from a dance partner, if he was not to be some other person who had not come?

Just as Lady Easton turned to her, Mr. Landon bowed and walked off. It was almost as if he understood Lady Easton's low opinion of his set of friends.

"Oh, he didn't," Lady Easton said, examining Caroline's card. "And for the first, too? At least it is not for supper. That really would be a step too far. I blame myself, I was too engrossed in hearing about Lord Jarden having lost his ear trumpet in the sea and Mrs. Gunn having dived in to rescue it. My dear, have a care around Mr. Landon. Richard believes him to have done something, well I do not know what, but more than unseemly and perhaps even shocking."

Caroline nodded. Bemmy had said as much too, but nobody seemed to know what it was Mr. Landon had supposedly done. Was it only debts, or was there something more? Did it even matter to her?

Lady Easton grabbed her hand lightly and Caroline turned to see what had startled her. The Regent, flanked by Lord Alvanley and a second as yet unknown gentleman, headed straight for them.

"Lady Easton, Miss Upton," the prince said. "How pleased we are that you could attend us."

Caroline curtsied and Lady Easton did too, though she knew the lady would rather not.

"Your Royal Highness," Lady Easton said pleasantly.

Lord Alvanley said, "Miss Upton, may I?" reaching out his hand for her card.

Caroline handed it to him as the Prince laughed. "Really,

Alvanley. Getting your name down before poor old Mushy has even been introduced?"

"In the race to secure the prettiest lady of the evening," Lord Alvanley said gallantly, "I wait for no man. Especially when supper is conveniently still open."

Caroline smiled but was certain Lady Easton was steaming beside her. It was precisely what she did not wish for.

"I make no argument against it. Miss Upton, Lady Easton," the Regent said, "may I present Mr. George Mushkell. We call him Mushy on account of his coloring being rather like a mushroom. He is one of the thousands of distant cousins that Alvanley seems to be always pulling out of his pockets."

"Or, to be more precise," Lord Alvanley said jokingly, "he is one of the *two* distant cousins, along with Mr. Landon. This one has just arrived and I cannot afford more than that—they stay at my house and eat my food, you know."

Mr. Mushkell was a rather ordinary looking fellow, or per-haps Caroline might describe him as *medium*. He was of medium height and had medium brown hair and medium brown eyes. His coloring *was* rather mushroom-like. There was nothing at all to put one off, and nothing at all to pull one in.

Mr. Mushkell bowed and said, "Alvanley conveniently forgets that it is always my pleasure to impose on a cousin. Miss Upton, may I?" Caroline nodded and he took her card from Lord Alvanley. He wrote himself in for the fourth.

The Regent was then called away, and Lord Alvanley and Mushy followed him like two moths chasing a flame.

"It is most aggravating," Lady Easton said. "That is three of that ridiculous set on your card now. Who on earth is Mr. Mushroom, I wonder?"

"They are only dances, though," Caroline said, looking to soothe the lady.

"Even so. I only wish Richard were here. He might stand right by us and those sorts would stay well away. They naturally avoid men like Richard, it is too likely he would expose them as juveniles by comparison."

Only a week ago, Caroline would have laughed into her sleeve over such an assessment. Now, however, she rather agreed with Lady Easton. Still, it *was* only a few dances.

Other gentlemen, who Lady Easton found she favored far more, approached and put their names down. Caroline's card was filled and she need not have worried about arriving late. There were plenty of people still arriving, and so Lord Easton had been right—Lady Easton might wish to express her displeasure by way of tardiness, but she could not bear to take the thing past a few minutes.

RICHARD WAS NOT so lacking in self-awareness that he did not see what he was doing just now. He was stewing and brooding. When had he become a stewer and brooder?

He did not have to be at the Regent's ball to know well enough what was happening there. He'd seen Miss Upton leave the house; it was all a foregone conclusion.

She had looked marvelous. He was certain she'd looked far more marvelous than any other lady who would attend the ball. They would all be in pastels of sky blue or seafoam green. But then, some modiste or other had decided to dress Miss Upton in an indigo silk whose matching sequins and stones positively glowed in the candlelight. She would be a star in the heavens and the rest of the ladies would be washed up on the beach. That dress, and that face, would tell the tale.

Why had his aunt allowed it? As they were walking into a veritable lion's den, why had not Lady Easton dressed Miss Upton in something more frumpy?

Frumpy would have been ideal. Dowdy, even better.

He supposed Alvanley and Landon and Pierrepoint and the rest of them were circling her like sharks in the water.

He'd not even had a chance to warn her off Landon. He'd hinted to his aunt, but he'd not been specific. He'd not told her that Landon had got a scullery maid with child. It seemed a subject Lady Easton would have recoiled from hearing.

He'd thought of warning Miss Upton directly, but then his apology had come off so well that he hadn't wished to ruin it by going back to lecturing.

Maybe he should have gone to the ball after all.

But no, it would have been foolish. He was not meant for such places, where the very air was committed to jokes and levity. There he'd have been, stern-faced and with a black eye. He would have been the subject of weak jokes from Alvanley, which all would have laughed at because they were secretly afraid of becoming the man's next joke. He would not fit in or blend in. Miss Upton might even have found him silly.

He did not find that reason for staying away a very satisfactory explanation for himself. He really should not have made his decision based on his personal comfort. He should have done what was needed, despite whatever cost to his pride.

Now, Miss Upton was exposed to what he considered unsavory characters.

Especially Landon.

He thought that reprobate took a particular interest in Miss Upton. And no less of an interest in her father, Baron Dunn. Landon had hinted he wished to go into business with the baron and had come right out and asked him if he could arrange an introduction. He was a second son and would avoid the clergy or the military. He wished to have a career in horses. Who better to align himself with than the daughter of the premier horseman in England?

That scoundrel, that reprobate who, upon discovering he'd impregnated a poor maid had told her she could *dance on a table and shout it to the world.*

Richard gulped down his brandy. Dance on a table. That was what Miss Upton had been accused of doing when the rumors went round about Alvanley's party.

Was that a coincidence? Or had it been Landon that had started the rumor?

One would think a gentleman would not spread such a rumor about a lady he admired. And, of course, a *gentleman* would not. But Landon was no gentleman.

Perhaps he thought to weaken Miss Upton's position so that she would be grateful to a man who did not condemn her. Perhaps a baron might be willing to connect himself to a second son who was willing to take on a scandalous daughter.

He would not put it past Landon to try such a gambit. After all, was not the idiot hoping his older brother would kill himself driving his phaeton? And not even afraid to express such ideas to a gentleman he did not particularly know?

Miss Upton might be in real danger of being tricked into marrying that clod.

She could not be allowed to marry him. Of course she could not.

Richard slammed his empty brandy glass on the table. Edgar leapt up and looked around for the alarm.

"Bramley!" he shouted. "Tell Kingston I need my dress clothes this instant!"

⋙⋘

THE MUSICIANS HAD been tuning their instruments for some minutes and now the Regent signaled the dance would commence. How he signaled it had caused Caroline to bite her lip lest she laugh at the sight. The Prince led the duchess, who was just now swimming in brocade and sprouting ostrich feathers out of the top of her head, to the top of the first set.

The duchess held her head high, looking for all the world as if she were on her way to her coronation. Caroline thought her rather wonderful. She was further amused by the looks on the faces of Lady Easton and Lady Heathway, gazing down from the gallery. It was a very studied aloof indifference.

Mr. Landon led Caroline to her place and said, "I see the old dragon deigns to be led by a Prince."

"If you refer to the duchess, she is anything but a dragon," Caroline said. "She is only very forceful."

"I'll say," Mr. Landon said laughing. "She has given me such blistering glances on the street that I am surprised I have not gone up in a puff of smoke."

"Well, yes, I could see that," Caroline admitted. "I do not believe she is very approving of your set of friends."

"Or of me," Mr. Landon said ruefully. "Fortunately, I have not a care for the duchess' opinion. My only interest is in Miss Upton's opinion."

Mr. Landon led her forward to begin La Dorset and Caroline gratefully glanced away. She was not at all certain whether he was simply making glib conversation, or whether that comment had been a hint of some sort.

She had come close to convincing herself that if Mr. Landon were to pursue her, she must accept. It had all seemed so rational—her father would like him, he wished to make his business horses, and he saw no reason why a woman must be kept out of it. She must marry and so why not to a gentleman with like interests? And then, he was very pleasant.

That had all changed though. She could not consider it. Not when she spent so much time thinking about Lord Bertridge. The *new* Lord Bertridge who'd attempted to rescue her and followed it up with an apology. Or if he were not new, then the more clearly seen Lord Bertridge.

It was stupid, she was well aware. A brave action and a few kind words did not signify anything other than that he was a fine man with solid principles.

And yet, she understood now that she would not accept Mr. Landon if he asked.

They had returned to their place and the lead couple began

La Victoria.

"I've not made it any secret, Miss Upton," Mr. Landon said, leaning close to her ear, "that I admire you exceedingly."

Caroline was afraid Mr. Landon was on the verge of going somewhere she did not wish to go, but how to stop such a thing? Nobody had ever told her that.

"As well," Mr. Landon continued, "I am very keen on horses and believe I could do very well."

"I'm sure you will," Caroline said noncommittedly.

"And I also imagine we might do very well together. Only think, with your father's skill and reputation, and then a younger man coming in to boost the whole operation—"

"Mr. Landon," Caroline said, "I cannot influence my father in any way."

"Surely, if we were to marry, he would—"

"But we are not to marry," Caroline said. "I am very sorry, but we are not."

The man was extraordinary. He had not even asked her to marry, he'd just taken her acquiescence as a foregone conclusion and was talking of what would come after.

Mr. Landon looked deeply surprised to hear they were not to marry. "Do you intend to become a spinster then?" he asked.

"A spinster? No, I do not," Caroline said, not having the faintest idea how he'd made that leap.

"Miss Upton," Mr. Landon said, in a tone as if he were talking to a small child, "your reputation is in tatters. Who else would consent to marry you? I felt I was being rather liberal in overlooking—"

"Overlooking? You know perfectly well that none of that talk was true. You were there!"

"Ah, well, that hardly matters, does it? Talk becomes its own sort of fact."

It was their turn to step out and dance La Victoria. As Caroline did so, avoiding Mr. Landon's eye, she thought he could not be right. The dust had settled on those ridiculous rumors.

Even if they had not, she would never consent to marry Mr. Landon. She had just seen a side of him that he'd have been better served to keep well-hidden. She was grateful he had not, though. She was grateful to have seen it, as it would save her any regrets she might have in the future if she did indeed become a spinster. Better alone than with him, she was certain.

He had presented himself so pleasant, but there was a calculating meanness to him. She had been made certain that Mr. Landon would not have stopped to give Miss Upton the time of day, had she not been the daughter of Baron Dunn. Had she not held the keys to his new proposed horse business.

La Moulinets and La Visites passed by with no further comments. As the tours of Les Lanciers became more intricate as they went on, Caroline put her concentration on the fifth and final of them, named after the dance itself.

They had nearly completed the steps and Caroline was looking forward to getting away when Mr. Landon said, "Do not be too hasty in your decisions, Miss Upton. I will give you time to reconsider."

"I thank you for the courtesy, but I do not require it," Caroline said.

"Of course you do."

As RICHARD WAS being dressed, his thoughts came at him fast and furious. They piled in, one after the other, rapid fire. It was almost as if they'd all been hiding together behind a veil waiting to make themselves known. Now, the veil had been lifted and he knew his purpose. How stupid that he hadn't known it all along.

Kingston had been roused from below stairs and had not made the slightest comment upon being informed that he would attend the regent's ball after all.

Bramley, on the other hand, was a different matter. As Richard came down the stairs, the butler was to-ing and fro-ing as if he did not know what direction he should go in.

"Lord Bertridge," he cried, "what about a carriage? Or should I send for your horse? It may rain so a carriage would be better, but then a carriage always takes longer. I've no plan in mind and it is very difficult to proceed without a plan! I must know the plan!"

"Get hold of yourself, Bramley," Richard said as Kingston disappeared down the stairs to the servants' hall to fetch a fresh neckcloth from the laundry. "It is not far; I will walk there."

"Walk?" Bramley said, staggering and then steadying himself with a side table. "Alone at night through this Godforsaken town? There may be footpads and murderers lurking about. We are at the seaside, there may even be pirates out for a press-gang! Lady Easton would be vehemently against it."

"By the time my aunt considers the idea, it will already be done," Richard said, pulling on his gloves.

Bramley looked wildly this way and that as if the footpads, murderers, and pirates had surrounded the house. He raced past Richard and stood splayed across the front doors. "I cannot allow it. Lady Easton must be my guiding hand and she would not allow it. What would I tell her if you were to go missing? Or turned up dead!"

Richard had come to the end of his rope with Bramley, his temper slipping out of its box and slithering through him, pumping his blood ever faster.

"Do you not see what's happened, you fool?" he shouted.

Bramley looked around the hall for what happened but appeared quite at a loss. "What has happened?"

"I've deceived myself all along. It is Miss Upton. She is an impossible lady."

"You have said so many times, my lord," Bramley said, bravely refusing to relinquish his hold on the door.

"Yes, well, she is *my* impossible lady!"

Bramley's arms fell to his side. "Miss Upton? My lord, I really do not think Lady Easton would approve."

"Of course she would not, *I* do not even approve! Blast it, it would be a life of chaos, precisely what I did not wish for."

"But now you do wish for it?" Bramley said, beginning to look a little woozy.

"No, but what choice do I have?"

His valet hurried into the hall with his recently starched neck-cloth. To Kingston's never-ending credit, he set to tying the cloth with his usual skill and entirely ignoring the butler just now ranged across the door.

Kingston expertly finished the knot and Richard said, "Kingston, get Bramley off the door. Pry him off before I must do it myself. Then give him a glass of brandy so he may collect himself."

"In a trice, my lord," Kingston said, as if it were the most commonplace of activities.

Bramley turned out to have more spirit than would be expected. Kingston struggled with him to no avail. Richard tapped his valet on the shoulder so that he might step aside. Then, he picked Bramley up and set him down again away from the door.

Richard strode out of the house as Bramley was led away, Kingston assuring the butler that a dose of brandy would soothe his fears over murderers, footpads, and pirates.

• —— ⁘ —— •

CHAPTER EIGHTEEN

CAROLINE HAD BEEN relieved to be away from Mr. Landon and she did not care to ever be in his vicinity again. The dances following had been pleasant enough, but she really would rather be at home.

How funny she would think so, as it had never occurred to her that she'd rather be at home with a book than at the Regent's ball. She had pined to come when she thought she would not, and now she'd got here and found that she pined to be away.

She was beginning to think she was a rather contrary sort of person.

Mr. Mushkell was to collect her for the fourth though she had not seen him since their introduction. Or perhaps she had, but he'd just faded into the mushroom color of the plastered walls.

He did finally appear before her and led her to her place. The dance began and though he was not the most riveting person she'd ever met, she did not mind it. His conversation was commonplace and that suited her just fine. At the moment, she did not feel she could keep up with the wit of Lord Alvanley and did not know how she would get through supper creditably. Mushy's inquiries into how she found the weather were quite sufficient.

It was a country dance and there was ample time to stand about as they slowly made their way to the head. They finally did so and took their turn, ending up at the bottom again.

Very suddenly, Mr. Mushkell stepped out of the line and Mr. Landon stepped into it.

Amidst her confusion, she watched Mr. Mushkell hurry off with a small smile.

"What are you doing, Mr. Landon?" Caroline asked. She was furious. Lady Easton would be furious. It was outrageous and would prompt talk of there being something between them.

Mr. Landon only shrugged.

Caroline did not know what to do. Should she leave the dance, or would that cause even more talk? Would it look like some kind of lover's quarrel?

Or should she carry on and merely look disinterested. Perhaps if she did that, Mr. Landon taking Mr. Mushkell's place would only seem like some kind of joke coming out of Lord Alvanley's set.

She glanced up to the gallery and saw the looks of consternation from Lady Easton and her friends, but those looks did not tell her what to do. They did not signal for her to step away. Did that mean she ought to carry on?

She neared the head of the line, then they were next. She did not feel she could step out of her place now, not with so many eyes trained in her direction.

So many eyes upon her who may not have seen the switch, but were now remembering she started with Mr. Mushkell and had already danced the first with Mr. Landon.

She wished to grab the nearest Greek vase and clobber him on the head with it.

As they went down the line, Mr. Landon leaned close and said, "Do follow my lead, Miss Upton. It is for the best."

What did he mean?

They reached the bottom and he suddenly kissed her on the cheek and exclaimed, "I am the luckiest man alive! The lady says she will have me!"

Caroline pulled away from him in horror. While not everybody in the ballroom may have heard him, all in the vicinity had.

"I said no such thing," Caroline said loudly.

"Now my dear," Mr. Landon said smoothly, "you are overcome by this turn of events, most natural thing in the world."

He came closer and took her by the arm. "You must sit down and recover yourself."

"Take your hands off me!" Caroline shouted, attempting to struggle out of his grip. His hand was strong and his fingers dug into her arm painfully.

Mr. Landon did release her then, though not through any efforts of her own.

Lord Bertridge had him by the coat collar and lifted him off the ground.

The musicians one by one stopped playing, the music drifting off in bits and pieces. The dance petered out and the room grew hushed.

The lord threw Mr. Landon to the ballroom floor and said, "Do you dare get up again, you reprobate?"

Mr. Landon got to his knees, a smarmy smile on his face. "Now see here, Bertridge, the lady has consented to be my wife."

"I certainly have not," Caroline said.

"Of course she has not," Lord Bertridge said.

"What goes on here?" the Regent called from the gallery.

"What goes on, Your Royal Highness," Lord Bertridge said, "is Mr. Landon is a scoundrel who has left a scullery maid with child, and now attempts to force Miss Upton into marriage to gain access to her father's stud concern. Should that not work out, he's been hoping his eldest brother dies driving his phaeton. He is conniving, avaricious, and utterly devoid of morality."

"I don't know what you are talking about," Mr. Landon said, rising and dusting himself off. "Do you never tire of staring down your nose, old man?"

Caroline noticed Lord Bertridge's fists opening and closing.

In a low fury he said, "The scullery maid paid you a visit before the boxing exhibition. I heard every word, as did my valet."

Mr. Landon paled. He jutted his chin out and said, "Come Bertridge, those sorts will say anything for money, everybody knows it."

"No," Lord Bertridge said, "*you* will say anything for money. And by the by, I warned you not to rise."

Lord Bertridge punched Mr. Landon square in the jaw and the man fell in a heap to the ballroom floor.

The silence was almost deafening in Caroline's ears.

The Regent said, "Alvanley, you'd better take your cousins elsewhere. And do not bring them back."

It was clear to Caroline that while the likes of Landon might amuse the Regent, he did not care to be associated with the downright scandalous. As for who the Regent was to believe between the two men, it seemed *that* had not even been a question. Lord Bertridge might not entertain him, but his propriety and veracity were above reproach.

Lord Alvanley, to his credit, looked entirely shaken. He grabbed Mr. Mushkell's arm roughly and marched him over to where Mr. Landon lay on the floor.

"My apologies, Bertridge," he said.

Lord Bertridge only nodded.

Lord Alvanley and the cousin he had still standing dragged the cousin no longer standing out of the ballroom and beyond the doors.

"Well, what now?" the Regent said. "I grow tired of gentlemen toying with Miss Upton's reputation. It is very low."

"*I* do not toy with Miss Upton's reputation," Lord Bertridge said, folding his arms.

"No, of course you do not, Bertridge," the Regent said. "I cannot imagine that you even toyed with *toys* in your younger years. Do take Miss Upton to the refreshments room and get her something restorative. Let everyone understand that I back Miss Upton in this matter and I name Landon a scoundrel that nobody will receive. Now, carry on everybody. It is my ball, after all."

Caroline was nearly dizzy with confusion. Too much had

happened too fast. She had been dancing, and then trapped, and then set free again. Mr. Landon had got her in his grip, and Lord Bertridge had knocked him flat.

Lord Bertridge held her up by putting his hand under her elbow. It was the same arm that Mr. Landon had bruised. But, where Landon's grip was deep and digging and painful, Lord Bertridge's hand was gentle and steady. It was strong, but it was gentle. It was the sort of hand one might lean on all day.

"Come, Miss Upton," he said, glaring at the starers until they turned away.

She allowed herself to be led and they went to the refreshment room. There were those people in it who had not heard the goings on in the ballroom but had only noticed that the distant music had stopped.

Lord Jeffries stepped forward as they entered the room. "What now, Bertridge? Has Mr. Gow broken a string?"

"Get out, if you would be so kind," Lord Bertridge said.

Poor Lord Jeffries had not expected that answer. He said, "What?"

"Out, all of you. Miss Upton requires quiet to recover herself."

"Recover? Well, if we can be of assistance—"

"Out. Now."

The surprised party did file out of the room, avoiding Lord Bertridge's eye.

He closed the door. "Sit," he said.

Caroline did sit. Her mind was spinning but she was lucid enough to know that nobody would disobey Lord Bertridge in the state he was in. She certainly would not. She was rather admiring of his current state. His neckcloth had been rumpled and he had a bit of a wild look to him.

He examined the drinks on offer. Then, he took a bottle of Madeira and poured a large glass of it for her. Bringing it over, he said, "You ought to drink it all down. You've had a shock."

"Yes," she said.

"Now, Miss Upton," Lord Bertridge said, beginning to pace the room as she sipped her Madeira, "I have no wish to lecture you, nor do I think anything that happened this night can be your doing. Landon is an out-and-out rogue, though you could not have known it."

Caroline did not answer, but only nodded. Lord Bertridge was so very handsome, pacing around like that.

"I simply feel that you seem to always fall into trouble some-how," Lord Bertridge said. "Or rather, trouble seems to find you."

Caroline nodded. It was perfectly true.

"That must come to an end. You agree, do you not? It is just not practical to carry on like this. One must, in the fullness of time, set one's course in life. One must choose a direction. As it were."

Caroline had not the first idea which direction Lord Bertridge thought she ought to choose. She was far too busy admiring how dashing he looked. He'd just run his hand through his hair and he looked wonderfully disheveled. She supposed he looked like that in the morning before his valet was called.

She had a sudden vision of him sleepy-eyed and shirtless, with the sun just coming up and peeking through the curtains. Perhaps she was there with him. Maybe they were in Venice and soft breezes came through the opened windows. Perhaps she would lean toward him and whisper that the valet ought not to be called so soon. Nobody ought to be called at all.

She saw him in her mind's eye, leaning over her and then his lips touched hers…

"Do you agree then?" Lord Bertridge asked.

It appeared he'd been talking while she was admiring his mussed hair and picturing a bedchamber in Venice. Whatever it was that he thought she ought to do, she was perfectly amenable to it.

"Oh yes, of course I agree," Caroline said nodding, her mind drifting back to the bedchamber in Venice.

"You do?" Lord Bertridge said, halting his pacing. "Miss Upton…that is to say, Caroline…I will not let you down."

What did he mean? Let her down how? And did he just call her Caroline?

"I will do everything in my power, well, my dear Miss Upton, Caroline, of course you will always be cared for, I may not be the most amusing fellow on earth, but then I suppose one can pick up such things if necessary. But I think the important thing to note is you will always be cared for, always protected…"

Caroline leapt out of her seat. "Did you just ask for my hand?"

Lord Bertridge looked mightily confused. "You said you agreed."

She threw herself into his arms. "Oh Bertie, I was imagining you waking up in the morning because just now, with your hair mussed and your black eye, you look very much like a pirate. We were in Venice."

Lord Bertridge pulled her close and nuzzled her neck. "Am I now to understand you favor pirates? *Venetian* pirates?"

"Only this pirate."

Richard kissed her deeply. His lips were soft, yet forceful. His arms were gloriously strong, just as she imagined they must be, and he pressed her against his broad chest. She could barely breathe, but she did not care. Most delightfully, she realized that he was not the stickiest of the sticks in *all* areas.

"You must say it all over again," Caroline whispered. "Exactly how you asked me to marry you so I can hear it properly."

"I said, marriage seemed the most sensible course."

"Oh Bertie, you didn't. Say something else."

Richard tipped her chin up and stroked her hair. "What would you have me say? That I am mad for Miss Upton? That she unsettles me and is always in my thoughts? That she makes my heart pound and I have been wondering for the past ten minutes what her hair smells like and now I know it is a rather delightful lavender. That I had to knock my aunt's butler out of the way to get to her?"

"Yes, all of that," Caroline whispered.

She winced just a little as he pressed against her bruised arm. He pulled back ever so slightly and lifted her arm, kissing it from wrist to shoulder. As he reached her neck he whispered, "There is something you should know about me. You've already seen it. I have a temper."

"Indeed," Caroline whispered back.

"I keep it well under control though. At least, usually."

"Yes, the man that pummels a cruel hackney driver to save a horse and pounds a scoundrel like Mr. Landon. I am entirely undaunted by it.

"I won't ever be cruel to you. I have been, with that ridiculous speech I made that caused you to faint. But I will never be again. That I swear."

"Swear away, Bertie," she said, unknotting his cravat and kissing his neck.

He groaned and she looked up and traced the outline of his black eye. "But rather than make such a promise, I think you'd better let your temper out now and again or you will pop like a champagne cork at inconvenient moments."

"I really do not like to let it out," he said, nuzzling her neck. "I boxed it up long ago and I try to keep it boxed."

She kissed his lips gently and whispered, "But you might shout at the sky or lecture a fence post, and nobody minds."

"I suppose the sky and the fence post won't mind."

"Bertie," she said, pulling his neckcloth ever looser and kissing around it, "perhaps I might button up and you might button down and we can be buttons meeting somewhere in the middle. We should do, I think, or you will be forever scolding and I will be forever cross at your scolding."

"I do not wish to scold you, ever again."

"Then you must try, do try! I have undone your neckcloth, perhaps keep it undone in your mind."

"I imagine you're right. Just this evening I was wondering if I was becoming a bit of a stick."

"Only just now becoming?" Caroline said laughing. "Oh Bertie, you are the stickiest of the sticks. I quite adore it."

The door crashed open and Lady Easton was followed in by Lord Easton, the duchess, and Lady Heathway.

Seeing the state of her nephew and her charge, Lady Easton cried, "What in heavens!"

"We are to be married, Aunt."

"Married?" Lady Easton said breathless.

"You cannot think I would compromise Caroline in such a manner for any other reason," Lord Bertridge said cheerfully.

"I should say not, but Richard, marriage?"

"Congratulations, my boy," Lord Easton said.

"This is most unexpected," the duchess said.

"Well it wouldn't be the first such surprise," Lady Heathway said.

"But if I may be the voice of reason here, you are not at all suited," Lady Easton said. "Richard, you require somebody who is demure. Caroline, I am very fond of you, but you are not—"

"Aunt, I do not require *demure*. However, I *will* have to button down. You know, loosen my neckcloth, and ease my expectations of things."

"Excellent, just as I've forever advised, Nephew," Lord Easton said. "How clever of Caroline to help you see it."

"Your neckcloth has seemed to have already undone itself," Lady Easton said with a sniff. She paused, then said, "I do not at all see why you must button down. Why should you lower your standards of how things ought to be?"

"We've talked about it between us," Lord Bertridge said. "At the same time I'm buttoning down, Caroline intends to button up."

"I cannot be opposed to *that* notion," Lady Easton said with aspersion.

"And on occasion," Lord Bertridge said, "when perhaps my temper wishes to make an appearance, I am to shout at the sky or lecture a fencepost.

"The sky? A fencepost? Richard, you will seem a lunatic." Lady Easton sunk down in a chair. She eyed the glass of Madeira and then took it and drained it.

"Lady Easton," Caroline said, untangling herself from Richard and coming to grasp the lady's hands, "you have been too good to me."

"I rather think I have," Lady Easton muttered.

"And I know it must seem very strange to you that Bertie and I are suited, and yet it is so. We really are suited, though we are so different."

"Who is *Bertie?*" Lady Easton asked, looking around as if somebody else was set to make an appearance.

"Now, you know who she refers to perfectly well, my dear," Lord Easton said, laughing.

"But what about the duke's daughter, Richard? It was a set thing between us."

"I am afraid we have been a little *too* set in our plans. It seems unexpected things happen in life and there is little we can do to predict them."

"Oh, I do not like that notion at all," Lady Easton said.

"Nor I," Lord Bertridge said, "but there it is."

CHAPTER NINETEEN

Caroline and Richard walked back to the house, despite Bramley's fears of murderers, footpads, and pirates. Richard gently took her hand and they walked along the road that ran beside the sea. The waves gently rolled in as they discussed their future.

"I suppose I do not have the slightest hope of a set menu each week," Richard said.

"Ah, similar to Lady Easton's schedules. I do not see why not," Caroline said. "We shall have surprise on Mondays, wonder what it is Tuesdays, far too spicy Wednesdays, you'll never guess Thursdays, astonishing Fridays, alarming Saturdays, and shocking Sundays. You'll always know what to expect."

"I am entirely resigned to it."

"Or, I can simply see what you like best and what I like best and plan accordingly."

"I like *you* best. I could care less what's on the table unless it's you on the table."

"I find that rather shocking, my lord."

"Do you?"

"No, not really."

Caroline squeezed his hand. For all his blustering, she was becoming more and more convinced that Bertie was rather a soft touch. And very deep, with his ideas about what ought to be on a table.

"I suppose you'll be redecorating the whole place," Richard said. "We'll have plaster dust and workmen and chaos for months."

"Oh no," Caroline said, laughing. "I will only go bit by bit so you will hardly notice. One day you will set your tea down on a table in the drawing room and think, were not those curtains green? Or have they always been yellow?"

"If you are on the table, I will never notice the curtains."

"Then you may expect to find me on tables all over the house, as I have particular ideas about curtains."

Richard nodded and said, "Now, children. I only have my own childhood to reference and that only tells me what I do not want. I am determined that my children grow up in a steady sort of house—no unwelcome surprises, no upsets. It must be calm and ordered and predictable. It must be the solid ground beneath their feet."

"Perhaps we might add into that recipe a dollop of fun and joy, with the occasional hi-jinks?"

"Yes, I suppose so. Now you see that's the sort of thing I don't have experience with. You'll guide the fun, I expect."

"You'll catch on to it quick enough."

"I suppose you'll want piles of pin money to buy all sorts of fripperies. My house will overflow with ribbons."

"Probably," Caroline said, laughing.

"Then it is fortunate that I'm very rich. My cheesemaking shall pay for your bonnets."

"I shall be interested to hear more about the cheese."

"Will you? Will you be as interested as you were the first night we met, where I believe I went into some detail about it? And where I also believe you may have been on the verge of laughing?"

"Now it is to be my husband's cheese. I can assure you that is an entirely different matter."

"We are well-suited somehow, are we not?"

"I rather think so."

They had come to the house, and perhaps lingered out of doors for longer than was strictly necessary.

Richard banged the knocker to alert Bramley before opening the door himself.

Caroline was surprised to see that it was Richard's valet who came to take their things.

"You may tell Bramley, wherever he may be," Richard said, "that the night has been entirely devoid of footpads, murderers, or pirates."

"I wouldn't bother telling him anything just now, my lord," Kingston said, looking meaningfully at Richard.

"The reason being…" Richard asked.

Kingston glanced nervously around and then in a low tone said, "He was overwrought about the murderers and such and so did have a large glass of brandy. Our man is not much of a drinker, as it turns out. I left him in his bed singing tavern songs."

Caroline covered her mouth to stop her laughter. She might have thought Bertie would take a very dim view of a singing butler and was surprised when he laughed too.

"Poor Bramley," he said. "Does Lady Easton know?"

"No she don't," Kingston said. "I told my lady that Bramley was struck down by a headache."

"Good man," Richard said. He turned to Caroline and said, "It's late, we'd best go up."

"Rather scandalous to go up the stairs together," Caroline said.

Richard nodded and they walked up, leaving the slack-jawed valet behind.

They stopped at Caroline's door. Richard leaned over her, his hand on the doorframe. "My valet does not yet know we are engaged and likely thinks he never knew me at all and that I am secretly a seducer to be taking you above stairs without escort."

"Well, he ought to know that the good Lord Bertridge would never be a seducer until after he is married. Then, one hopes, he may seduce all he likes."

"And so he will," Richard said. He kissed her forehead and said, "For now though, go to bed. Even upright Bertridge has an end to self-control."

Caroline thought that idea rather marvelous, though she did not dare test his limits. She slipped in her door and closed it behind her.

Bemmy sat by her bedside next to a lone candle. "I told ya, didn't I? He was in your pocket all along." She stretched her legs and let out a satisfied yawn. "Fancy types, they do take the roundabout way to the races."

Caroline bit her lip. Bemmy could not be more right about *that*.

⇒⟫⟪⇐

THE LADIES OF the society had gathered before noon in Lady Easton's drawing room. If they had not witnessed what had occurred at the Regent's ball, they had heard of it. Nobody in Brighton talked of anything else.

If Lady Easton must come to terms with this disturbing development, at least she was surrounded by friends to bolster her up.

When she'd woken, Lady Easton almost thought it could not have happened, it must have been a dream. Her nephew, who was meant to marry a duke's daughter, could not be engaged to Caroline.

But then she'd been informed by her lady's maid that Bramley had fled the breakfast room because Richard and Caroline had been caught kissing there. The couple had since gone out to nobody knew where.

Kissing. In her breakfast room. It was as if Richard was under some kind of spell.

"What I fail to understand," Lady Heathway said, "is how we never see these things coming. I cannot imagine any couple less suited."

"That's what I said," Lady Easton murmured, "and yet they say they *are* suited."

"I do not think it is a case of they are suited, but a case of they will be suited through their own determination," the duchess said. "They outright said that Bertridge intends to button down and Miss Upton intends to button up. Frankly, it won't do your nephew any harm to loosen the stays a bit."

"Loosen the stays?" Lady Easton asked, the incredulity of her tone apparent to all.

"I think what the duchess means," Lady Redfield said, "is that he is very…what shall we call it? Exacting, perhaps? A wonderful quality of course, but I suppose one can have too much of anything."

Lady Redfield looked at her friend hopefully, no doubt wondering if the notion had cheered her. Which it had not.

"I'm sure it's all for the best," Lady Mendleton said. "Remember, Clara, I was entirely set on Lady Annabelle for Jasper, we all were set on it. And then he married Georgianna. I was shocked at first, but I do so like having a daughter. We are exceedingly close, you see. Now Caroline will be like *your* daughter."

"Yes, I suppose," Lady Easton said grudgingly. "I am fond of her, do not mistake me on that."

"And she plays beautifully," Lady Heathway said. "Just as my Grace plays. Of course, we never did have the chance to hear Miss Wilcox at the instrument, but one hopes that day will soon come."

Lady Mendleton glared at Lady Heathway. Lady Easton ignored them both—it was well settled that Miss Wilcox, now Lady Langley, likely could not play a note. Penelope was only determined that Louisa admit to it, which she never would.

Bramley came in with the tea and looked decidedly under the weather. Lady Easton was certain he must still have his headache.

"Bramley," she said, "do have some of my laudanum for your

headache. It always does me a world of good. Now, did Richard and Caroline say where they went? Or when they would be back?"

Bramley sniffed and said, "They've taken horses, they go to post a letter to Miss Upton's father, and then…"

"Yes?"

"Then," Bramley said, as if he were reporting to a court, "Lord Bertridge said they were going *wherever the wind takes them.* They packed a lunch. As you might surmise, I am at a loss to understand precisely when the wind intends on bringing them back."

Bramley marched out of the room and closed the door with a decided thump.

"It's happening already," Lady Easton said quietly. "This is Caroline's influence. Richard has never in his life allowed the wind to set his course. I only wish Bemmy would consent to stay on as Caroline's maid. She is such a rational influence."

"Bemmy was a lucky find," the duchess said.

"A treasure, I think you've said," Lady Redfield added.

Lady Easton finally noticed that Lady Featherstone had not said a word since she'd arrived and in fact appeared to be dozing off. The lady absentmindedly fingered her beloved emerald brooch and her eyelashes fluttered.

"Anne," she said. "What has made you so tired that you are nodding off in my drawing room?"

Lady Featherstone roused herself and said, "It's the fisherman's missing nets. I was on to some clues and following them right to the end but as it turns out, Dr. Merrigan was not the thief."

"Dare I ask," the duchess said, "why a physician would make off with fishing nets?"

"He recommends fresh fish to all his patients," Lady Featherstone said. "He says it strengthens the blood. I thought, how is one to get fish without a net? I did some sleuthing and asking around and it was confirmed that Dr. Merrigan has never been known to have nets. Then I instantly deduced he would have need of them. So why not buy them? Perhaps his practice was suffering because he was always recommending fish but had none to give. It all started to fall into place."

Lady Easton did her best not to allow her eyes to roll back in her head.

"As it happens," Lady Featherstone went on, "he just tells his patients to go buy fish, as he informed me directly in the strongest terms. Rude terms, if I do say so. In any case, I had to start over and I studied my list of clues until dawn. I am determined to get to the bottom of it and report my findings at the criminal society next season. The fisherman who lost the nets has said I ought to give it up, but I said no sir, I will have my man!"

Nobody cared to comment on Lady Featherstone's unique deductions, not even Lady Redfield, who almost always could think up something pleasant to say.

"Well ladies," the duchess said with her usual vigor and practicality, "I suggest we view this outcome as a success. We were faced with the herculean task of launching a girl in Brighton and we did it. Our goal was to get Miss Upton creditably married, and she is engaged to an eminently suitable gentleman."

Clara sighed. It was all well and good for the duchess to view the thing with equanimity. But for herself, it was a blow. First, her husband had transformed himself into someone difficult to manage. Now, her dependable nephew planned to transform himself too. It meant that she'd lost one of just two people who understood her attachment to clocks and schedules. Now, it was down to only her and Bramley to carry on and keep the world in order.

BRAMLEY TOOK LADY Easton's advice and dosed himself rather liberally with laudanum. It was as effective as she had claimed, and he felt his spirits returning.

It was true that he had failed to stop Lord Bertridge from daring the dark and dangerous streets of Brighton.

It was true that he'd drunk a glass of brandy though the stuff always seemed to strike him hard.

It was true that he'd got maudlin in the drawing room and told Kingston about his dear departed mother.

It was true he'd suddenly cheered up and allowed Kingston to help him to his room as he found he could not get there under his own power.

It was very unfortunately true that he had vague recollections of laying in his bed and singing *A Fox May Steal Your Hens, Sir* and *The Bailiff's Daughter of Islington*.

And of course it was true that he had a rather loud singing voice and so might have serenaded the entire staff.

However, it was also true that Lord Bertridge had not been robbed, killed in the streets, or pressganged onto a pirate ship. It was also true that nobody in the house would think much about his own activities with all tongues wagging about Miss Upton and Lord Bertridge.

And mostly it was true that the clocks were in order and a pineapple had been served.

Whatever had occurred the night before, nobody could take that from him. He was the server of a pineapple, and always would be.

RICHARD HAD POSTED the letter to her father, which he had stayed up late writing. Between kisses in the breakfast room, Caroline had peeked at it before he sealed it. It was just as formal as anyone would imagine Lord Bertridge to write. Her fine qualities were extolled in laborious fashion, he described his seriousness about marriage and his ability to properly care for a wife. He proposed exceedingly generous terms regarding pin money and a jointure amount that far exceeded her dowry. Further, his estate was not entailed and he planned to set aside a sizable portion of it in case he died before there was an heir.

It was practical and thoughtful and it was Bertie through and through. She suspected her father would be delighted with it. Baron Dunn had sent his daughter away so that she might meet a more elevated fellow than a stable hand, and she presented him with a most elevated fellow indeed.

They'd since ridden past the church and Caroline admitted that Richard had indeed spotted her that one day. But he'd not spotted her on the other days that she'd been there with her maid. She had viewed him shirtless any number of times.

He was not cross about it, and only said, "I knew it."

They'd since made a mad gallop across an expansive sheep down with those creatures grazing across the green and not bothering to look up. Mr. Landon might have had an interest in horses, but Bertie was a master on horseback. Her father would be further pleased with that. *She* was very pleased with that.

They stopped under an old chestnut tree and Richard unpacked the panniers.

After the picnic was laid and the wine was poured, Caroline said, "I must admit, I always did think that I aggravated you."

"As did I," Richard admitted. "But I realized that I was only unsettled. I had imagined that when I married, there would be no disruption. A very quiet and unobtrusive lady would take her place in my house and everything would stay just as ordered as it has always been since my parents' passing."

"Demure," Caroline said. "And here I am blowing into your life like a gale force wind."

"True," Richard said. "But it is not the same chaos that my parents brought with them. That is what I've always tried to avoid."

"You should know, I am not usually as much trouble as I have been. My father has always found me a delight."

Richard laughed and took her in his arms. "And now I am to be delighted."

"You should also know," Caroline whispered into his neck, "that while you were being unsettled by me, I was being unsettled by the stickiest of the sticks."

"I *am* a stick, I am afraid."

"Well, it seems I am rather fond of sticks, then."

The afternoon wore on and there was shockingly little eaten from the picnic. They only rose and packed up their things to return to the house when it seemed even upright Lord Bertridge might need some cold water thrown on him.

Caroline thought that whatever this marriage would be, it would surely be full of passion. She had wondered about it between her parents, and now she would experience it for herself.

CHAPTER TWENTY

NEWS OF WHAT had unfolded at the Regent's ball had spread like a fire throughout Brighton, eventually made its way to London, and then set off for distances as far as Falmouth and Inverness. There were even a few letters sailing to Boston and New York about it.

Lord Bertridge had been seen by all of society as the stickiest of the sticks. But then, as many people now said, still waters often did run deep. It seemed the lord was of a passionate nature, hidden behind a costume of caution and reserve.

Those lucky enough to have witnessed the events firsthand were sought out in drawing rooms to tell the story. As all stories were prone to do, the tale grew in excitement each time it was told.

In the end, the facts had been settled upon to everyone's satisfaction. Lord Bertridge had been in a wild passion. Miss Upton had been a beautiful damsel on the verge of a kidnaping. Mr. Landon was the vilest of creatures and had slunk back to his father's house, where he would stay, being received by no respectable person.

As for Lord Alvanley, he was generally excused, as everybody privately thought of their own distant cousins who might not be quite up to snuff. Alvanley, himself, grew far more cautious about who he allowed into his circle, and downright wary about who he let into his house.

Not much was ever said about Mr. Mushkell's role in the events of the evening. But that was perhaps one of the advantages of fading into the cream-colored plaster like a mushroom. He was entirely forgettable and everybody save Alvanley forgot he'd ever been there.

What the tale did not include was some particulars that were arranged in the following days. Lord Bertridge hired a man to track down the poor scullery maid that Landon had compromised. Annie was found easily enough, begging on the street so she might raise enough money to follow Landon out of town.

Richard convinced her to give up the chase, and convinced her that if she ever caught Mr. Landon, she would not like what she'd caught. He set her up as housekeeper to an old great-aunt in Derbyshire who mostly just required company and was delighted to have a baby in the house. Annie would go on to marry a local tradesman and do very well for herself.

BRAMLEY'S SUMMER IN Brighton had, he thought, added to his grey hair significantly. Never had he imagined that he could survive such chaos. He did survive, though.

Unfortunately, though he and the mistress had hoped it was a passing phase, it turned out that Lord Easton was determined to keep having ideas and opinions. They were never very convenient and usually upset well thought out schedules. Lady Easton had, to Bramley's admiration, drawn a line at Brighton. If her lord were insistent on going again, he must go alone.

This turned out to be a successful gambit as the lord did go and it gave his lady some quiet months to recover from a whole season of opinions and ideas. It was in those months that he and his mistress were able to freely follow their own inclinations of quietly ticking clocks and a regular schedule.

Then, of course, there was always the comforting memory of the pineapple. He reveled in visiting his exclusive London social club that was restricted to only the most senior servants and finding himself asked about the pineapple. He delighted in commenting whenever a large dinner was planned by a fellow butler. He would ask about the presence of a pineapple and whether it would be eaten, and then condescendingly sigh at the inevitable response. He was only sorry he'd never bothered to actually taste the fruit, as he was often pressed to describe it. He'd finally settled on "otherworldly."

OVER THE YEARS, Lord Bertridge took his wife's advice and did uncork himself from time to time, shouting at the sky or giving a fencepost a bracing lecture. His children would hang out the nursery windows and listen to their father rail to the moon against one too many unpleasant surprises in a day. They were never frightened of him, as he was a kind and even-tempered father who only ever roared at the sky or berated a fencepost.

Lord Bertridge's Christmas '22 explosion became family lore. After a day of mayhem which had seen a carriage wheel broken, curtains set afire in the drawing room, a shoe eaten by one of the dogs and then helpfully regurgitated in the library, Lord Bertridge had found himself on shaky ground. Then, the Christmas roast came up from the kitchens burned to a cinder.

According to the butler, Cook had imbibed too much holiday cheer and was snoring on a bench and the kitchen maid had been terrified to make a move without direction. So, while she peered into the oven from time to time and knew the roast should come out, she did not take it out. The result was like shoe leather and after Lord Bertridge attempted to saw through it unsuccessfully, Lady Bertridge had suggested he'd better go out and give the sky a talking to.

That he did and stood out in the snow demanding the heavens tell him why he was doomed to live in such chaos. After he'd run out of shouting, Lady Bertridge went out with a generous glass of brandy and led the exhausted lord back into the house. Having uncorked himself on Christmas, he was far more cheerful the following day and the servants' party went off without a hitch.

The children had been vastly entertained by the Christmas explosion and used the phrase to express their displeasure about any and all things. It was not unusual to hear distant echoes from the nursery of some young person plaintively cry, "Why am I doomed to live in such chaos" and then the hearty laughter that accompanied it.

For all their amusement, they did not ever purposefully provoke their father and often hid some mishap or other that might shake his equanimity. It was some years before he discovered that one of the dogs was regularly chewing up his books, as the evidence of mauled covers and torn pages was always speedily disposed of. He only found it out when there began to be large empty spaces on his bottom shelves.

Lord Bertridge did find that unboxing and uncorking himself now and again did not signal the end of civilization, nor did the unpredictability of his daily life kill him. Though, he did notice that the unpredictability of his day had increased in direct correlation to how many children and dogs were roaming the house. His wife, like Lady Dunn before her, seemed always to be blooming.

For all the noise, chaos, and hijinks that went on, Richard was determined that his children never live the life he had lived with his rash and careless parents. *These* children were provided a steady home with sensible routines and they flourished. Their father might always retain a bit of stickiness in him, but he was a stick the household could rely on.

Though she would not own it publicly, it had taken Lady Easton a number of years to thoroughly approve of the match and to get used to her nephew's new, and rather more relaxed, habits. Over time, though, she did get used to it.

She particularly found herself approving of Richard's good influence on his wife, as she noticed when she visited that Caroline's attention to clocks was vastly improved, though she remained unaware of how this was accomplished. Lady Bertridge was invariably running behind, but rather than stew while he paced the drawing room, Lord Bertridge changed the clock in their bedchamber so that when she came flying down the stairs ten minutes late she was precisely on time.

Lady Easton did also, over those years, become rather more fond of Caroline herself. After all, the dear girl seemed to be able to provide her with no end of grandnieces. These young ladies always found it a special treat to come to London and stay with their great-aunt. It became a wonderful game among them to try to make each other late to the drawing room and the excitement of getting there with just seconds to spare was thrilling.

Lord Easton was, not unexpectedly, a very jolly great-uncle. He regularly slipped marzipan wrapped in paper under their pillows and could be counted on for a wink when Lady Easton became too stern.

As for Caroline's own parents, Lady Dunn liked Lord Bertridge well enough, but then she generally liked everybody as she was too distracted by her overflow of children to spend any time disliking a person.

Baron Dunn, much to Caroline's delight, hit it off famously with her new husband. The baron found his son-in-law rational, careful, and well-equipped to take good care of his eldest daughter. In truth, the baron considered that Caroline had made a far more sensible choice than he would have thought.

Bemmy did indeed marry Jimmy and they made a great success of their cheesemaking operation. Such was the renown of their blue that Lord Bertridge even invited the couple to Hertfordshire for a week to discuss his own efforts. He gave them a charming cottage on the grounds to stay in and what with Bemmy admiring the place so much and Jimmy impressed with the size of the cheesemaking concern, one thing led to another. Before the week was out, Jimmy had handed over his father's farm to his brother to manage and had taken over Lord Bertridge's much larger operation.

As the couple were paid generously, Bemmy became known in the neighborhood for her unique style in dress, generally favoring elaborate bonnets with large feather plumes or over-layed netting dripping with colored glass. She was also admired for her interesting ways of working round situations, though whether they be wise or ill-advised was always up for debate.

Bemmy became a great favorite with the children, as they liked to visit her cottage for a confidential cup of tea. Caroline thought it best, for her own peace of mind, not to dwell on any naughtiness Bemmy most likely encouraged them to. Caroline may have buttoned up, but Bemmy's buttons remained just where they were.

RICHARD, HIMSELF, FOUND various methods of easing himself through all sorts of mishaps and his railing at the sky and lecturing of fenceposts dwindled.

He often found it helpful to just stare at his wife when things were going too far awry. Caroline nearly always could put things to right, or if not, at least convince him that she had.

He also found that if he imagined the worst each day, then if the worst happened it did not sneak up on him and if the worst did *not* happen he was pleasantly surprised. Though most would find always imagining the worst not particularly cheerful, it cheered Lord Bertridge quite a bit. Lady Bertridge found the habit amusing, as her lord would often take her arm into dinner and say, "Well, my darling, I suppose this could be the night Cook finally kills us off." Having survived dinner, he was sanguine for the rest of the night.

Lady Bertridge did button up a bit, less because her lord would like it and more because she'd made some unbuttoned mistakes and they'd stuck with her. Throughout her life, she never did lose her admiration for her lord's care of her and her children. She heard, from time to time, the results of a lady having made an unwise choice of husband, whether it be financial ruin, emotional cruelty, or worse. She had made no such mistake.

She did not button up too far though, and if the children wished for something they ought not have, or had done something which they must confess, they went straight to their mama, tiptoeing past their father's library.

It was just as well that Lord Bertridge remained in the dark about some things. He need not know why two of his girls were determined to wear their bonnets in the house for a full six months, as the hair they'd cut eventually grew back and the bonnets came off.

Nor was it necessary for Lord Bertridge to contemplate why a certain governess decamped, she being an unpleasant woman and the boys deciding to haunt her dreams by awful scratchings in the night. Or that on the final night she was in residence, that they'd tied a string round a chair leg in her room and then when the moon was full had eerily dragged it across the floor.

He certainly would not like knowing that there had been for quite some time a fox living in the nursery. It seemed the kit had been abandoned, its vixen likely killed by a hunter. It had wandered out of its den and forlornly cried. Well, young Caro hearing it, what could be done? Of course it must be brought inside and fed drops of milk and wrapped in a warm blanket in front of the nursery fire.

The new governess reported the creature to Lady Bertridge immediately, but her mistress said to let it be, the fox would leave when it reached a certain age and heard the calls of another. Miss Jenkin was not at all approving, but the fox did not cause much trouble in those early days. As it got older though…

As Lady Bertridge had predicted, the creature did leave eventually, and not quietly either, racing round the house and looking for a way out one early evening. Lord Bertridge, upon viewing the sight of a fox running past his library's doorway, was left with the impression that the fox had somehow got in, not that it had been in all along and now attempted to get out.

Fortunately, Lady Bertridge ordered all the doors open and forbid her lord from getting his gun as she would not have gunfire in the house. The fox shot out into the moonless night and was never seen again, though Lord Bertridge never understood why his children all called out from the nursery windows.

"Bye, Scruffs!"

"Good luck, Scruffs!"

"Cheerio, Scruffs!"

For all the chaos that her lord hid from in the house, it turned out he was not opposed to some chaos in the bedchamber. Caroline could not fathom how he'd ever thought he ought to marry a demure lady. The wild beating heart and ungovernable nature that she'd hoped for on that very first night at Portland Place had been there all along. It only turned out to be a *private* wild and beating heart, meant for her alone.

It was rather wonderful to observe the buttoned-up face he showed to the world and know what he was *really* like.

Some weeks after they returned from Venice for their wedding trip, Lady Easton wrote Richard some interesting news. Lady Redfield had daringly crossed Lord Skeffington and demanded to take charge of his ward for the season.

Lady Arabella Beresford, who had so far been confined to an estate in Cornwall, would arrive any day. The Society of Sponsoring Ladies were already making arrangements for her launch, and they would pull together as they always did.

This news seemed almost incredible. Not the news that a certain Lady Arabella would arrive, but that Lady Redfield had been daring and crossed somebody.

Upon hearing of it, Caroline only hoped Lady Arabella was sensible and would bring with her a sensible maid. For the sake of that marvelous group of matrons.

After all, hope does spring eternal.

The End

About the Author

By the time I was eleven, my Irish Nana and I had formed a book club of sorts. On a timetable only known to herself, Nana would grab her blackthorn walking stick and steam down to the local Woolworth's. There, she would buy the latest Barbara Cartland romance, hurry home to read it accompanied by viciously strong wine, (Wild Irish Rose, if you're wondering) and then pass the book on to me. Though I was not particularly interested in real boys yet, I was *very* interested in the gentlemen in those stories—daring, bold, and often enraging and unaccountable. After my Barbara Cartland phase, I went on to Georgette Heyer, Jane Austen and so many other gifted authors blessed with the ability to bring the Georgian and Regency eras to life.

I would like nothing more than to time travel back to the Regency (and time travel back to my twenties as long as we're going somewhere) to take my chances at a ball. Who would take the first? Who would escort me into supper? What sort of meaningful looks would be exchanged? I would hope, having made the trip, to encounter a gentleman who would give me a very hard time. He ought to be vexatious in the extreme, and *worth* every vexation, to make the journey worthwhile.

I most likely won't be able to work out the time travel gambit, so I will content myself with writing stories of adventure and romance in my beloved time period. There are lives to be created, marvelous gowns to wear, jewels to don, instant attractions that inevitably come with a difficulty, and hearts to break before putting them back together again. In traditional Regency fashion, my stories are clean—the action happens in a drawing room, rather than a bedroom.

As I muse over what will happen next to my H and h, and

wish I were there with them, I will occasionally remind myself that it's also nice to have a microwave, Netflix, cheese popcorn, and steaming hot showers.

Come see me on Facebook! @KateArcherAuthor

www.ingramcontent.com/pod-product-compliance
Lightning Source LLC
Chambersburg PA
CBHW071232210726
48293CB00002B/678